KILLER TIED

KILLER TIED

LESLEY A. DIEHL

W RLDWIDE

TORONTO • NEW YORK • LONDON
AMSTERDAM • PARIS • SYDNEY • HAMBURG
STOCKHOLM • ATHENS • TOKYO • MILAN
MADRID • WARSAW • BUDAPEST • AUCKLAND

WORLDWIDE™

ISBN-13: 978-1-335-29990-1

Killer Tied

First published in 2018 by Camel Press, an imprint of Epicenter Press Inc. This edition published in 2020.

Copyright © 2018 by Lesley A. Diehl

This edition published by arrangement with Harlequin Books S.A.

For questions and comments about the quality of this book, please contact us at CustomerService@Harlequin.com.

Harlequin Enterprises ULC
22 Adelaide St. West, 40th Floor
Toronto, Ontario M5H 4E3, Canada
www.ReaderService.com

Printed in U.S.A.

ACKNOWLEDGMENTS

My high school English teacher, Mrs. Webster, and my college English professor, Dr. James Graham, encouraged my creative writing efforts at a time when I was more interested in studying science than the writing arts. Their words of encouragement came back to me when I retired from academic life, and I found I couldn't ignore the insistent whispers that I should indulge my love of cozy mysteries and pen a few of my own. These early writing mentors might be disappointed that I took so long to come to where I am today, but they wouldn't be surprised at how much I love conjuring up a good murder.

ONE

I LOOKED AROUND the old detective's office. The top of the desk no longer overflowed with paperwork, the floor was as clean as a heavy-duty cleaner could get it, and the paperwork was neatly filed away in the cabinets. I knew Crusty McNabb would hate what I had done to the space, but he had told me to make myself at home while he was gone. He was visiting his daughter, whom he hadn't seen in over a year, and wouldn't return for a few days. I was his apprentice now, somewhat eager to learn the private eye business, and I had the blessing of all my family—my grandmother Grandy, her husband, Max, my husband, Sammy, and our three adopted sons—Sammy's orphaned nephews—Jason, Jerome, and Jeremy. Even my best friend and business partner, Madeleine, and the police detective Frida Martinez had blessed my PI career path.

The only one with misgivings was me. I still wasn't real keen on the use of firearms, although I had been going to the gun range to practice with the pistol Crusty loaned me. My instructor there said I'd soon be a crack shot, no problem, but, he added, opening my eyes when I fired the durn thing might help my aim.

Well, I lied about me being the only one with doubts about my new career path. So did my friend Nappi Napolitani, who was a mob boss, or that's what we all thought—I mean, how do you ask a mob boss for his crime credentials to determine if he's genuine? Anyway, it seemed clear to me that he had something he wanted to say to me about my PI license but hadn't gotten around to saying it yet. And then there was my ex-husband, who worried I'd take this opportunity to pistol-whip him or arrest him for transgressions against me while we were married. There were many, but getting revenge for those wasn't a priority right now.

I heard a knock on the door and turned to see a man peering through the store window. He rattled the knob.

"Sorry, the office is closed until the end of this week. Mr. McNabb will be back on Friday."

"Are you Ms. Appel?"

This was silly, having a conversation through the closed door. I walked over and opened it. "I'm Eve Appel, but I—"

"Then you're the one I'm looking for. They told me next door I'd find you here." He smiled and held out his hand. "Henry Montrose."

He was a slender man with thinning, brownish-gray hair. He wore a beige knit shirt, khaki pants, and sneakers. I noted the beiges did not work together. That was just me, quick to make a fashion judgment.

I shook his hand, curious about his reasons for seeking me out.

"If it's detective work you need, I'm just Mr. McNabb's apprentice. I don't do cases on my own, so you might want to come back when he's here. Like I said. End of this week."

"I need someone to find my daughter."

"Have you reported her missing to the police?"

"Well, no. You see, I'm not certain where she's missing from. Or whether she just moved away. We lived in the Northeast, but we left. But not all together."

He wasn't making a lot of sense, and as he talked, he began to show signs of distress. His voice was shaky, and he twisted his hands so tightly together I thought he'd remove the skin.

"Maybe you should sit down for a minute." I offered the usual but seemingly useless glass of water. He collapsed into the chair in front of Crusty's desk.

"What police department do I notify? The one up North or the one here? See, I know my daughter was headed here."

"So you've heard from her?"

"No, but this is where she'd come. I told her that her mother might be dead, but my daughter insists she's still alive." He shook his head. "That woman, my wife, has nine lives, it seems."

I was more and more confused by his tale. "Uh, I have a friend on the police force here. Maybe she could help. I can call her, if you'd like."

Frida might be able to make better sense of his story than I could. And she'd know the legalities of missing persons.

Someone walked past the front windows and caught the attention of my visitor.

"No, never mind. I have to go now." Without another word, he jumped up from the chair and ran out the door, stopping on the sidewalk, looking in both directions and then running toward the street. I lost sight of him when he turned left into the alleyway at the end of the strip mall.

Weird. Just plain weird, but Crusty said that PI work

could be unusual, although he warned me that most of it was just plain boring.

I shrugged and decided to tackle cleaning the tiny bathroom. It looked as if Crusty hadn't taken a brush to the toilet bowl since he'd moved in. As I scrubbed— with rubber gloves on, of course—I thought over my decision to move from Connecticut to rural Florida.

I'd chosen to open a consignment-shop business with Madeleine Boudreaux Wilson, my best friend forever and forever. The shop was here, right next door to Crusty's detective agency. Some might question why I'd located a consignment business specializing in high-end fashions and classy home goods in rural Florida, where you're more apt to run into a live alligator than a designer alligator bag. We set up our shop to remedy that, not by doing away with the alligators, but by buying apparel and furnishings from the matrons of West Palm Beach, who rarely wore their clothes more than once or twice. Since none of these wealthy ladies would consign their items close to home for fear of someone recognizing the merchandise, we stepped in to take anything they no longer wanted off their hands. They liked having "mad" money to use any way they pleased without conferring with hubby or leaving a credit card trail for him to grump about. To our surprise, our consignors often slipped off the coast and visited our shop just for the fun of it. They didn't buy much. They preferred to sell, but they liked to pick up tips about where they could find entertainment not offered in upscale West Palm. Nothing kinky, you understand. Just good old country two-step in our local bars with some mighty handsome cowboys or airboat rides with a member of the Miccosukee Indian tribe piloting the boat (that would be my husband, more handsome than any cowboy). I'd also turned the gals on to a local dude ranch. They sometimes dragged their husbands along for a trail ride.

So why was I in training to become a PI? Was selling used items too tame for me? Well, yes and no, and that's a long story, but here's the truth. I am a snoopy gal. I get it from my grandmother, who is the queen of curiosity. Over the years I've "intruded" in a number of murders in rural Florida—at least that's the word you'd hear used to describe my investigations by my family, friends, and Detective Frida, who is also a friend of mine when she's not moaning about my interfering with her cases. From my perspective, I've been more than a little helpful tracking down clues and bringing the bad guys (and gals) to justice. A former lover and private detective Alex Montgomery thought I had a nose for murder and the brain to match wits with any killer. Although he resented my meddling in his business, he respected my sleuthing instincts so much, he suggested I get a PI license by learning the trade from Crusty.

My life was so full of family and business that the very last thing I needed was to learn the professional sleuthing trade, yet the restless side of my nature was intrigued. With Grandy helping Madeleine at the store and Shelley McCleary, our new dressmaker, assuming a growing role in the shop as tailor and junior partner, I figured I had time to try my hand at the detecting business. I yearned to sink my teeth into a big murder as my first case. Why waste my skills on small potatoes? When I excitedly talked with Crusty about murder investigations, he laughed.

"What you get in the private-detecting business is routine: surveillance of cheating spouses, insurance fraud, and some work for the police department when they need to hire out part of their investigation. Most of the work entails a lot of sitting on your butt in a car. I sure hope you don't have a tiny bladder."

I reminded him that I'd been key in solving several murders in the county.

He did a dismissive flap with his hand. "Well, maybe you've taken out all the bad dudes in this county, and the rest of us will be left in peace."

I squeezed some bleach gel into the sink and began to scrub at the grimy brown stains. I ran water and rinsed out the bowl. When I turned to extract a new bar of soap out of the cabinet behind me, I bumped into the person standing there. I jumped.

Damn. I'd forgotten to lock the front door. A fine detective I'd make.

The person standing inside the entrance of the small bathroom was a tall, slender woman with long frizzy brown hair. She looked somehow familiar, although I'd never met her before.

She smiled sweetly. "Hello. I'm your sister."

TWO

I OPENED MY MOUTH to reply, to let her know she was mistaken, but she stepped closer and said, "I know you don't believe me, but it's true. We've never met, but we have the same mother. Different fathers, of course." She spoke with firm certainty.

I finally found my voice. "How old are you?"

"Younger than you. You could say I'm your kid sister." She continued to smile.

"How old?" I persisted, because she looked to be at least a decade younger than me. She stood uncomfortably close. I moved forward, thinking I could move her back. She didn't budge.

"You're upset, aren't you? This is something I shouldn't have sprung on you without some warning."

"Eve?" Grandy called from the front of the office. "Are you here? Someone is looking for you."

"It seems she's found me." I put my hands on the young woman's shoulders and steered her out of the bathroom. The smile on her face stayed put, but she let me walk her toward Grandy.

"Hello," she said to Grandy, who was inspecting the newly clean and organized space.

"Hi there. I'm sorry, Eve. I didn't know you were here with someone."

"You said someone was looking for me."

"I meant a man was looking for you. He seemed

to be interested in investigative services." Grandy's gaze took in the woman. "You're busy, Eve, and I'm interrupting. I'll leave you two alone to get on with it."

"Oh, I don't want to hire Eve or anyone to do investigations. Well, not now, anyway. Maybe later. I just dropped in to say hi. I'll just leave and be back some other time."

Before I could stop her, the young woman slipped around Grandy and made for the door. As she opened it, she waved a cheery goodbye and was gone.

"Wait a minute," I yelled and tried to run after her, but when I threw open the door, she had disappeared.

"A reluctant client, I see," said Grandy. "I guess people do sometimes change their minds about hiring a PI. Do you think she'll be back? I hope I didn't chase off your first client."

"I hope she's gone for good. She's not who stopped by the shop to see me?"

"Nope. Like I said, some guy. Older man, slim, kind of nondescript-looking."

"Yeah, he was in here, too, but left in a hurry. They both took off without explaining why they were here. Although the woman had some weird story about being my sister. She said we shared a mother. Mom would have been…uh, gone before she was born."

Grandy dropped her gaze, shuffled her feet, and finally shook off whatever had made her uncomfortable. "Well, Crusty did tell you that some of his clients were a little odd."

"I guess I should have expected one of the weird ones would show up when he was gone. I'll make a note on the calendar."

"What you've done to this place makes it look a

lot more professional and welcoming. It doesn't smell like cigar smoke anymore," said Grandy. "I can see the desk's surface."

"Crusty will hate it, and when my back is turned, he'll be smoking up a storm and playing havoc with the file cabinets."

"Listen, honey, I'd better get back to the store. Shelley's there, but she has some alterations due tomorrow, and we've got customers to wait on. Are you coming in soon?"

"Yep. I've done all I can here. It does smell better, but I had to use some heavy-duty cleansers and air deodorizers to get the smoky smell out, and they're getting to me. I'll leave a window open to air it out." I looked around the office, pleased with my work, though my visitors were still on my mind. Two weird people in one afternoon. What were the odds of that, even with Crusty's warning that PI's worked with unusual folks?

"Eve. Eve!" said Grandy. "Did you hear me?"

"Sorry, Grandy. My mind was elsewhere."

"Thinking about the return of Sammy's father from a thirty-year absence in the swamps, weren't you?"

I shook my head. "No, I was thinking I don't believe in coincidences, and having two spooky folks in here the same day doesn't bode well. What were you saying?"

"I said, don't forget to come back and close the window before we leave for the night. Crusty's files contain confidential information that should remain under lock and key. There's no sense in inviting a thief in with an open window."

"Good point."

"Well, here's another point you should consider. I know everybody is excited and thrilled to have Sammy's father back, and I know I should be giving him some latitude when it comes to his adjustment period among all of us, but that is one strange dude, Eve. He acts particularly creepy when he's around you."

"'Strange' and 'creepy' are pretty strong words to use, Grandy."

"Maybe they're not strong enough. I get crawlies up and down my spine when he's around. I know he must feel out of place after not being around other humans for so many years, but...."

"Give him a chance." I was surprised at Grandy's attitude. I'd never known her to be so judgmental. She gave everyone a second chance, and a third. Especially someone in Mr. Egret's unfortunate circumstances. I followed Grandy out the door, then locked it behind me.

"Well, I'm just going to say it, then. I don't like him much. He frightens me, with his never-smiling face and that wicked big knife always at his belt. It's as if he thinks someone is out to get him and he needs to be armed at all times. He gives me the willies." Grandy pulled her sweater around her as if a cold wind had come up.

"I feel..." I began, but a shadow fell between Grandy and me.

"Am I interrupting?" It was Lionel Egret, Sammy's father, materializing as if out of the ether. I hoped he hadn't heard what Grandy had said, and I was glad I hadn't replied because I also found his presence unsettling, and I felt guilty about not being able to warm up to him. I had to try for Sammy's sake and for my sons, his grandsons.

"Mr. Egret. I didn't know you were going to pay us a visit today. Come on into the shop, and I'll make you a cup of tea."

His lips moved slightly with what I hoped was an attempt at a smile, but it could as easily have been a frown. He wasn't as tall as his son, his long black hair was streaked with white, and his face seemed to be perpetually set in stone. Sammy's features resembled his father's, but where Sammy was considered handsome, his father was not. His countenance was almost frightening. Sammy was known to be a generous man, but his father had lived for no one but himself for too many years. His dour face, his off-putting manner—it was all perfectly understandable. He had taken to the swamps to live alone, punishing himself for what he perceived as his responsibility for a friend's murder. The man was hard on himself. There seemed to be little warmth in him. To his credit, however, my sons adored him, and he returned their affections, taking them out in the canoe and on hunting expeditions into the swamps, even attending their school events.

"You've had a number of visitors today," he said.

"Potential clients," Grandy interjected.

"I don't think so. I think they are troublemakers. I'd be careful."

Without another word, he began walking away. Grandy and I looked at each other, and both of us shrugged. When we turned our heads to watch him walk off, he was gone.

"What the hell?" said Grandy. "Where did he go?"

"It's as if he's still hiding out in the swamps. He seems to appear and disappear without warning."

Grandy and I walked the short distance to the consignment shop in silence, both of us spooked by Mr. Egret's peculiar behavior.

She opened the door to the shop and ushered me in. "That's what I mean. The guy is strange."

"Who's strange?" asked Shelley, the young woman who did the tailoring for our shop. Shelley had lost her mother over a year ago and had come to work for us shortly after. She was attending a fashion institute in West Palm at night and working here a few days a week. Madeleine and I both thought Shelley might become a partner in the business one day. With my taking on the PI apprenticeship, we needed to lay out some concrete plans with Shelley, but we were waiting until she got her degree and was in a better position to consider her future. For all I knew, she wanted to leave the area. Her mother's murder and a love relationship that didn't work out may have convinced her that the memories here were too unpleasant for her to stay put.

Grandy and I both avoided answering her question. Shelley returned to the backroom where she did her tailoring and then brought out two of the items she was working on. The gal was a whiz at alterations.

"What do you think?" she asked, holding up the dresses.

Grandy and I both expressed our admiration. I wanted the best for Shelley and would support any decision she made about her future, but I also knew it would be hard to replace her if she decided to leave.

"I see we're down in inventory again," I said. "It's difficult keeping merchandise for both this store and our store on wheels, and we've been moving clothes into the RV on the weekends when we take it to the flea market on the coast and then moving them back here early Monday morning."

The three of us talked shop, discussing when we should go to West Palm for more inventory and who should make the trip.

Before moving into this location, we'd operated solely out of an RV we'd converted into a shop on wheels. Now, with Madeleine's family responsibilities, both shops, and my work with Crusty, we were struggling to keep everything going. Grandy helped out when she could, but I knew she and her husband, Max were eager to get back to Key Largo to run their charter boat business for casual fishermen. Max was recovering from a heart attack and had turned the business over to another captain while making it clear that the arrangement wasn't forever.

"I need salt air, not swamps," Max had declared, although he enjoyed fishing the Big Lake for speck, catfish and bass in his time here.

We heard rapping on the glass door. It was Madeleine with her twins. "A little help," she called through the door.

I held the door open while Grandy helped move the baby stroller over the threshold. Both twins were sleeping.

"I thought I'd take the babies out for some fresh air. It's such a nice day. Did I see Sammy's father walking across the parking lot? Was he here?"

"Yes and no," said Grandy. "Other than to deliver an ominous warning about several of Eve's potential clients, he went on his way. That's just fine with me."

I gave Grandy a warning look.

Madeleine looked puzzled for a moment, but her attention was distracted by Eve, her daughter, who awakened with a gurgle that erupted into a loud cry.

"Just as in-your-face as her namesake," said Madeleine.

"And the boy is so good," said Grandy, looking with affection at both children. David, the other twin, was named for his father, and was the kind of baby parents dream of having. He slept through the night and rarely cried. His good behavior was offset by his sister's fussing.

"Why don't you hold her, Eve? I'll get her bottle." Madeleine handed the wriggling, bawling baby to me.

Everyone wanted me to hold babies, especially Madeleine's babies. Oh, I got it. They thought having three sons wasn't enough. After all, my boys were children when Sammy and I adopted them. Grandy and Madeleine thought I needed to mother a tiny, helpless baby, but I knew the motherhood gene had passed me by. Eve continued to cry in my arms, her usual response to me, quieting only when Grandy took her and gave her the bottle. Baby David continued to sleep, undisturbed by his sister's yelling.

"I think you should wake him up and feed him, too, so he can put on some weight to catch up with his big bruiser of a sister," I said.

"He'll grow," said Grandy.

"I hope so. Who would want to try out for basketball and find his sister played center for the women's team while he was the water boy?" I saw the look of hurt in Madeleine's eyes. "Sorry. I was joking, honey."

"I know, and I was worried at first, too, but David is growing faster than she is. He's longer now, and she's chunkier." Madeleine took Eve from Grandy, burped her, and put her back in the stroller. "Say, I passed by the beauty salon at the end of the mall just now and saw the oddest thing. There was a young woman there who had just gotten her hair dyed blonde, and she looked like you, Eve. Your doppelganger."

THREE

I FELT A wave of anger envelope me, powerful enough that it threatened to knock me off my feet.

"Is there something wrong, Eve?" asked Grandy.

I shook my head and slammed out the door, running down the sidewalk in front of the mall. I pushed through the doors of the hair salon. A stylist was finishing a cut and applying gel to a customer's hair, coaxing it into spikes identical to my own.

"Who the hell are you?" I said to the young woman in the chair.

"Do you like it?" she asked, holding up a mirror to admire the back of her new do.

"Of course I like it. It's my hairdo."

"Now it's mine, too," she said, that irritating saccharine smile still plastered on her face.

"The two of you look enough alike to be sisters," the stylist said.

"No we don't," I insisted.

"But we are sisters. I told you that."

"Finish up here. We need to talk."

She paid her bill, and I grabbed her by the arm and propelled her out of the shop and down the street to the consignment shop.

"You're hurting my arm," she complained.

"And you're annoying me with your silly story." I shoved her through the doorway. There was a collective sharp intake of breath as Grandy, Madeleine, and Shelley stared at her.

"Because you're family, I won't have to introduce you. You must know everyone here." Sarcasm fairly dripped from my voice.

She kept up the idiot smile and held out her hand to Grandy. "You're my grandmother. I wanted to tell you when we met earlier, but I chickened out."

"I don't remember.... Yes, I do. But you looked so different. You reminded me of Eve when was she was younger, before she got her spiky blonde do."

"Grandy!" I said. "Just because she's got my hairdo doesn't mean a thing. Anyone can do that." I stopped talking because Grandy approached the woman and scrutinized her.

"I can't believe my eyes," Grandy said. There was a look of surprise on her face and something else. Was it fear?

"She told me the oddest story when she came into Crusty's. She said she was my sister. Now, isn't that just the dumbest thing you've ever heard?"

Grandy seemed to recover her composure. "That's impossible. Eve's mother has been dead since Eve was nine years old and that's long after you were born, my dear. What are you trying to pull?"

The smile slipped from her face, and her eyes filled with tears. "My father told me not to come here. He said you wouldn't believe me."

"Of course we don't believe you, because it's a lie. You'd have to be much older for Eve's parents to be your parents as well," Grandy said. Her voice was tense and angry, but her eyes remained round with worry.

Through her sobs, the young woman repeated what she had told me earlier. "Our fathers are different."

"Now you're accusing my dead daughter of being unfaithful to her dead husband. You're delusional, girl." Grandy was working herself up to a real mad, and when she got into that state, it was better to get out of her line of fire.

The young woman looked at each of us and saw that our initial shock had been replaced by full-fledged anger.

"I should never have come here." She turned and ran out the door.

"What's happening, Eve?" asked Madeleine.

"I wish I knew. Do you?" I asked Grandy.

"Of course not. It must be someone who heard about your involvement in solving crimes around here and thought she could wriggle her way into your good graces by making herself up to look like you." Grandy smiled. "Kind of like a rock groupie, only she's a crazy crime groupie. Forget about it." Grandy began rearranging clothes on the rounds, but I caught a glimpse of her face before she turned her back. Her brow was furrowed in worry. Did Grandy know something she wasn't telling me?

At Grandfather Egret's that night, the family gathered around the table to eat his famous rabbit stew. Only Grandfather and I knew the secret to his stew: it wasn't rabbit at all. It was made from chicken.

"Rabbits used to be plentiful around here," Grandfather had told me, "but the recent invasion of Burmese pythons into our swamps has wiped out the populations of rabbits, raccoons, and other small mammals."

"So I was right when I said your stew tasted like chicken," I said one night when I was helping him put the dish together.

He made a shushing sound with his finger to his mouth, and we laughed. Chicken in the stew was fine with me. I didn't like the idea of bunnies with their little pink noses and cute tails appearing as stew on my plate.

Tonight Sammy and my sons surrounded their grandfather and begged him to tell them more about his life in the swamps. To the boys, the idea was exotic, and anyone who could survive such a life was a hero.

Our youngest, now almost six, had been an unhappy, anxious boy when he came to us, and who could blame him? His mother had died of cancer, and not long after, his father had been killed. The boys had adjusted well to having Sammy and me as their parents and Grandfather Egret as their great-grandfather. The return of Sammy's father to our family was another source of joy to them. Maybe Grandy was right about his being an odd duck, but none of his distancing behavior showed itself when it came to his grandsons. It seemed as if he couldn't get enough of their company. He might treat me with suspicion, but he was loving and kind to them. Perhaps because of his own self-imposed isolation, he seemed to understand how much they needed to be enveloped in love and acceptance and to have people they could count on to support them through their grief over the loss of their biological parents. Sammy and I were grateful to have yet another person around to love the boys.

Grandfather Egret served a spiced pudding for dessert; then we shooed the boys off to bed. They had school the next morning, and supper had been late. We took our coffees and sat in chairs in front of the large fireplace.

"Dad told me you had some odd visitors today at the store," said Sammy, returning from the bedroom where he'd tucked the boys into their sleeping bags. Grandfather's house was small with only one bedroom, which had been Sammy's growing up. Whenever the boys got to do a sleepover at Grandfather's, they spread their sleeping bags in Sammy's room. Sammy's father used the single bed in the bedroom while Grandfather slept where he always had—on a small cot he set up each night near the fire in the main room of the house. The boys, Sammy, and I were still living at my place, but we had plans to build a house on the property near Grandfather's, adjacent to the airboat business Sammy and Grandfather ran.

I had hoped to tell Sammy about the young woman and the man who came to Crusty's while I was cleaning the office. Now his father had beat me to the punch line, and I was resentful. The news was mine to tell. Not his. Or was I overreacting?

"Just some loonies who wandered into Crusty's looking for a PI. That's all." It wasn't the truth, but I didn't want to air my worries with anyone but Sammy.

"You are wrong. They mean you harm. Even I could see that," said Sammy's father.

Sammy looked at me, one eyebrow raised in curiosity. "Is that true. Eve? What did they say?"

I sighed. Now that Sammy and Grandfather had half the story, I decided to tell them the rest. "The woman said she was my sister. She looks like me. But of course, that's impossible."

"And the man?" asked Sammy.

"He was a lot older. He said his daughter was missing. He didn't make a lot of sense, but it sounded as if she'd left home up North and headed down here looking for her mother. He seemed to believe the woman was dead, but his story was disjointed, and he fled before I could make sense of it."

Grandfather puffed on his pipe, then laid it on the floor beside his rocking chair. "Did he hire you to look for her?"

"No. He just ran out of the door and disappeared. I didn't know what to think of either of them. And Grandy seemed a little upset by the young woman and by...."

"Yes?" said Sammy's father.

"Nothing." I could hardly tell him her concern included his odd behavior.

"I saw the young woman," said Sammy's father, "and him. I think she's his daughter."

"Really! Did they see each other?" I asked.

He shook his head. "The last thing you need for my grandsons is some crazy relatives in their lives. It's unsettling and not good for them. Keep them away from my grandsons or I'll...."

Grandfather raised his gaze from the flames in the fire. "What will you do?"

Sammy's father shook his head. "The boys don't need disruption from this woman's family. That's all."

"I'm sure they're not, uh, she's not, my family." I couldn't keep a note of defensiveness from my voice. How could he think I didn't know what the boys needed?

His gave me a hard, challenging look, but then dropped his gaze and said, "Of course."

Sammy slipped his arm around me. "Do you think she's trying to pull something?"

"Probably, but what?" I leaned into his embrace.

We dropped the topic for the evening, but I could tell everyone was thinking about the woman's strange story. Was she some kind of a threat to me? Or was she just a lost soul latching on to me as some kind of an idol as Grandy had suggested? I wanted to meet her again and get the real story. This time I wouldn't let her go so easily.

"It's time we got home," Sammy said. "I'll be back early tomorrow to drive the boys to school, and we can take the airboat out together and see how you like the business, Dad."

Sammy was still working David Wilson's game reserve part-time, and if his father took to the airboat business, he could run it along with Sammy. Though Grandfather Egret still sold tickets, he no longer ran the boat. When the winter visitors flooded into the area, the business got busier, so the family was considering running a second boat.

Sammy and I waved goodnight and headed for the truck. As Sammy started the engine, he said, "You should have told me about your unusual visitors, Eve. I worry about you."

"When did I have time to tell you before your father announced it to all of us and then made it sound as if I were to blame?" I felt my face heat up.

"What is it with you and my father? He's only interested in our welfare, you know."

"Maybe *your* welfare and that of the boys, but not

mine," I shot back. I was sure he could hear the edge in my voice.

"You need to understand what he's experiencing. He thought he'd lost his family, and now he has it back. He's protective. That's all." Sammy's words were clipped, and now he sounded as defensive as I had.

"He *chose* to spend thirty years in the swamp. His family didn't abandon him." I should have left it alone. Sammy and I were having our first fight, and it was over family. I was on thin ice here.

There was a knock on the passenger side of the truck. I jumped and looked into the face of Sammy's father. Although the window was rolled down, I hadn't heard him approach. I guess that was good for tracking animals in the swamp, but it came off as sneaky when you did it with humans.

"I'm taking the boys on a camping expedition into the swamps this weekend. I forget to tell you."

That little announcement added fuel to the fire of the argument Sammy and I had begun in the truck. I felt he should have cleared it with us before making those plans, but Sammy was thrilled he was taking the boys on a swamp adventure. By the time we got back to my house, we weren't speaking. We always said, "I love you" before we fell asleep, but tonight it sounded forced on both our parts.

SAMMY HAD LEFT to pick up the boys by the time I awoke the next morning.

I had two items on my to-do list for the day. First I needed to find Sammy and apologize for not being more understanding of his father's difficulties in adjusting to life out of the swamps. Second, I had to find that young woman who said she was my sister. I needed to lay my anxiety to rest. I had more important issues to deal with in my life than a silly, delusional woman.

I stopped by the airboat business and found that Sammy and his father were out on the boat with a load of customers.

Grandfather Egret sat in the chickee where tickets were sold for the boat rides. He looked bored, but his face lit up at my greeting.

"I was hoping I'd find Sammy here. I need to talk to him."

"I'm guessing it's about last night. You had a disagreement."

In the earlier years of our relationship, I would have asked him how he knew, but now I accepted that Grandfather knew things others did not. I wondered if the swamps sent him messages on the wind.

"Did you know his father meant to take the boys to the swamps this weekend?"

"No, but if that's what's bothering you, who else would know how to protect them in the swamps better than he would?"

"I know. It's not that. I just wish he had talked to us first. We are their parents."

Grandfather hesitated before responding. "He can be a difficult man, Eve. He was always stubborn, making decisions on his own, never letting others in on what he was doing or thinking. But I think his pigheadedness is what kept him alive all these years. And now he's met you."

"*I'm* the problem?"

Grandfather held up his hand. "The two of you are so alike."

"We're *what*?" I sputtered.

He smiled. "Think about it."

"I will not. I am nothing like that man. He does his own thing, is in-your-face, sticks his nose into others people's business...." I heard my description of him, stopped talking and laughed. "You're right, but please do not tell me I should be more patient around him. That's a virtue neither he nor I possess."

"One of you needs to develop it, then, or there's trouble ahead."

I heard the airboat in the distance.

After the passengers left, Sammy and I wandered off down the canal.

"I'm sorry about last night," I said.

"So am I."

"The boys will be thrilled to go into the swamps with their grandfather."

"Of course. Maybe you could tell him that?"

Okay, I would. I was pretty sure he didn't much care for me, but he was family and I had to learn how to get along with him.

FOUR

Madeleine, Grandy, Shelley, and I had arranged to meet at the shop early in the morning before we opened, so I gunned my car out of the airboat-business parking lot to make certain I wasn't late. We had decided it was time to talk about the future of our two stores. I had grown fond of the RV because it allowed me alone time to think when I drove it over to the coast to open shop on the weekends, but we had to address the issue of merchandise and what sold best where. We couldn't continue to offload our items on Sunday night from the RV and then reload some of them into the rig early the following Saturday morning when we drove to the flea market in Stuart. It was too much shuffling around of goods.

I tried to watch my speed as I drove down the highway into town, but I heard a siren and saw lights in my rearview mirror. I looked down at my speedometer and noticed I was going five miles faster than the posted speed limit.

"Oh, fish heads," I said to myself in disgust. I pulled over and watched the driver of the police car behind me walk up to my car. It was my friend Frida Martinez, a homicide detective with the Sabal Bay Police Department.

"I thought you were interested in dead people, not those alive enough to be driving on our roads," I said.

"And I was only going a few miles over the speed limit. Does the city need the revenue that bad?"

"I have no idea how fast you were going. Since I spotted your car, I decided to take the opportunity to stop you so we could have a word. But since you've confessed to an infraction, I'll have to write you a ticket."

"You're kidding me."

She pushed her dark curls off her face and leaned on my car door. "Is now a good time to talk?"

"No, I'm on my way to the shop. I've got an important meeting. Can we do this some other time?"

"Name it."

We agreed to meet for a late lunch at the diner on the main street of Sabal Bay.

"By one thirty, most of the lunch crowd will have dispersed, and we'll have some privacy," Frida said.

"Can you tell me what's up?"

"Can you just be patient?"

That word again. No I could not be patient. I shook my head.

"Well, learn a lesson from today," Frida said.

"What lesson?"

"Don't admit to anything around an officer of the law. Here's your ticket. The instructions for settling up are on the back." She gave a cheery wave and left.

I yelled out my window, "Lunch is on you."

She replied, "Let's not make trying to bribe a police officer yet another charge."

I heard her chuckle as she got into her car and drove off. The ticket was blank.

"You're late," said Grandy, handing me a cup of coffee as I entered the backroom of the shop.

"I got stopped by a cop. It took time." I threw myself into the desk chair.

"Let Madeleine have the comfortable chair, honey. She's been juggling babies this morning." Grandy took my hand and pulled me into one of the folding chairs she'd set up for our meeting.

"Thanks, Eve." Madeleine sank into the chair with a sigh, followed by a moan. "Both of them were up most of the night. Eve woke up baby David. She's got a set of lungs on her."

All eyes turned on me as if it was my fault the kid wouldn't let her brother and parents sleep.

"Hey, she's my namesake, something I never agreed to. I don't send her telepathic messages telling her to misbehave."

Everyone looked skeptical.

"Grandfather hasn't taught me how to do that yet," I joked.

"Of course not, Eve," said Grandy. "Oh, before we begin, I have a message for you. Crusty McNabb called after you left this morning and said to tell you he's returning today, a day early. Apparently, the visit with his daughter did not go as well as anyone would have liked."

It was my turn to groan and sigh. I had hoped to call him and let him know, gently, that I'd done some light cleaning in his office. I didn't want him confronted by a surprise that I knew he'd find less than pleasant. Crusty seemed to thrive on chaos, and I'd relieved him of a habitat that looked as if a Category 4 storm had hit it.

"I'll call him on his cell after our meeting."

"Good girl." Grandy knew what he was like. "I told

him you had a surprise for him, but I didn't say what, so he's somewhat prepared."

No, he wasn't. A "surprise" to Crusty meant a new ashtray or a month's supply of cigars or a new roll of toilet paper in the bathroom—nothing as radical as soap and water, room deodorizer, and a new arrangement of his files.

"Let's get things rolling here," I said, eager to leave the Crusty issue behind.

"Maybe I don't belong in this meeting," said Grandy. "I'm not an owner, and I'm not even a paid employee. I've been working the shop floor in return for Max and my room at Eve's. Soon we'll be heading back to Key Largo and the boat, and that's the end of my involvement in the shop."

"How long before Max decides to return to the fishing boat?" I asked.

"I'm not certain. He was eager to go a few months back, but now he just keeps going out with his friend, Captain Jack, and fishing the lake every day. I may be more interested in having us return to the Keys because I'm sick of cleaning his catch every night."

"Yeah, and my freezer is full of bass, more than we can eat. We may have to open a fish store along with the consignment shop and sell speck, bass, and catfish," I said.

"Why don't you see if you can get an answer out of Max about his plans? When we know whether or not you'll be with us, we can plan accordingly. Meantime, we need to discuss how we're splitting the merchandise between the two shops. What sells best where?" I asked.

"I've been running through our receipts," said Madeleine, "when I can't sleep, and we sell clothing well on the coast, but not our used household merchandise like furniture and decorative items. I think we should focus on clothing and reserve the other for here."

"Good idea. It saves moving heavy items in and out of the rig. That is, if we want to keep the rig. What do you think?" I asked.

"That still depends upon sales personnel. We need to know Grandy and Max's plans," said Madeleine. "We love having you here, but we understand you need your own life."

Madeleine and I could have gone ahead without considering Grandy, but neither of us wanted to do that. I wasn't about to shove Grandy out of my house and the store if she and Max were not ready to leave.

I looked at my watch. "That's all we have time for now, except to say that your future plans are important also, Shelley. Do you have any idea what you'd like to do?"

Shelley looked reluctant to say anything.

"Honey, I know you see yourself as our tailor, but you're much more than that. You're an integral part of this operation. This is as good a time as any to suggest you begin thinking about whether you'd like to come into the business as a partner and part-owner," I said. Madeleine nodded her head in agreement.

"I don't know. I always dreamed of going to New York City and apprenticing to some designer there. I'd have to think about staying here and what it would mean."

"Whatever you decide, you know we'll back you one hundred percent," I said.

As we began putting the chairs away, there was a

banging on the front door of the shop. I stuck my head around the door to see who was there. It was the crazy woman from the other day. Seeing her head of blonde, spiky hair so like my own was freaky, especially so early in the morning with just a half cup of coffee in me. Maybe I was experiencing caffeine-deprivation hallucinations. Nope. The banging continued, followed by her yelling.

"Let me in. I need help."

"Oh, for heaven's...." I went to the door and opened it. "You're just the person I wanted to see."

She stumbled into the shop. "Really?"

"No, not really, but we should talk. I think I deserve some straight answers." I didn't know then that I wouldn't like what I heard.

MADELEINE AND GRANDY worked the store while the young woman and I headed toward the back. Grandy grabbed me before we went into the office.

"Are you certain you want to talk with her? She sounds demented to me. And she may be dangerous."

"I'm bigger than she is. And I'm almost a PI. I think I can handle her."

Grandy gave me a skeptical look. "Whatever you think is best."

"Is there some reason you don't want me to talk to her?"

Grandy seemed both surprised and annoyed at the question. "No, of course not."

My doppelganger, as Madeleine had called her the other day, told me her name was Eleanor Montrose, and she had lived most of her life in Upstate New York with her father and mother. "Several weeks ago," she said, "Mom left home very upset. She said she wanted to hide out from the men after her, then she changed that, saying she had to warn my sister of danger. She seemed almost hysterical." Eleanor's face was flushed and she seemed about to cry, but she took a deep breath and recovered herself.

"Mom was always a bit odd, wary of others and trusting only Dad. Now I think Dad is holding something back. I'm pretty sure he knows something about Mom's past, but he wouldn't tell me. About two weeks after she left, I received a phone call from her, telling me she was in Florida and had located my sister in Sabal Bay, but didn't know if she should contact her. After that call, I heard nothing more and decided to follow her to Florida, but not before talking with Dad. He confessed that he and Mom were not married."

Eleanor continued with her odd story. "He told me that she couldn't marry him because she was still married to another man. She told Dad her husband might come after her and kill her. That would be your father, Eve. I think he found her and she had to leave."

"That's absurd. My father is dead. He died in the same boating accident my mother died in." *What a loony story.*

"No, no. That was a cover. Our mother made it look as if she drowned in the accident. She assumed her husband had perished, so for a time she felt safe. But the boat was never recovered and neither was his body."

"'Felt safe.' From what?"

"From him. From your father—he was a violent man. Didn't you know that?"

I wanted to toss her out of the shop, but I also needed to hear the end of her insane tale.

"Go on," I forced myself to say.

"Mom met Dad, and they had me. We moved around Connecticut and then to a small village in rural New York. She thought she was free of your father, but recently someone had been calling and hanging up, and she'd received threatening letters in the mail."

"Did you see the letters or hear the hang-ups?"

Shaking her head, she continued, "Mom and Dad realized that your father wasn't dead. That he had found her and was going to kill her. And he probably would kill Dad and me too."

"What do you think I can do?"

"Don't you see, Eve? If he's after us, then your father will try to find you, too. We're all in danger. I don't want to put you in jeopardy, but you're a PI, and I read stories in the newspapers that you helped catch some murderers. We can use your help."

"And how did you find out about me? You were in Upstate New York. I can't believe you were reading the Sabal Bay newspapers."

"Dad told me about you, so I googled you."

There was no privacy anymore, not even in the wilds of rural Florida.

"Where is your father now? Did he come here with you?" I knew the answer, of course. Henry Montrose, my other strange visitor, had clearly been her father.

"I don't know. I think he might have followed me here, but he would have been very circumspect about that, not wanting to alert your father about…."

Oh, like that would help. If she found me through an internet search, so could anyone.

I did not believe her story, but what seemed obvious to me was that she did believe it. I needed to talk to Grandy. I knew this woman had upset her some-how yesterday, and I was determined to find out why. For now, I wanted Eleanor out of the shop and gone. But gone somewhere I could find her. I didn't believe my father had returned from the dead to hunt anyone down, but from the fear in her eyes and her voice, I knew she was terrified that someone was after her. She didn't know where her parents were. She was all alone, and I knew what being alone was like.

"Where are you staying?" I asked.

"At the Rimside Inn."

Yikes. That had to be the worst motel on the canal. But it was cheap. And who would look for a young woman there? On the other hand, with her spiky do, she would attract as much attention as I had when I arrived in town. People were used to me by now, but what would they think of my clone?

I couldn't be certain she wasn't a bit crazy and maybe dangerous, so moving her in with any of my friends was out of the question. If there was someone after her or after her parents, she needed to stay out of sight. She could use a place she would be safe in and one where she could cook her own meals, do her laundry, and chill for a time. Until I could figure out what was going on.

"I'll need to take a look at those threatening let-ters. Do you have them with you or can you get them?"

"Mom burned them."

Well, of course she did. Nothing was going to be simple here. There was no proof that anyone was after this family, only the word of the people in it, and they seemed to be an odd lot. I wondered if the mother was as weird as her daughter and the father. But where to stash this frightened young woman? Where had the man who'd approached me at Crusty's disappeared to? He told me the mother was dead. Was she? My head was aching.

As if in answer to my question, my guardian angel entered the shop—Nappi, my mob-boss friend. If anyone could protect Eleanor and keep an eye on her, it was Nappi Napolitani, and I would be calling on him yet again for a favor. He always came through, and my debt to him grew ever larger. Sometimes I wondered if it was a smart thing to be so beholden to a man with ties to organized crime.

"Stay right there," I said to Eleanor.

"Nappi," I greeted him with a hug.

"My lovely Eve," he said, taking my hand and kissing it in the old-fashioned and gentlemanly way he did when greeting me, Grandy, and Madeleine. Grandy and I loved him for many reasons. Madeleine, like Frida and some of my other friends, had her doubts. Grandfather Egret seemed to think he was just fine, and that was better than good enough for me.

"She's in a pickle," said Grandy. "She has this nut job in the office who's saying something crazy about Eve's parents. I'll let her tell you all about it, but I'll bet she wants you to solve the problem for her."

"As in remove this person?" asked Nappi, guardedly.

"As in put her someplace for safekeeping," I said.

"A bad idea," said Grandy.

"Her life could be in danger," I said.

"Well, not from your father," Grandy said, "unless you believe in ghosts."

"You were listening, weren't you?"

"Of course I was. She's a crazy person. You need to be protected."

"I only want to find out about her story."

Grandy gave me a look I'd seen few times on her face before. The corners of her usually happy mouth drooped, a sign she was disappointed in me. "You believe her story? You think I lied to you?"

"I know you did not lie, but perhaps you didn't tell me the entire truth. Perhaps you wanted to protect me."

"I can't believe you'd say that. I thought you trusted me. Maybe it's time Max and I went back to Key Largo." She turned her back, grabbed her purse from under the counter, and left.

Family—family on both sides, mine and Sammy's—was becoming a problem.

And of course, Madeleine weighed in. "Aren't you going after her, Eve?"

"I'm going to...."

What was I going to do? I had no idea. A disturbance at the door distracted me from considering my actions.

"Eve Appel Egret. What the hell did you do to my office?" Crusty McNabb yelled from the entrance of the shop. "It looks and smells like a girl's room."

I MANAGED TO settle Crusty down a bit, promising I would never use room deodorizer in his office again if he promised not to smoke his smelly cigars in there. He'd made that promise before and hadn't kept it, but I think I convinced him that paying clients would be put off by the smell if they knew a woman PI occupied the space with him.

"Damn nuisance, having a girl, er, gal, uh, woman

on the payroll," he muttered as he strode around the office, waving his arms like a windmill. He was so short he looked like a fat elf on speed. He and I made quite a team of detectives.

After he calmed down a bit, I ran back to the shop and asked Nappi if he had any properties in Sabal Bay.

He gave an elaborate shrug. "I have properties everywhere. Why not here?"

I introduced him to Eleanor, told him her story, and asked if he would put her up in a rental, if he had one.

He looked a little exasperated with me for not being more specific. "I have one, two, and three-bedroom units. What area of town are you looking for?"

"Somewhere near my place, so I can look in on her," I said. "And on the bus route so she can get into town to buy groceries."

"Maybe she shouldn't be taking public transportation. I'll have Jerry give her a ride when she needs one," Nappi offered.

Jerry was my ex-husband, not one of my favorite people, but he was a gofer for Nappi, so I tolerated his presence in my life. He was a lot easier to take now that we weren't married.

As if the sound of his name had been shouted out the door, Jerry popped into the shop.

"Hiya, Ev..." he started to say. I knew he was about to call me "Evie"—a name I hated and he knew it—but he couldn't seem to help himself. When he saw Eleanor, he stopped mid word and stared.

"Wow, she looks just like you. You could be—"

"I know. Please don't say it."

Nappi gave Jerry his marching orders, and Jerry seemed pleased with the duties he was assigned. Eleanor seemed just as pleased. *Oh, please*, I prayed to whatever gods favored me at the moment, *please, please don't let them have a thing for each other. That would be just too, too creepy.*

FIVE

I THANKED NAPPI for letting Eleanor move into one of his rentals. He didn't ask who would be paying the rent. I assumed it would be me, and I hoped she wouldn't be staying there long. For a gal who prided herself on being savvy about others, I was a little at sea here. Was taking on Eleanor's problems wise? I dismissed the thought, and true to my impulsive nature, plunged in.

After Jerry left with Eleanor, I warned Nappi that he should keep an eye on the two of them. "He thinks he's getting a younger version of me. Eleanor's very vulnerable, and I don't want Jerry taking advantage of her."

"Your problem, Eve, is that you think all young women on their own are vulnerable. Maybe she'll surprise you," Nappi said.

"Do you know something about her that I don't?" I never like it when others see something I missed.

Nappi shrugged. "She seems a little, uh, on the edge."

"Yeah, on the edge of sanity," said Madeleine. "Grandy just stormed out of here when Eve insulted her by saying she wondered if Grandy told her the whole truth about her parents. Bad form, Eve."

Madeleine was peeved at me too. Great. Just great. At this rate I wouldn't have a friend or relative who would speak to me.

Nappi laid a hand on my shoulder. "I think you could use some of Nappi's fine Italian cuisine. Perhaps tonight? Linguine with calm sauce? That should smooth over things between you and Grandy."

I was enough of a coward when it came to Grandy that having Nappi run food interference for me tonight seemed better than a confrontation. I said yes, and then remembered all the fish in our freezer and our recent diet of fish from the lake. "How about something that isn't related to fish—fresh water or salt water?" I asked. We agreed on Bolognese sauce.

AT HOME THAT NIGHT, I didn't have to apologize to Grandy at all. She left me a sweet note saying she and Max had gone back to Key Largo, to the boat. She said she'd be in touch. When I called her cell, it went to voicemail. I didn't know what to say, so I left no message.

After dinner, with the boys in bed, Nappi, Jerry— who crashed the event, saying he was just checking in with Nappi—Sammy and I settled into the living room with our coffees. Nappi told me to let Grandy cool off. "She'll soon see how difficult it was for you trying to deal with this story about your parents. And she'll understand how frightened Eleanor is."

"I like Eleanor," said Jerry.

"You do not," I said.

Jerry looked hurt. "It's more than her looks. Ellie is a smart gal, and she has class."

"Don't call her Ellie."

"That's what she said."

"'Evie,' 'Ellie.' It makes us sound like children."

"Sorry." Jerry leaned back into the couch and sipped his coffee.

"Are you certain you want to get involved in her problems?" asked Nappi.

"Oh, I do," Jerry replied.

"I think he meant me," I said.

"I understand Eve wanting to get involved. It's about her parents. I understand about losing a parent," said Sammy.

I reached out and grabbed his hand. "I don't really think my parents could be alive, but how could I live with myself if I don't look into her story? I would always wonder. My curiosity over this young woman and her parents is also part of why I am looking into this situation."

AFTER EVERYONE LEFT that night, Sammy and I lay back in each other's arms in bed and gazed out my sliding glass door into the branches of a live oak at the edge of my property. A herd of cows grazed in the adjacent field, and although we couldn't see them because the night was so dark, we could hear them crunching the cattails at the edge of a small pond.

"Will you mind moving from here when we build our house out by the airboat business?" Sammy asked.

"Not at all. It's quiet now that it's so late, but I prefer listening to the frogs and the gators in the canal out by Grandfather Egret's to the sound of cars on the road here."

"Good," he said, kissing me lightly on the lips.

"I assume your father will move into your room in Grandfather Egret's house."

"He's there most of the time now because we've chosen to live here with the kids. There's no room in Grandfather's place for them." He hesitated a moment before adding, "Or my father could move in with us when we build the house."

That was something I had not considered and definitely did not want. I laughed and said, "That would mean a mighty big house to build. Think of all those bedrooms."

If I thought my clever reply would cover my feelings, I was wrong.

"You don't want him there, do you?" asked Sammy.

Were we going to have yet another fight? I felt too overwhelmed to argue tonight.

"I want what's best for the family," I said.

"You're right. We have to consider the boys and how to help them bond with us as their parents. It's best if it's just them and us in the house. Besides, their grandfather and great-grandfather will be close by."

I was relieved he understood, even if our agreement was based upon misinterpretations of what we'd said to each other.

I snuggled closer into his arms, and the next thing I was aware of was the light coming through the slider. Sammy's side of the bed was empty, but still warm. I heard the shower running, and I hurried to slip off my nightgown and join him. By the time the boys were up and looking for breakfast, Sammy and I were pruny from the water and making silly google eyes at each other over our coffees.

"Why do you two look at each other like that?" asked our youngest.

"It's because we're in love," Sammy said. "Someday you'll look at a woman that way."

The boys snickered and rolled their eyes.

I packed their camping clothes into backpacks,

which I promised to deliver to Grandfather Egret's so Sammy's father and the boys could leave from there for their weekend jaunt into the swamps. Mr. Egret knew the swamps like he owned them, yet I was uncomfortable having the boys out there with him.

Frida and I hadn't connected for lunch yesterday because something came up, so we'd rescheduled for today. Shelley was tending the store until noon, when Madeleine was to come in for the afternoon. I was on RV duty for the weekend. Grandy worked the store here in Sabal Bay on Saturday, but now that she and Max had returned to the Keys, I had to find a replacement for her. Shelley had a Saturday day-long seminar, and Madeleine needed time with her twins. I wanted to work up a mad over how Grandy left us high and dry, but I knew it was as much my fault as hers that she left in a huff. My choices for who to handle the store were few: Grandfather Egret or Jerry. It looked like a busy weekend for the airboat business, so I got in touch with Jerry on his cell and asked him to mind the shop. He was delighted to help. He liked hanging around wealthy women, and I knew Saturdays were the days the matrons from West Palm chose to "slum" in the swamps of rural Florida. This weekend I liked the idea of getting him away from Eleanor before he could put the moves on her. And I knew he'd do just that. Jerry couldn't resist coming on to women. He'd done it to all my friends when we were married. Seduction was like a drug he was addicted to. He wasn't good at it, either. He had no smooth lines, no finesse. His best was "How do you like me, babe?" followed by a goofy grin. It was so bad that no woman took him seriously and he was so bumbling that no one got mad at his attempts, not even me. It took me years to divorce the guy, and I still felt responsible for him when he got into trouble. I'd felt more like his mother than his wife. I still did.

I spent the morning in the shop, then left for my lunch engagement with Frida. Shelley came in to do alterations and assured me she could also handle the customers until Madeleine arrived.

Frida slid into the booth I'd nabbed for the two of us at the diner. I checked my watch. "You're late. You're never late. Something big must be afoot at the station."

"We've hired a new officer who served with the West Palm Police Department for a number of years. The captain is thinking of moving him off patrol into Linc Tooney's place as my partner."

Linc had been with Frida for years. The two of them had a good working relationship, so I was surprised he was being replaced.

"What's happened to Linc?"

"He's been wanting to move to a larger department, so he's taken a job on the coast. I'll miss him."

The waitress bought us water, and we ordered. Frida continued, "I'm mentoring the new guy. His name is Reginald Butler. I'm not sure this is going to be a good match. He's pretty arrogant about his experiences in West Palm. He seems to think all of us here are country hicks, and he calls me a 'girl.' I was talking to the captain about my reservations. The guy may not work out, and if he doesn't, we'll have to hire someone else."

A tiny smile lifted one corner of her mouth.

"Wanna be a cop?" she asked.

"Good God, no," I said. "I'm not even certain I want to be a PI."

"Still having trouble keeping your eyes open when you fire your pistol, are you?"

"How'd you know about that?"

"Word gets around." She mouthed the name "Crusty."

"So what's up other than having hired a sexist cop?" I asked.

"This guy came into the station the other day. He said he'd talked to you, and you thought he should talk with the police. Thanks for that, Eve. He's kind of squirrelly."

I held up my hand. "Say no more. I know who you're talking about. His name is Henry Montrose. I kind of know his daughter."

"He's the one. He's looking for her. I had no idea where she might be because she hasn't come to our attention. You solved my problem for me, Eve. I'll get him on his cell and tell him you know her."

"You'd better let me call him. The story about his daughter is kind of complicated."

"Anything I should know about?" asked Frida. Our food had arrived and Frida took a big bite of her cheeseburger.

"I don't think so. But here's her story." I shared what I knew about Eleanor Montrose.

"Odd. The missing piece here seems to be the mother. Well, keep me posted. I gotta run back to the station. My new partner awaits me." Frida wrinkled her nose in distaste, then grabbed a handful of fries and ran out the door. I looked at the uneaten fries she'd left, reached over and dumped them onto my plate. I've always had a giant appetite and never gained weight, although I've been warned it will catch up with me someday. I was still skinny and still waiting for that first pound.

The waitress brought the check. I was wrong. Lunch wasn't on Frida. It was on me.

NEXT, I DROPPED the boys' camping gear at the airboat business. Grandfather Egret offered me a cup of tea.

"A quick one," I said. "I know Madeleine has to bring the babies into the store with her this afternoon because David's cutting brush on the reserve." Madeleine's husband, David, owned the game reserve and hunting ranch Sammy worked on as part-time manager. David had inherited the ranch from his father, but was no longer interested in hunting and was trying to sell. So far the only bite had been several years ago from someone now in prison for murder.

Again I wondered how I could fit in my PI apprenticeship with work in the shop without inconveniencing everybody.

"Take a deep breath," Grandfather Egret said to me. "Grandy will rethink what was said. The two of you are too close for one argument to destroy your relationship."

I felt a presence behind me and turned quickly with a smile on my face, thinking it was Sammy. Instead it was his father who stared down at me.

"She is like all white women. She thinks only of herself, when she should be respecting her elders and considering how her words can hurt them. Is this how you will raise my grandsons, with angry words and insolence? It would be better if they were with their own people."

The man seemed to know how to get under my skin.

I wanted to lash out at him, but that would be buying into what he accused me of. Instead, I held my tongue for a moment before I spoke. "Sammy and I want our sons to feel at home in both worlds. We want them to know both worlds. That's why we're pleased you are taking them into the swamps this weekend."

He looked at me with his black, angry eyes, and his expression never softened.

Grandfather stood and placed a hand on my shoulder. "This woman's spirit is large, of this place and of her own home. She will lead your grandsons down a path of love and of acceptance. Do you not feel that?"

Sammy's father lowered his gaze, not out of shame, I guessed, but to keep his thoughts veiled. "I don't think I feel anything." He grabbed the camping gear and walked off toward the canoe, which was beached in the reeds near the airboat landing.

"It must be hard for you, Grandfather, to see the swamps return such an unhappy son."

"He was unhappy when he entered the swamps. That has not changed."

"While I have you alone, do you have Renata's telephone number?" I asked Grandfather.

Renata was Sammy's mother and Mr. Egret's white wife. She now lived in Las Vegas. I had met her once and liked her. The engagement ring Sammy gave me came from her.

"She might be helpful to you, but you're right not to mention her name around my son. I'll get you her number."

I thanked him and said goodbye, waving a greeting to Sammy, who was returning to the dock with an airboat full of passengers.

"I'll see the boys off this afternoon with Father. Don't worry about them. I'll make certain they have everything they need for this weekend," he called to me.

I reminded myself that Sammy's father was master of the swamps, but I still felt anxious about the trip. Was I becoming an overprotective mother?

BACK AT THE consignment shop, I noticed a familiar car parked out front. I walked through the front door and saw Grandy at the cash register. Madeleine, assuming we might have things to say to each other, made herself scarce in the back office.

I ignored Grandy's and my recent unpleasant exchange. "How's business today?" I asked, slinging my purse underneath the back counter.

"Good. I understand I missed a great supper last night. Nappi cooked?"

"Yup. I'm sorry you weren't here, but there are leftovers in the fridge." Our conversation was strained. We were avoiding what needed to be said.

I sighed. I might as well get to it. "I'm sorry for doubting your word. You're my rock, Grandy."

She threw her arms around me. "These people coming into our lives…why now? Why does it have to be when everything is going so well?"

"At least it's not another dead body," I said, trying to lighten the mood.

She nodded. "I wouldn't lie to you, Eve, not about my own daughter, your mother. She is gone, and so is your father. I was so furious at that man and his daughter bringing up painful memories for both of us."

Uh-oh. I'd have to tell her I'd taken Eleanor under

my wing, and that would upset the peace we'd just established.

We continued hugging each other until we heard the bell on the front door jingle, announcing a customer.

It was Eleanor. *Oh, hell.*

Grandy held on to her composure, and so did I. Eleanor believed what she had been told, and I could understand that. Regardless of who her mother was, she was almost hysterical over her disappearance. We walked her into the office, and Madeleine nodded her head toward the door to signal she'd leave us alone, but I shook my head.

Eleanor repeated her story again for us. Grandy was silent after Eleanor finished telling her tale.

"Have you located your father yet?" I asked, and told her he had visited the police headquarters and talked with Frida. "He left a cell number with Frida. I was going to call it, but haven't yet. Why don't you give him a call?"

"I've never known him to have a cellphone. He must have purchased it recently."

I gave her the cell number, and she tried to connect, but shook her head. "It goes to voicemail. Where is he?"

Well, this is what detective work is all about. "I'll check the motels and hotels around here. You can help, Eleanor." I handed her the phone book.

I let her use the desk in the office to make her calls. Grandy, Madeleine, and I conferred out of her hearing at the counter of the shop.

"This is pretty crazy, but I'm going to be doing detective work on my own case. I've got to find out why these people think my dead mother and father are alive and part of their lives."

"I've got an idea," Madeleine said.

"What? Aside from the obvious. I need to find Eleanor's father and question him. And maybe I'll have to take a trip to New York and interview the people in that town where Eleanor was raised."

"You could do a DNA test. You and Eleanor," said Madeleine.

Brilliant. Maybe Madeleine should be the PI.

FRIDAY NIGHT AND Saturday passed without incident. On Saturday Grandy accompanied me in the RV to the coast. En route, I worked up the courage to tell Grandy I had settled Eleanor in one of Nappi's rentals. Her response was to shake her head and stare out the RV's passenger-side window. While we greeted customers at the coast flea market, Madeleine took the hunting ranch's truck, accompanied by David and the twins, and picked up furniture from the West Palm area. Jerry handled the shop. I expected the boys back sometime Sunday afternoon, but the phone rang Saturday evening as Sammy, Grandfather, Grandy, Max, and I were eating a meal of frog legs and bass at Grandfather's house.

Frida was on the other end of the line. "I don't want you to get upset, Eve, but I'm out here in the swamps near the fishing pier. Your sons found a body while camping."

SIX

I RAN OUT the door and toward the airboat landing. Sammy was close on my heels, followed by the others. I heard the sound of a boat motor before I saw the craft emerge from the mist rising off the canal waters. Our sons were huddled in the rear, wrapped in blankets. There was no sign of Sammy's father, only Frida and two uniformed police officers.

The boys ran into Sammy's arms. We hugged them to us. I could feel my youngest trembling. The other two, however, tried to act as if they could handle the situation. They couldn't. I could read panic in their eyes. Even the oldest seemed to have difficulty maintaining a brave face.

"Where's my father?" asked Sammy. I was glad he was the one to ask the question, because it was the next thing on my mind. Someone was dead, and that was a tragedy, but Mr. Egret was responsible for the safety of my sons, and he seemed to have abandoned that job.

"We don't know," said Frida. "We got a call at the station about an hour ago. It came from a cell number. The caller was male. He told us there was a dead body near the fishing pier down from the boat launch into the river. That's all he said. When we got there, we found the body and your boys, but no Mr. Egret. They were pretty shook up, so I held off questioning them in any detail. I thought they needed their parents. I can talk with them later, tomorrow maybe."

"My father doesn't have a cellphone. He couldn't have made that call," Sammy said.

"But he did call," said Jason, my oldest son.

"Let's get the boys into the house," I said, "then we can sort this out."

"I left an officer on duty out there, but I've got to get back to meet the crime scene team," Frida said.

I steered her away from the others. "Do you know who it is? It's not Mr. Egret, if he called it in. But whose cellphone did he use?"

"I've got no identity for the body, but I'm curious why Mr. Egret wasn't there with your boys." Frida leaped back into the boat and headed back down the canal.

The boys were tired and scared. We hustled them into Grandfather Egret's house and made hot chocolate for them. I didn't want to press them with too many questions, but Frida's concern about what had happened to their grandfather bothered me. I knew Sammy was keeping a lid on his feelings for the sake of the boys.

Grandfather had said nothing since the boys arrived, but now he spoke, so softly I could barely hear him. "He's gone. Again."

I turned on him, furious. "Is that what he does best? Disappears when there's trouble? I wish he'd never come back here in the first place. Right now, I'm concerned how this will affect Sammy and the boys as well as you, Grandfather."

Sammy reached out and pulled me to him. "You're

scaring the boys, and they've already had a difficult evening."

I pulled back, knowing Sammy was right. I was lashing out at the wrong party. "I'm sorry, Grandfather. I know it's not your fault, but I'm so angry he didn't take care of them."

"He did take good care of us," insisted Jason. "He taught us how to find the best wood for a fire and how to catch frogs. He warned us to be careful near the canal because of the alligators. When Jeremy went off to play and was gone for so long, he found him and brought him back to our campsite. Then he told us to wait by the fire to keep warm and safe. He told me to take care of my bothers. That we would be just fine."

"That's all?" I asked. "Did you see the man who was, uhm...?"

"The dead guy? Nope," said Jason. "We did what we were told. We sat by the fire and waited, although...."

"Although what?" asked Sammy.

"Nothing. It was a little scary, I guess. Are we gonna go to the police station now?"

"Later," said Sammy. "Right now I think all three of you should get some rest. Did the police let you take your sleeping bags with you?"

The boys nodded and trooped off to the bedroom. Sammy and I followed and tucked them into their sleeping bags with a hug and kiss for each of them.

Grandfather Egret sat in front of the fireplace, puffing on his pipe. The smoke swirled around his head, a metaphor for the churning confusion in my brain. My anger at Sammy's father still lingered, ameliorated somewhat by my relief that the boys were safe.

"There's a good explanation for why he left the boys

there," said Sammy, joining Grandfather and me in front of the fire.

"Really? What would that be?" I asked. Despite my attempt to contain my rage, the words sounded shaky. I was acting like an enraged mother protecting her cubs.

"I don't know, but I'd guess that your friend Frida has already developed a theory about the situation."

I caught the undertone of anger in his voice. "You think because she's a cop and he's Miccosukee that she thinks he's responsible for the body. We don't even know if foul play was involved. Maybe he just drowned or was attacked by an animal."

"Because he was going for a stroll out in the swamps? Don't be silly." Sammy picked up the fireplace poker and stirred the embers, then slammed it back into its holder.

"What do you think, Grandfather?" I asked.

He stood and removed his pipe from his mouth, then tapped it against the brick floor in front of the fireplace. "There are winds blowing out of the north, cold winds. I'm glad the boys didn't spend tonight in the swamps. A storm is brewing."

I looked into his face, lit by the firelight. I'd never seen him look so tired, so defeated, so without hope. His emotional state was far from being about the weather. There was something disturbing about this situation that I sensed too.

"We're all tired and should sleep," Grandfather said. "What are you going to do about the boys? Leave them here with me for the night, or do you want to take them home to Eve's house?"

"I don't think they should be awakened," Sammy said. "I'll sleep on the floor beside them. I've got an old sleeping bag around here someplace. Eve, you can take the single bed in the room."

No more was said about Sammy's father, the dead body, and the boys' frightening experience that night, but I might as well have been lying on a cold, stone floor, for all the sleep I managed.

I GOT UP at first light and found Grandfather already awake, making coffee. The boys awoke soon after and came out of the bedroom, followed by Sammy. No one said much as they ate the oatmeal Grandfather prepared for them. I decided not to drive the rig to the coast today, even though it was one of our coast flea market days. I wanted to be close for the boys.

The phone rang as we were finishing breakfast. It was Frida.

"No sign of Mr. Egret?" she asked.

"None."

"Does Grandfather or Sammy have any idea where he might have gone or why?"

"Ask them." I handed the phone to Sammy. He had the right to put his own spin on his father's disappearance, although I might not agree with him. Sammy talked with her for a few minutes. He indicated that he thought his father might have gone off into the swamps for good reasons, although he couldn't say what they might have been. He didn't mention his suspicion that because he was Miccosukee, he might have feared the authorities would view him as a suspect in the death.

"Okay," he said, ending the conversation. Turning to me, he added, "Do you think we can bring the boys into police headquarters today? Frida would like to talk with them some more."

The boys couldn't hide their excitement over being interviewed at the police station. For them, the fear of last night had passed, and now they were only looking forward to taking part in a criminal investigation, like "Detective Mommy."

I groaned at their description. I wanted them as far as possible from any criminal matters I might be involved in.

In Frida's office, Sammy and I listened as she ran through questions about last night's events. The boys told their stories again, all identical to what they had told us last night.

As we left, Frida pulled me aside. "Would you do me a favor, Eve? We're doing the autopsy on the body today, but we still don't have an ID."

"How can I help?"

"The light was bad last night, so I couldn't be certain, but I thought I recognized the guy. I took another look this morning, and I believe he was the one who came into the station looking for his daughter. You saw him at the office. I thought you might be willing to take a peek at the body before I call the daughter in. If you think it's her father, you could accompany her."

I was shocked. The man was dead? Out in the swamps? If it was him, his daughter would be shaken. To look for her parents and then find one was dead and the other had disappeared?

Frida saw the expression on my face. "Here's the worst part. It wasn't accidental. He was stabbed with a big Bowie knife, like the one Mr. Egret wears in a scabbard on his belt."

And there it was. Sammy was correct. The authorities would suspect his father, and not without good reason.

I swallowed hard. "I'll come back in after I get the boys home and make them lunch. Sammy's out at the airboat business today, but Grandy's back now, so she can take care of them for the afternoon."

"I didn't know Grandy was gone."

"Uh, yeah. She and Max had something they needed to do on the boat. It was just a quick overnight." I wondered if Frida could tell I was sidestepping her comment about Grandy.

"Good. And Eve…?"

"What?"

"Don't say anything about the manner of death to Sammy. Let's keep that between us for the time being. Okay?"

Smart gal. She knew Sammy would be furious at the police for suspecting his father. She was buying herself some time and space before she went public with her case.

"When do you want me to take a look at the body?"

"How about now? Maybe Sammy can take the kids home, and I can give you a ride when we're done here."

I let Sammy know Frida needed my help and why, then followed her down the hallway into the morgue. It took only a glance for me to recognize the man as Eleanor's father.

"It would make more sense for you to call Eleanor. You know her. You may be related to her," said Frida, then caught what she had said. "Sorry. We don't know that, do we?"

"No, and why should I make the call? Isn't that police business?" I knew I was being difficult because I hated Frida's comment about Eleanor and me.

"Think about it, Eve. She's alone here and searching for her parents. She thinks they are in danger from someone, and that's why her mother left home to begin with. And…."

"Right, right. You're right." I used my cell to contact her, and Jerry answered. I was not surprised that he was giving her his full attention. Well, then. How fortunate is this? I wouldn't have to break the news to her. He could tell her. And yes, I was being a coward.

Jerry didn't want the job either. "I can't tell her that. That's awful. Besides, she's still asleep."

"Were you there all night?"

There was a moment's silence.

"Uh, yes."

"Jerry, she's a vulnerable young woman. You need to be careful how you treat her. Did you sleep with her?"

Again, there was a moment's silence.

"What do you mean by 'sleep'?"

"Oh, for heaven's sake. Just wake her up and get her dressed and down here as soon as you can. I'll be waiting."

Frida had listened to the conversation. "What made you think Jerry would make a good babysitter for Eleanor?"

"Lack of good sense on my part?" I ventured.

ELEANOR IDENTIFIED THE body as that of her father, then broke down in Jerry's arms. He drove her back to her place after receiving a warning from me to "keep your testosterone-laden paws off her." He shot me a hurt look.

This awful day had started with my sons' appearance at police headquarters after their camping trip ended with the identification of a dead body. This was not the way I wanted my Sunday to go in any case, but it was about to get worse—much worse. Frida dropped me off at my house as she'd promised. I hoped Sammy and I could rescue the remainder of the day by taking the boys to a matinee, although it appeared that we were more in need of distraction than the kids were. They seemed like their usual selves, just excited about going to a movie.

"Can we have large popcorns, not those small bags?" begged Jerome. "We're finished with the little ones before the movie even comes on."

As we were about to leave, the phone rang. It was Frida, and she wanted to talk with Sammy. Judging by her tone, she wasn't eager for the conversation. She added, "It's police business."

Sammy listened for a few minutes. I watched the muscle in his jaw begin to twitch and knew something bad had happened. He slammed the receiver into the base. "I've got to go down to the station."

"They found your father? Is he all right?"

"Frida wants me to look at the knife that has been identified as the murder weapon. She thinks it's my father's."

"I'll come with you. Grandy and Max can take the boys to the movies."

"No. You take them. They need their mother, whether they know it or not."

He was right. The boys' lives had been hard, enough so that they'd learned it was best to put a good face on things. They were doing that now, and I had missed it.

I kissed him goodbye. He didn't lean into my embrace as he usually did. I knew he was both angry and afraid. His people hadn't been treated well by white authorities in the past. I just hoped he didn't see me as being in league with those white people who saw only an Indian in front of them. He had to know I didn't feel that way, didn't he?

THE BOYS ENJOYED the movie, and I fed them as much popcorn and soda as they could hold, even if it meant upset stomachs tonight. My eldest turned to his brothers when he thought I wasn't listening and said, "Wow, if this is what finding a dead body gets us, I want to do it more."

I gave him a gentle cuff on his arm to let him know I'd heard. "It's not funny stuff, you know. It's serious. That man was a friend's father."

So was that what Eleanor was? A friend?

"I'm sorry," he said.

I hugged him to me and saw his eyes were shiny with tears. I knew what I said reminded him of the loss of his own father and mother. "It's okay. Sammy and I are here for you, and we always will be."

Could I make that promise to my sons and keep it? I was certain my parents would have made the same promise to me if they could, but they were taken by the sea. I knew they were gone, yet some tiny piece of me wanted Eleanor's story to be true, even if it meant my parents weren't who I thought they were. Eleanor had given me hope they were still alive. I'd deal with the consequences of that somehow. I shook off the thought. Maybe I could sort out having my parents alive, but what role could Grandy have played in all this? No.

No. I had to believe they had died as she said—at sea, years ago, in a boating accident.

The sound of a vehicle pulling into the drive interrupted my thoughts. It was Sammy back from police headquarters. I looked at my watch. He'd been gone all afternoon and most of the evening. The boys were in their room, and Grandy and Max, leaving the house to us, had gone out to eat.

I tried to judge his mood as he came through the door. He tossed his keys onto the table and stuck his head in the refrigerator, his face hidden. I knew better than to inundate him with questions.

"I'm starved. It took longer than it should have." He grabbed cold cuts and bread from the cabinet.

"I could heat up spaghetti from the other night, if you'd like," I said.

"I don't want any damn spaghetti." He slammed the refrigerator door closed, then flung himself into a kitchen chair and dropped his head into his hands.

I went over and began to massage his shoulders. "Tell me."

"I'm sorry, Eve. I shouldn't take any of this out on you. It's just that I've been here before, with Grandfather being accused of a murder. And now Father. Why do the authorities always pick on us?"

I sat down in a chair beside him and took his hand. He raised his head and looked into my eyes. Despair had replaced the anger on his face. "I guess I know why they picked on us this time. I told Frida I was not certain if I'd seen the knife before. She was kind enough not to accuse me of lying, but of course I was. Instead, she suggested we take a ride out to Grandfather's to see what he had to say about it. I could tell where all of this was heading, but what could I do? Grandfather identified the knife responsible for the murder as my father's. Frida asked for something from the house that might have Father's fingerprints on it so she could compare them with those on the murder weapon. You know they will find a match. Oh, Eve. I don't know what to do." He put his arms around me and we hugged, finding some comfort in each other's physical presence.

"I guess I'm not as hungry as I thought. I'm going to bed." He rose and started toward the bedroom, then turned back to me. "I just found him again. Why would he do this?"

I found Mr. Egret to be difficult, but even though the meaning of Sammy's question had more to do with what his father was doing to Sammy and the boys, I considered another aspect of the question. What possible motive did Mr. Egret have for killing Eleanor's father? He didn't even know the man. Did he?

Sammy went to the boys' room to say goodnight. Then, kissing me goodnight, he headed to our bedroom. Grandy and Max came in shortly after that, and I followed Sammy to bed an hour later. Questions about my parents and Sammy's father swirled around in my head. I slept poorly and awoke with a headache and a stomach upset enough that I ran to the bathroom and threw up.

Well, enough of that, I thought to myself as I gargled with mouthwash and prepared to step into the shower. I was a take-action gal, not one who did well wringing her hands in despair. It was time to get Eve Appel, newly minted PI, on the case.

SEVEN

As DETERMINED AS I was to shake off my lethargy and take charge, I felt tired and achy, and my stomach was too unsettled to eat. I got the kids ready for school and let Sammy sleep in, since I knew he didn't need to open the airboat business early and wasn't working at David's ranch today. Grandy accompanied me to the shop, where I told her what had happened yesterday.

She seemed withdrawn and worried, and I wondered if she still felt betrayed by my concern over Eleanor's story as well as my putting my wannabe sister up in a rental.

"Grandy," I told her as we straightened the shop for the morning opening, "I'm so glad you're here. I'm sorry I doubted you."

"It's okay. I know you'd like to believe your mother is still alive. I'd give that to you if I could, but it's just not true."

"I believe you." I pulled her plump body into my skinny one and gave her a hug. I must have been more distraught over our disagreement than I thought. My body began to tremble like an earthquake was shaking it.

"Uh, Eve," Grandy said, breaking the hug, "your cellphone is...."

I gave a small, embarrassed giggle. "I forgot I put it on vibrate." We both laughed.

It was Grandfather Egret. "The police think they've

found their man in this murder, but I know otherwise. My son may be a recluse and more than a little odd, but he's not a murderer. Sammy and I have talked. We know the authorities will not go beyond the evidence they already have."

I was about to interrupt, to assure him that Frida was fair and would pursue other leads, but even I had my doubts. She might want to look further, but would her boss let her?

"Don't tell me about your friend Frida. She's a good cop, but why would she stick out her neck for an Indian, especially one no one understands, not even his own family? Who knows what such a man is capable of?

"We need your help. We want to see if Crusty will take this case for us. We know he'll want you to do the work, so that's why I'm alerting you first."

I felt alive with anticipation. This was what I was destined to do: track down murderers. As quickly as a tingle went up and down my spine, a lump formed in my stomach. Did I believe Mr. Egret was innocent?

"Meet us at Mr. McNabb's office. We've got an appointment there in fifteen minutes." He disconnected.

I told Grandy what was up.

"You're going to have to go at this investigation the hard way, Eve."

"What's the hard way?" I asked.

"You know this better than I do. You'll have to go to the town Eleanor's parents lived in and where she grew up."

I groaned. "But that's in New York State. I can't leave everything here—the boys, Sammy, the store, you, Madeleine, everyone. What will Sammy say about my leaving now?"

"Sammy knows that if you work this case, he'll have to pitch in here. We'll take care of things on this end, Eve. And you know we'll be waiting when you get back."

Get back? It seemed it was a done deal that I was leaving for Eleanor's hometown.

"One more thing," Grandy said with a smile. "I think you should take someone as backup."

Before I could consider who that might be, Grandy had already sprung into action. "I have just the person in mind. Don't worry. I'll get in touch with him. You mosey next door to your meeting."

It seemed Grandy had put together some kind of plan. Whatever she had up her sleeve, it lifted her spirits out of despondency. She almost shoved me out the door.

"YOU THINK YOU can handle this one, Eve?" asked Crusty. Grandfather Egret, Sammy, and I were conferring with him about how to proceed with the case that was shaping up against Mr. Egret.

"No charges have been filed against him yet," said Crusty, "but it's only a matter of time. He fled the area, the knife has been identified as the murder weapon, and Mr. Egret is the owner of that knife. If the fingerprints can be determined to be his, the case is all but over. We need to move fast, and we don't have much information to work with. If you want me to take on this matter for you, then we'll need a contract, and then I'll need your help."

"What kind of help?" Grandfather Egret asked.

"Everything about your son is relevant here. I know he's been living in the swamps for years, but I need to know what he did before he left, what he did there, and what he's been up to since he returned. And any ideas you might have about where he might be now." Crusty gave Grandfather and Sammy a stern look. "I mean *everything* on the man."

Sammy and Grandfather exchanged looks and nodded.

"I'll be looking into Eleanor and her family," I said.

"Doesn't that hit too close to home, Eve?" asked Sammy.

"Just as your father's life does for you, my love," I said. "Everything about this case is personal, whether we know it or not."

"You'll be going to New York then," Sammy said. "By yourself? Isn't that a lot to take on? I'd feel better about your leaving if you had someone to go with you."

The door to Crusty's office opened, and the person who would serve as my guardian angel walked in.

"Nappi." I smiled, knowing that Grandy had called him to accompany me. Who better than a mob boss to ferret out family secrets?

FRIDA CALLED LATE in the afternoon to say that the authorities wanted Mr. Egret for questioning in Mr. Montrose's murder and that the fingerprints on the murder weapon matched those found on the comb in his bedroom. An APB had gone out an hour earlier. I doubted the authorities would find him or that anyone would spot him, not unless they were willing to search the swamps.

"There are other prints on the knife, too," said Frida. "Some from a small hand, perhaps a child's. Your boys said nothing about handling the knife to me. Did they say anything to you, Eve?"

"Now you think my sons might have killed Mr. Montrose?"

"No, of course not. They might have asked to see the knife, and he let them. I just can't understand why the kids wouldn't have said anything to you."

"Well, they didn't, and they're not liars, you know." I gritted my teeth, trying not to sound irritated at her insinuations.

"I'm sorry, but I had to ask." She paused for a moment. "I got word that Grandfather Egret and Sammy hired Crusty McNabb to look into the case. I assume that means you'll be involved."

"I will be, but I won't be intruding into your case. I'll be looking into the other side, trying to figure out if there was a connection between Mr. Montrose and Mr. Egret. If he killed Mr. Montrose, there had to be a motive. What might that be?"

"So you'll be going to New York to look into the Montrose family there?"

"Isn't that something the authorities should be checking into also?" After I said it, I wanted to bite my tongue. It was a dig at how the police were handling the case, but I'd also revealed to Frida how our family was going to proceed. Was that something a PI should keep to herself?

THAT NIGHT GRANDFATHER, Sammy, the boys, Grandy, Max, and I had gathered around the fire outside Grandfather Egret's place. Sammy and I had told the boys

I would be leaving in the morning for a few days and reassured them I would be back.

"It's for a short time, to help your grandfather out," I said.

"Where is he?" my oldest asked.

"He's somewhere safe," Sammy answered. I hoped he was right.

Sammy wasn't happy that my companion for the trip north would be Nappi, but he was convinced I needed someone to accompany me, and I knew he trusted Nappi to take good care of me. Like my friend Madeleine, Sammy had reservations about my hanging out with mob bosses, even though Nappi had proven to be a true friend. Earlier I had called Madeleine and David and apprised them of my plans.

"What kind of case, Eve?" asked Madeleine.

"I can't give you any details," I replied.

"Humph," she said. "I'll bet I can guess. It's all about the recent murder and your newly found relative."

"I don't have any new relatives," I insisted.

"Right. Sure you don't." It was clear she didn't believe me.

"You know Grandy would know if there was any doubt about the death of my parents."

"I know. I'm sorry. I just can't get over how much Eleanor looks like you. It's uncanny. Well, good luck on your first case. And be careful."

I heard one of the babies crying in the background and wished for a minute that my life was as simple as Madeleine's—that is, if you can call the demands of two infants simple.

As Grandfather stirred the fire and the boys made

their s'mores, I considered what Madeleine said about the resemblance between Eleanor and me. It bothered me too. Grandy intruded on my thoughts.

"Eleanor is an odd one, don't you think?" she said. "Poor girl losing her father and not being able to locate her mother. I have no reason to doubt she believes the story about her mother being your mother, Eve, but I think you should push for a DNA test."

"What's the point if the story is false? And it is." I was surprised at Grandy's suggestion.

"It will settle things and reassure all of us, particularly you, Eve."

"And shatter Eleanor's life. She's kind of got her hopes wrapped around our being sisters. She just lost her dad. For now, I'd like to hold off. I know what the truth is and so do you. We'll let it stand like that for the time being." My tone of voice carried conviction, but there was still a part of me that wondered, that wanted parts of Eleanor's story to be true. "I need time to think about this." I left the fire and walked along the canal, taking in the stillness of the water, broken only by several fish coming to the surface to feed.

I knew Grandy was right. I was entertaining a fantasy, one that needed to be put to rest. A DNA test would do that. Maybe there was a way to do the test without Eleanor's knowledge. I punched Jerry's number into my cell. "Is Eleanor with you?"

When he said she wasn't, I told him what I wanted him to do.

"Ah, Eve, I don't want to do that. That's sneaky."

"Since when don't you do sneaky?"

"I'm trying to be a better person."

"You can do that after you get some of Eleanor's hair and send it off to the lab for DNA analysis. I'll text you the address. Be sure you get roots or it won't work."

"Ah, Eve," he said again.

I ended the call. There. That was done. I hoped.

NEXT MORNING, WE headed north in Nappi's black SUV, a more comfortable and luxurious ride than my Mustang. We took I95 into South Carolina then cut west, staying overnight in North Carolina and driving the Blue Ridge the next day into Pennsylvania and north to New York State. I hadn't experienced early summer in the Northeast for several years, but the lush green foliage of the mountains and river valleys was as beautiful as I remembered and salve for my anxieties about this case. By the time we reached Eleanor's hometown of Tillahook at the edge of the Catskill Mountains, it was dark. We found a mom and pop motel just off the main street next to a diner, where we ate dinner then retired for the night.

Nappi was surprisingly quiet during the ride, and I suppose I was too. I did learn that he had attended cooking school at one point—in Connecticut—a gourmet spin on what he had learned in his mother's kitchen. For a while we talked about movies. He liked noir movies from the forties, and I was more a fan of comedies.

The next morning Nappi made inquiries at some of the stores, including a ski shop where Eleanor said her dad had worked for several years. I headed for the high school. While I flashed my newly minted PI card, Nappi would be flashing his award-winning smile. If I thought my credentials might get me some traction with the principal, I was wrong. He was suspicious of my inquiries and told me he knew little about Eleanor's family since he hadn't been principal when she was in school.

"I'm sorry, but I can't help you," he said, rising from his chair in a move of dismissal.

"How about any of her teachers?"

He shook his head. "I don't want you bothering my staff. Now please leave. Our students' records and their time here is confidential. You should know that."

"Look, Mr. Albert, I appreciate your need to protect your students, but Eleanor's father has been murdered, and her mother is missing. You can appreciate how upset she is. Don't you want to help her?"

He paused for a moment, then sat back in his chair. "You're working for whom?"

"I can't tell you that, but I can say that Eleanor is aware I'm here and looking into the case."

"If this request was coming from the police, I might be forced to cooperate, but you're only a PI."

Only a PI? Until recently I was simply a snoopy gal. Would he be more impressed with that?

"I need your help so Eleanor can have some peace. And there's the matter of her mother. This is the best place to start looking for her." I tried for my best pleading look, and it must have worked.

He sighed and sat forward. "I'll take you to the library. You can look through the yearbooks there. Maybe they will be of help. But that's all." He signaled me to follow him out of his office. We headed down a hallway and then up a flight of stairs. A bell rang, signaling the end of a class period. Doors opened, and students streamed out into the hallway. Mr. Albert said something to me, but his words were lost in the din.

"Do you understand?" he asked.

I nodded agreement to whatever he had said. I was anxious to begin my work. He opened a door and ushered me into a room filled with shelves of books and about twenty tables, each one with seats for eight students.

"This is Mrs. Falco, our librarian. Ms. Appel is interested in looking at some of our yearbooks." He did not explain why I needed the yearbooks, but Mrs. Falco, an older woman with curly gray hair, nodded and showed me to a table.

"I'll find them for you. What years?"

I told her.

"I'll leave you to it. Just remember what I said," he said.

"Of course."

Mrs. Falco returned with the yearbooks, and she and Mr. Albert spoke for a moment. With a final warning glance, he left.

"You must have worked here for a while. It didn't take you any time to find those books," I said.

Her face softened a bit at my compliment.

"Yes, for thirty-five years. I'm retiring this coming year." She looked around the large room with nostalgia. "I'll miss it."

"I'll bet the kids will miss you. Did you ever think of how many children you touched in all those years? The woman who was the librarian in my school turned me on to Agatha Christie. She's still one of my favorites."

This time her face lit up with a smile. "Oh, I love

her too. I reread her when I have the time. I guess I'll have more time soon."

A student approached us and tapped her on the shoulder. "I can't find this book," he said.

"Did you try the return cart, Donald? I remember it just came back in this morning." She scurried away to help the student locate the book.

I had guessed correctly at Eleanor's age, and the yearbooks chronicled her journey from freshman to senior. Or, I should say, *would* have chronicled her journey. The years were correct and her class pictures were there each year, but as for any school activities, Eleanor was missing. Individual pictures senior year listed club memberships, offices held, and one-line predictions for the student's future such as "most likely to become a millionaire" or "headed for Hollywood." Under Eleanor's picture there were no club memberships or offices and the odd prediction, "When Turtle Girl comes out of her shell, what will she be?" I assumed she had kept to herself and was shy. Well, if she had come out of her shell, she'd emerged as a very odd girl indeed.

A shadow fell on the page. It was Mrs. Falco.

"I see you're interested in Eleanor Montrose. Principal Albert told me."

"Yes. Did you know her?"

"I think I knew her better than anyone here." She sighed and looked out the window. "But then, no one really knew Eleanor."

EIGHT

Mrs. Falco told me she had been warned by Principal Albert to be wary of me. "I don't trust him," she sniffed. "Too rule-bound."

I confessed to her who I was, and what I was doing. Not everything, of course. I left out that Eleanor thought she and I shared the same mother.

"Can you help me? I need to know as much about Eleanor and her family as I can."

She nodded. "Not here. I leave the school grounds for a lunch break in the park a block away. Meet me there at noon. Mr. Albert advised me you weren't to wander around the halls talking to anyone, but I'll bet you lose your way and find Amy Winthrop's office. She's the school counselor. I don't know if Eleanor talked with her or if she would be willing to say anything about Eleanor, but turn left out of here and her office is the first door on your right."

I looked both ways to make certain Mr. Albert wasn't around, then I dashed down the hall and knocked on Ms. Winthrop's door. Amy Winthrop was a petite woman dressed in casual slacks and a white blouse. With the exception of her short haircut, Amy reminded me of Madeleine—perky, a twinkle in her eye, and an open nature that made you want to tell her everything about your life.

"Ms. Winthrop," I said and held out my hand to shake hers.

"Actually, it's Doctor, but around here we're informal, so it's Amy to you and the staff, students, and parents. What can I help you with?" She gestured me toward a chair, and she took the one nearby. No hiding behind her desk. I liked that.

I introduced myself, told her I was a PI exploring the murder of Mr. Montrose, and of my discussion with Mrs. Falco.

"I heard about Mr. Montrose's death and have been worried about Eleanor," she said. "We got word her mother had gone off somewhere. Before we go on, I must tell you that I can't say much about Eleanor because—"

"Confidentiality. I know."

"That, and the fact that I don't know much about her. She never came to my office to seek my counsel."

"Yet you seem to be worried about someone you don't know. Can you tell me why?"

"Let's just say her mother was an issue."

"Her mother?"

Amy stared out the window for a moment, then leaned forward in her chair. "It's a matter of public record, anyway. Eleanor's mother came into my office one day, mad as hell. She accused me of advising her daughter to suggest she get professional help—the mother, I mean. Of course, I had nothing to do with that because Eleanor never came to me, but I'm pretty sure she did tell her mother to get help because she needed it. The mother wouldn't leave, was very agitated, and launched herself across the desk at me. I buzzed for security, and they came and escorted her off the school grounds. Well, actually, they had to wrestle her off the grounds. Her husband showed up and calmed her down. As I said, I never met Eleanor, but I felt sorry for that girl. That was one of the many times her mother contacted the school with some wild story. The police might be of help to you. I know these incidents came to their attention over the years."

No wonder Eleanor had kept such a low profile here. She'd been trying to fly under the radar in an effort to prevent her mother from making any more scenes and to save herself from the inevitable taunts of the class-mates who'd witnessed these unpleasant events. Poor Eleanor. Her mother was nothing like my mother, an-other flaw in Eleanor's story.

"You seem somehow relieved to hear about how unhinged the woman was."

"Oh, sorry. I was thinking of something else." I got out of my chair, thanked her, and left for the police sta-tion. I knew more about Eleanor's life now, but noth-ing seemed linked to my father-in-law. Perhaps there was no link. Regardless, the background I was putting together had to be relevant to Mr. Montrose's murder.

Nappi had dropped me at the high school and taken the SUV to make his inquiries. We were to meet later at the motel to exchange information. I checked my watch to make certain I had enough time before I was to meet Mrs. Falco for lunch. I could walk to the po-lice station and then to the park. I had plenty of time to stroll the tree-lined streets of the village.

The town was small and lovely, summer coming on in full force, the trees leafed out in dark shades of green. It reminded me of places in Connecticut where Madeleine and I grew up. The villages there were more affluent than this one, but it appeared the merchants here were attempting to attract tourists who might be coming through on their way to the resorts in the Catskills or heading north to climb the Adirondack peaks. The main street boasted a cute little coffee shop and several stores offering gifts and clothing. One shop featured equipment for camping, fishing, backpacking and displayed canoes and kayaks for sale and rent.

I'd read that the area had been flooded last fall by a hurricane that worked its way up the coast and stalled over parts of rural New York. We'd been spared the wrath of the storm in Florida, but its torrential rains had wiped out entire villages here. I could still see the water line on some of the buildings. The cleanup must have been overwhelming. I wondered how much damage the storm did to residences. Eleanor had said nothing about the storm, so I assumed her parents' house had been spared.

Tucked in between a hardware store and an eatery, the police station looked as if it had taken a hit from the fall storm. One of the plate-glass windows on the right side of the entrance was boarded up with plywood. I understood. Town budgets weren't equipped for many emergencies, especially damage from a hurricane.

The foyer of the station was anything but welcoming. There was a bench and a reception window with a sign on the wall beside it that read, "Ring bell for attention." I did, and a woman in uniform appeared.

Her smiling face lit up the cold room. "Can I help you?"

I told her I wanted to talk to someone about the Montrose family.

"Isn't that just awful? I heard about Mr. Montrose. Now all the daughter has for family is her mother." The

officer made a face, eyes wide with sorrow for Eleanor's loss but lips tight with disdain—I assumed for
the mother. I showed her my PI license from Florida.
She took it and said she'd be right back. I roved the
small area, reading the posters about bicycle safety
and a notice of a village board meeting tacked to a
bulletin board.

After a few minutes, the door to the right of the window opened, and the officer ushered me in.

"Chief Raleigh is through there," she said, pointing
toward a door. "Can I get you coffee?"

I shook my head and proceeded toward the door. Before I could knock, it opened, and a tall, sandy-haired
man gestured me into the room.

"Bunny offer you coffee? Bunny, could you get me
one? Thanks. Have a seat. You're here about the Montrose murder? Did the police department hire you to
look into it?"

"No, another party, and...."

"You can't say who. I get it."

"From everything I've learned, Mrs. Montrose
seems to have the temperament for murder, and she's
missing, you know."

Chief Raleigh looked at me in surprise. "I guess you
don't know everything about the family if you'd say
that. Mrs. Montrose would be the last woman to kill her
husband. He was the person she seemed to trust, the
one who could control her. With the kind of abuse Eleanor suffered at that woman's hands, I'd take a closer
look at the daughter. I felt sorry for the girl, but she
has to have stored up a lot of resentment with regard
to her mother over the years. It could have spilled over
to the father for not protecting her." He paused for a

moment, looking closely at me. "Say, you remind me of the mother a bit. Same blonde hair and blue eyes. If Eleanor didn't have brown hair, she'd look just like your sister."

"So people have told me."

The chief's friendly demeanor faded. It wasn't replaced by animosity or suspicion exactly, but he seemed less open and more cautious. "You aren't a relative, are you?"

"Certainly not. Lots of people have blonde hair and blue eyes."

"Sure. Now, how can I help you?"

I liked his forthright manner, so I decided to reciprocate by being truthful up front. It was the best way to get the most information from him. "You're right. I don't know much about the family. I only recently met Eleanor, and I must say, she's a little, uh, odd."

He gave a small laugh. "That she is, but it's understandable, with the mother she has. The girl had few friends because the mother embarrassed and humiliated her every chance she got."

"How do you know this?"

"I heard her do it. We'd get called in because of a disturbance at the school or in the local supermarket or even out on the street. It would be Mrs. Montrose ranting about something, often about how ungrateful the daughter was, how she should never have left her first husband and child, how perfect they were, compared to Eleanor."

"She was married before?"

"That's what she said. She would talk endlessly about living in Connecticut and sailing on the sound there. An ideal life, it seemed. Why she married Montrose, I can't figure, but he was a kind man and he tried to give her and Eleanor a good life. He just couldn't hold down a job, probably because he had her on his hands."

Sailing? On the sound? I gulped and gripped the arms of the chair.

"Say, you look kinda green around the gills. You're not going to faint, are you?"

"Certainly not. I've never fainted in my life."

And then everything went black.

I AWOKE LYING on the leather couch in Chief Raleigh's office. Someone was patting my hand, and someone had placed a cold, damp cloth on my head.

"Who hit me?" I asked.

The chief looked at me with concern. "No one. You fainted."

"Impossible. I'm not a fainting kind of person." I tried to sit up, and the world spun around me. My vision narrowed and I felt nauseated.

"Well, you are now, miss," said the female officer patting my hand. "You'd better rest here a minute."

The door opened, and Nappi walked in.

"How did you get here?" I asked.

"I saw you come in earlier. One of the officers said you were back here. What happened?"

"And you are…?" asked Chief Raleigh.

"My uncle and my associate on this case," I interjected.

The chief gave Nappi a serious once-over. "You look familiar."

"I'm a familiar-looking guy," Nappi said, introducing himself and shaking the chief's hand. "You know how it is, Chief. You live long enough, and everybody looks like someone you've met before."

The chief nodded, unconvinced.

"I think your niece could use a bit of a lie-down," said the female officer. "She still looks a little peaked. It could be a summer cold. It's going around."

I still felt shaky, but it wasn't a cold. It was what the chief had said about Eleanor's mother sailing on the sound. It hit too close to home, too close to what my mother did with my father, and—I reminded myself— how they died.

"I think I do need some rest," I said. I held out a hand, and Nappi helped me to my feet. We left police headquarters and got into Nappi's car parked outside. He looked at me closely as I buckled my seatbelt.

"Something's wrong," he said.

I told him about Mrs. Montrose's rants about living in Connecticut and sailing and of her first husband and daughter. All my attempts to reason away what Chief Raleigh had told me failed. Something seemed to burst inside me, and I gave way to tears. Patting me gently on the shoulder, Nappi let me have my hysterical cry, then handed me his clean white monogrammed linen handkerchief.

"I couldn't," I said.

"Take it. I have hundreds more, and it's far better that you get this one soppy than have snot running down your face. It's not a pretty sight."

I looked at him, thinking his comment was shocking and just plain mean, but he winked at me, and we both broke out in laughter.

"As if Eve Appel ever would stoop to letting snot

run out of her nose. You look appealing even when you cry."

"Really?" I said, glancing at my image in the rear-view mirror.

"No, but my lie got your mind off crying. I hate to ask and bring it up again, but what was that cry about?"

"Don't you see? It's possible Eleanor is right. Her mother was my mother. And Grandy lied to me. My mother has been alive all these years."

Nappi was silent, tapping his manicured nails against the burl-wood steering wheel. "So you're willing to believe the story of a crazy woman?"

"We don't know she was crazy. Maybe she was just stressed. If my father was a violent man and she ran away from him by staging that sailing accident, she must have been terrified. And if he wasn't dead, then she had to have lived in fear he would find her and her new family."

Nappi started the car. "We need to talk, someplace other than in front of the police station. Makes me nervous. Let's go back to the motel."

"I know what you're going to say. You'll defend Grandy, but she had to have known." I tried to put the brakes on thoughts that raced to grab onto the possibility my mother was still alive. I wanted that to be true. Or did I? It meant betrayal by the one who had raised me—Grandy.

"Look, Eve, if this woman did stage the accident and was running away from a man she feared, why would she let anyone know? If the story is true, Grandy wouldn't have known."

I thought about his words as we sped down the village streets toward our motel. He made sense. My heart was pounding out of my chest. I knew something was wrong with believing Mrs. Montrose was my mother. I couldn't imagine the woman I'd known as my mother embarrassing or abusing any child of hers. And my father, an abuser of my mother? That couldn't be. I felt nausea stirring in my stomach again.

"You okay, Eve?" asked Nappi. He reached over and patted my hand.

"Sure." But I wasn't okay. I might never be okay again. The wonderful world of just a few weeks ago with my husband, sons, and family had been broken by the loss again of Sammy's father and the possibility that he'd killed someone, and I couldn't shake this strange and upsetting story about my parents. I couldn't imagine how life could be put right.

"I CHECKED AROUND TOWN and found out where the Montroses lived. The property is being managed by a real estate agency. I've got an appointment to meet the agent. Mr. Montrose put the house in the agent's hands to look after when he left town to look for his daughter and wife. I talked the agent into letting me see the house this afternoon." Nappi leaned back in the upholstered chair in my room while I lounged on the bed.

I thought about what kind of talking he did with the agent. He could be very persuasive, I knew. I just hoped it hadn't entailed any physical threats this time.

"Oh, don't look so worried, Eve. The agent was a lovely woman, around my own age. We hit it off right away. It might be a good idea for all three of us to have dinner tonight. She's a treasure trove of information about his town."

When he said "treasure trove of information," it brought to mind my own treasure trove, Mrs. Falco.

"What time is it?" I asked, sitting upright and looking at my watch. "I've got an appointment at noon."

Nappi jumped out of his chair and pushed me back into the pillows. "You're not going anywhere."

"I feel fine now." I told him about Mrs. Falco.

"I'll drive you there and come with you."

"You can drive me, but I think it would be better if I talk to her alone. She might be put off by your smooth sophistication."

Nappi smiled knowingly. "You mean she might think I look like a mobster."

I gave him an appraising look. "No, I meant what I said. You look like an urban sophisticate—you know, sophisticated in a 'connected' sort of way."

"And she'll think I look like a mobster. I'll sit in the car and wait for you, out of sight."

NAPPI DROPPED ME at the entrance to the park. I spotted Mrs. Falco on a bench near the fountain, sitting in the shade of a maple tree and eating her lunch. She greeted me, and I joined her on the bench.

"Nothing for lunch?" she asked.

"I'm not hungry." Hmm, I wasn't hungry—an odd experience for me. I always wanted to eat.

Once Mrs. Falco got to talking about the Montrose family, she provided more details about Eleanor's odd mother. As Chief Raleigh said, the mother couldn't seem to appear in public without causing some kind of a scene. Usually it took the form of yelling at someone, a store clerk or a passerby, and accusing them of trying to "take her back."

"What did that mean?" I asked.

"No one got it at first. I think we all thought she was talking about ghosts or something trying to carry her off to the world of the dead, but Mr. Montrose told a friend of mine that his wife had been in a mental hospital and didn't want to go back there. It explained a lot."

"What hospital?"

"Mr. Montrose didn't say. I think a number of people thought she should be committed, but he wouldn't hear of it. He seemed to be able to calm her down, and he was the only one who could. She seemed to despise Eleanor. 'That hateful child,' she always called Eleanor. I know County Social Services was notified on occasion, but when a social worker came to the house, Mrs. Montrose was always calm and Mr. Montrose didn't want their help. I guess they figured he was able to handle his wife and protect Eleanor. Aside from Mrs. Montrose's public displays, no one saw much of the family. They kept to themselves."

They were hiding something, something I needed to know.

"They lived here for how long?"

"Since Eleanor was in high school. I don't have any idea where they moved here from. Maybe the school records would say."

"I'd sure like to see those records, but I'd be the last person the principal would show them to." I looked imploringly at Mrs. Falco, who understood what I wasn't saying.

"You think it's that important?" she asked.

"I'm sure it is."

She crumpled up her sandwich wrappings and rose to her feet. "Well, then, I guess I'll have to have a talk with the principal's secretary, Mrs. Dorren, about making certain his office door isn't left unlocked the way it is in the late afternoon when he walks the halls checking the classrooms."

"A wise precaution," I said.

"Mrs. Dorren agrees with me. She thinks the principal is a bit of a pill also. We can trust her."

We walked to the park entrance and stopped there. I spotted Nappi's car parked around the corner. Mrs. Falco assured me she'd get in touch tomorrow evening. She turned to walk down the sidewalk, while I started to step off the curb to cross the street. I waved to Nappi, a spring in my step. With those school records, I might be able to track down Eleanor's past, a past she had been reluctant to talk about. I heard the squeal of tires on the pavement and spotted a blur of black as a car careened around the corner from my left. I heard Mrs. Falco cry out and then felt someone grab my arm and pull me back onto the curb. I stumbled and fell as the car roared past me.

"That driver tried to run you down," said Mrs. Falco, helping me to my feet. "Are you hurt?"

I looked down and saw a ripped knee in my jeans and one of my classy red stiletto-heel shoes lying crushed in the gutter. Some blood trickled down my elbow from where I'd scraped it on the pavement.

Nappi rushed up to me, saw the look on my face, and followed my mournful glance as I assessed my mangled shoe.

"That could have been you," he said.

NINE

"You know this man?" asked Mrs. Falco, giving Nappi a stern look.

"He's my associate." The close call with the car was beginning to sink in, and I felt an attack of the jitters coming on. "I think I'd better sit down." I collapsed on the curb and tucked my head between my knees. *Damn.* This fainting thing was getting too familiar.

"I'll call the police," said Mrs. Falco, extracting her cellphone from her purse.

The spinning sensation stopped, and I lifted my head, noting Nappi's discomfort at the prospect of Mrs. Falco calling the police.

"A bad driver. He took the corner too fast, that's all," said Nappi.

"No he didn't. It was deliberate." Mrs. Falco turned away to complete her call while Nappi and I exchanged knowing looks. Someone didn't like all the questions we were asking and had decided to let us know that. Did the driver intend to run me down or just frighten me?

"I'll be fine. I just need to lie down for a bit." It seemed I was doing a lot of lying down today. I hoped it wouldn't become a habit or I'd be the only PI who investigated crime from her bed.

A police car pulled up, and Chief Raleigh jumped out of the passenger seat. The look he gave me was filled with concern for my wellbeing, but his wrinkled brow also expressed something else. Suspicion.

"It seems as if you're having a bad day in our little town. First a visit to my office and you faint, and now someone tries to run you down. Or more likely, they were aiming for your associate here." His glance took in Nappi.

"What?" I said. "He was in his car over there, not here."

"Perhaps your hit-and-run driver targeted you as a warning to pick better associates."

"Now wait a minute, Chief. This man is both my friend and my associate. We've been acquainted for years and—"

"Not your uncle?" he said with an edge of sarcasm. "I assume you're aware of his connections?" Confronting Nappi, he added, "I thought I recognized you. You were one of the people arrested several years ago in connection with a crime syndicate in the Boston area."

"I was released," Nappi said. "No charges were filed."

"I know all about Nappi," I said. Well, really I didn't. In fact, I'd made a point of not knowing about Nappi. I knew his generosity and his sense of loyalty to his friends. Other than that, I stayed out of his business.

The chief gave me a long stare. "Okay. We'll let it go for now. Did anyone get a license number of the car?"

We all shook our heads.

"Can you describe the vehicle?"

"It was black, or dark blue, I think," said Mrs. Falco.

Nappi stepped forward. "It was a black SUV, much like mine." He gestured toward his Escalade. "I didn't see the driver's face."

"And you're sure it was intentionally trying to run down Ms. Appel?"

"Yes," said Mrs. Falco.

"It seemed that way," said Nappi.

The chief looked at me. I was still sitting on the curb, gazing sadly at my ruined shoe. "What do you have to say about all of this, Ms. Appel?"

I gazed up at him, too tired and nauseated to be of any help. "I just want to lie down."

The chief's face softened for a moment. "You need a doctor?"

"No, I'm just a little disgusted with how people drive in your town," I said. "All in all, this hasn't been a good day for me."

The chief held out his hand and helped me to my feet. "I can assure you that most of our citizens don't target visitors for a hit-and-run. I'll put out an APB for the SUV. It was an SUV, Ms. Appel?"

"I didn't see it. I was busy kissing the curb." Well, at least my sense of humor had returned. "Nappi, could you take me back to the motel now?"

The chief got back in the police car and left with a backward look that said he'd prefer we finish our business here and leave town as soon as possible.

"The chief doesn't like you," said Mrs. Falco to Nappi. "He's worried you've come here to cause trouble. Have you?"

"No. I'm here to help my friend, and that's all."

I saw Mrs. Falco think about what he said for a minute, and I worried I'd lost the chance to get those school records on Eleanor.

"If she trusts you, I guess that's good enough for me."

"I'll drive you back to the school," offered Nappi.

Mrs. Falco shook her head. "I think it would be better for me not to be seen with you. No offense."

"No offense taken. You're being smart," said Nappi.

"And you'll be of more use in my investigation if you fly under the radar," I said.

"Oh, yes," Mrs. Falco agreed. From the barely suppressed delight in her voice, I realized Mrs. Falco was having a fine time being witness to a crime and an undercover informant to my investigation.

"Do you know Betsy Morelli?" asked Nappi.

"The real estate agent. Of course," answered Mrs. Falco. "Why do you ask?"

"I was thinking we all might like to get together tonight at the Dancing Bear Inn. I hear the food is quite good. I would be delighted to have yet another lovely lady join us for dinner if you're free."

Out of the corner of my eye, I caught the look on Mrs. Falco's face. It was the usual response Nappi got when he turned on the charm. Her smile was so broad, I worried the corners of her mouth would be permanently fixed in a silly grin.

"You're something, you are," she said. I was certain I heard her giggle. Nappi had that effect on women, and he never engaged in false flattery to win their affection. Mrs. Falco, with her gray curls and dignified way of carrying herself, was indeed "lovely." She agreed to dinner.

Nappi wanted to drive me to the emergency room, but I was adamant. I was fine, just a little tired. He walked me to my motel room and let me know he had other errands in town to attend to. I told him to go ahead and didn't inquire what he meant by "errands." I knew he'd tell me after he did whatever he was going to do. I hoped it didn't involve breaking any laws. With the police chief already suspicious about us, any crime around here, including jaywalking, was likely to be laid at our feet. If Nappi acted menacing while extracting information from a source, that might land him in jail. Of course, Nappi's menacing usually took the form of a smile so cold it could reverse global warming.

I assured him I felt fine, and I did. Well, I was a little shaky, but anyone would be after almost being run down. And my stomach continued to jump around. I grabbed a coke from the minibar to settle it.

I sipped my soda and felt better. Now that the chief had identified Nappi, I figured our information-gathering in town was almost at an end. The chief of police wanted us gone, and the principal hadn't liked me from the start.

I thought about Mrs. Falco and the real estate agent. I was anxious to get those school records. I hadn't had the opportunity to talk with Nappi about what he might have gleaned from his meeting with Ms. Morelli, the agent, but dinner tonight should prove interesting. A little food and a good bottle of wine plus Nappi's charm could loosen any woman's tongue.

I called Grandy and Sammy to see how things were going back home. They had nothing new to report about Sammy's father, but were anxious to hear how Nappi and I were faring. I knew better than to mention the hit-and-run incident. Grandy would have been on the first plane up here, accompanied by Sammy, and they would have hauled my butt back to Sabal Bay.

"How's Eleanor?" I asked Grandy. "I wish I'd had more time to talk with her before Nappi and I headed up here."

"She and Jerry seem to have gotten very close," Grandy replied.

I groaned inwardly, but tried to put the best spin on it I could. "Maybe Eleanor has confided more about her past and family to him."

"Do you want me to have a talk with him?" Grandy asked.

"No. I'll give him a call and see what I can find out."

Sammy sounded hopeful that his father might walk out of the swamps any day as he had done before. "I take the canoe out each night after I close down the air-boat business, in case he wants to make contact with me out in the swamps. So far there's been no sign of him."

"I don't think he trusts anyone, certainly not white people, and he may feel you've been corrupted by white culture." When I said "white people," I meant me. I heard Sammy sigh at my remark.

"You're right."

"I've got an idea," I said. "Call your mother in Las Vegas. She might have some ideas on how to approach him." I had meant to get in touch with Renata, but hadn't had time before Nappi and I left for New York. Having Sammy call her might make him feel as if he was helping his father. It was a long shot. Sammy's father and mother had been married for a short time before he took his long trip to the swamps. I'd met her once, and found her to be a savvy woman. We had to use all the resources we could think of.

My suggestion met with silence.

"She's white, too. If Dad got wind of my talking with her and asking all kinds of questions, it might drive him away from me."

How Mr. Egret might find out about Sammy contacting his mother, I couldn't imagine, but it wasn't worth running the risk of alienating him.

"You're right," I said. If I thought she might provide us with any insights into Lionel Egret, I could still make the call.

In the background, I heard the boys clamoring for a chance to talk with me. Sammy gave up the phone to them, and we talked about school and the upcoming junior rodeo that all three boys were taking part in. They had been practicing riding and calf roping at their cousins' ranch over on the Brighton Seminole reservation.

"You'll be back to see us ride, won't you, Mommy?" said my youngest. This would be the first year he could take part in real rodeo events. In past years he had been too young and could only enter the "mutton busters" competition at the annual rodeo. The year before last, he'd won by riding the sheep for several seconds beyond the buzzer. He slid onto the sheep's underside halfway through the ride, but he hung on to the belly until they pulled him off. Determined little guy. This year he saw his previous victory as "kids' stuff," and announced he was ready to take on the grownup events.

I promised I would be at the rodeo, and then made smacky-kissy sounds on the phone when we said goodbye. Sammy took over again and told me he loved me. I said the same and asked him to tell Grandfather hello.

"He's worried about you, Eve. He thinks something bad might happen to you."

I forced a laugh, guaranteed him I would be fine, and said I would call tomorrow. Disconnecting, I looked across the room at my shoes lying on the floor, one of them smashed flat. Maybe Grandfather had a right to be worried.

I decided to check with Jerry to make certain he had gotten the DNA analysis rolling.

There was a note of caution in his voice when he answered my call.

"I know I'm not your favorite person, Jerry, but something's up. What is it?"

"Nothing."

"Don't lie to me. I can always tell."

"Eleanor's right here. Do you want to talk to her?"

"No, I want you to tell me what's going on."

"Just a minute."

I heard noise in the background and then Jerry's voice. "I had to step outside for better reception."

"Okay. What is it you don't want Eleanor to hear?"

"I didn't do that DNA thing."

I sighed. "You're testing my patience, Jerry. I ask you to do one little thing and you refuse?"

"I told you. I'm trying to be a better person, and Eleanor thinks I am an okay guy. I'm not going to go behind her back."

"Now is one heck of a time to decide to improve your character."

"Gotta go, Eve."

"Jerry!"

He was gone.

I heard a light tap at my door. "Are you awake?" It was Nappi. I got out of bed, noting how stiff I was, and opened the door to let him in.

"Did you manage to sleep any?" he asked.

I shook my head. "I talked to Grandy, Sammy, and the boys."

"You look angry. What's up?"

"I talked with Jerry, and he was his usual annoying self." I waved my arm. "It was nothing." I'd find another way to get DNA from Eleanor.

Nappi hesitated, waiting for me to explain further, but I shook my head and gave him a smile of encouragement.

"I stopped by the police station to talk again with Chief Raleigh," Nappi said and confirmed what I had guessed the chief was thinking about the two of us. Nappi continued, "He thinks the attempt to run you down was a warning meant for me. He'd prefer we move on. He'll investigate the incident, of course, but he's certain whoever was involved had to be *my* enemy. His reasoning is that it was my presence that provoked the incident. An old vendetta against me is his take on it. According to his theory, if we leave, we'll take my connections with me, and his town will be safe."

"Could he be correct about someone wanting to pay you back for something?" I asked.

"We both know whoever tried to run you down did it because we're snooping into Mr. Montrose's murder. It has nothing to do with my 'Family' connections."

"It was a long shot, but you tried to talk with him."

"He's just protecting his town. I understand. I stopped by to see how you're doing. Your color is better."

"I feel just fine except for a little stiffness. Don't you have an appointment this afternoon with the real estate agent?"

He nodded.

"I want to come along."

"Are you sure?"

"You're not leaving me out of that meeting. It is my investigation. You're along for support. You're not supposed to be doing most of the work."

He gave a heavy sigh. "Somehow I knew you'd say that."

"Good. I'll grab another pair of shoes and meet you downstairs."

He left with a wave. I picked up my ruined stiletto heels, gave them a final sad look, and tossed them into the garbage.

Nappi had gotten the Montroses' home address from Betsy Morelli, who arranged to meet us at the house with the key. We found the address on a street lined with small houses built after World War II. Most of them were well kept, yards mowed and flowerbeds starting to show the colors of blooming hydrangea, iris, and recently planted petunias. We parked out front until Ms. Morelli pulled in behind us. The Montroses' house was one of the small bungalows, but unlike its neighbors, it was in need of paint. One of the front window shutters hung at an angle, waiting for a strong wind to tear it off. All three of us stood for a moment looking at the house. Nappi introduced me to Betsy, then we headed up a broken concrete sidewalk for the front door. It was ajar.

Nappi stepped in front of Betsy and motioned me back. "Wait here, and if you hear anything or I don't come back out, call the cops." He entered the house, and we waited.

In several minutes Nappi appeared, signaling us to enter.

"Oh, my heavens," said Betsy. "Someone's been here and—"

"They searched the house. Every room is like this." Nappi gestured toward the living room. All the furniture had been turned upside down, the upholstery ripped open, books in the bookcase taken out and opened, then tossed on the floor.

"The office is worse," Nappi said. "All the desk drawers were pulled out, the file cabinet there gone through. Anywhere something could be hidden has been examined. A very thorough search. When was the last time you checked the house?"

Betsy pulled her organizer out of her briefcase. "I was in the house a week ago Saturday. I picked up the mail. They don't get much. Mostly bills. I put them on the kitchen table." She walked into the kitchen. "They're gone."

"Can you remember anything other than bills?" I asked.

Betsy thought for a moment. "There was a statement from the bank."

"I think whoever was in here was looking for a number of things, including a clue about the Montroses' present location. A credit card bill and a bank statement might provide that, but those items were in plain sight. From the extent of the search, the intruder or intruders wanted something else. I think we can be sure they now know where the Montroses went. Now we have to wonder if the intruder or intruders followed the Montroses to Sabal Bay, and did they find what else they were looking for?" said Nappi.

"Could they have been responsible for Mr. Montrose's death? And why?" I asked.

"The police couldn't have done this, could they?" asked Betsy. "When we heard Mr. Montrose had been killed, I notified the police that he had asked me to look after the house."

"This is not the way police conduct a search," Nappi said.

"Maybe our hit-and-run driver also has a penchant for breaking and entering," I suggested.

"Hit-and-run?" asked Betsy.

Nappi told her about my close call earlier in the day.

"Well, I guess we'd better call the police," I said.

"If you don't mind, Betsy, would you call them? I think they've had enough of Eve and me for one day."

Betsy, being the smart lady she was, nodded. "I'll say I was checking on the house. I won't mention you."

As Nappi and I drove out of the neighborhood, I examined the houses to see if anyone was at home. When the police responded to Betsy's call, they'd be certain to talk with the Montroses' neighbors, who might report another car besides Betsy's at the house. Chief Raleigh would probably enjoy bringing Nappi and me in for questioning about the Montrose break-in.

"We're all still on for dinner tonight. We can pool our information then. I'm curious what Chief Raleigh will think of this turn of events." Nappi chuckled.

"What do you find so funny? He'll blame us," I suggested.

"He might like to, but he's too smart for that. He'll call Frida for sure, since it's certain he learned about Montrose's murder through the Sabal Bay Police Department."

"Wouldn't it be nice if she recommended he work part of the case through his end, like bringing us into it once he takes a look at the house," I said.

"Not likely," Nappi replied.

DINNER AT THE Dancing Bear Restaurant that night was everything we'd been told it would be: great ambience provided by a view of a stream cascading over boulders lit by outdoor lights, excellent service, and an extensive menu of steak, chicken, and seafood items. My stomach was back to its normal state of growling for large portions of protein and the desire to cap it all off with something chocolate.

We chatted through our before-dinner drinks and appetizers and were awaiting our salads when Mrs. Falco tapped me on the shoulder,

"I could use a visit to the facilities. How about you, Eve?" She signaled me by moving her eyes toward the restroom that she wanted a private word. Neither Nappi nor Betsy gave much notice as we left.

In the restroom, Mrs. Falco removed a file folder from the large purse she was carrying. "That hit-and-run worried me. It felt like someone didn't want you to look too closely at the Montroses, so here you go. Can you read it tonight and get it back to me in the morning so I can return it to the office first thing?"

"Of course." I took the folder and tucked it under the sweater I wore.

"I feed the ducks in the morning before school. Same park," she said.

I nodded and took her arm as we left.

Nappi and Betsy looked up at us as we returned to the table.

"Girl talk," I said.

Nappi winked at me.

As WE LEFT the restaurant, Nappi told me to buckle up and hold on.

"What's going on?" I asked as he slid around a corner and accelerated, then stomped on the brakes and steered into an alleyway, turning off his lights as he did so. In the rearview mirror, we saw an SUV similar to Nappi's drive past. We waited a few more minutes, then backed out of the alley. The SUV was gone. Nappi continued toward the motel.

"I thought I spotted someone tailing us to the restaurant. Smart of you and Mrs. Falco to have your girlie pass-off alone in the ladies room instead of at the table."

"How did you know?" I asked.

"You made crinkling sounds when you got back. I guessed you might have something up your sleeve. Or somewhere on you." He smiled.

"Very funny. I stowed it there so it wouldn't get béarnaise sauce on it."

"Thank you for your culinary sensitivity." He checked the rearview mirror once more. "All clear."

Back in my room, I took a quick look at the files Mrs. Falco had passed me, but I was too stuffed with food and too exhausted to examine them closely. I brushed my teeth and fell into bed. The next thing I knew it was morning. I turned on the in-room coffee maker and jumped into the shower.

I DRESSED AND was about to leave to meet Mrs. Falco in the park when the phone in my room rang.

"This is Chief Raleigh. We're at Mrs. Falco's house. Her neighbor called us about an hour ago saying he had heard loud noises coming from her place. We responded and found her tied up in her bedroom. The house has been ransacked."

"Is she okay?" I asked.

Before he could reply, my cell rang. "Hold a minute, would you?"

I looked at the cell and recognized the number as Jerry's. That couldn't be good. I answered. "This is a bad time, Jerry. I'll call you back."

"I can't find Eleanor. She's run away."

TEN

"RUN AWAY? YOU were supposed to keep an eye on her,"
I yelled at Jerry.

"I know. I know."

"How long has she been gone?"

There was silence from Jerry.

"Well?"

"A few days after you left for New York, she told
me she needed some space."

"So, days then? And you are just now letting me
know?" I was about to ask him if he'd called Nappi
to tell him Eleanor has skipped, but realized Jerry
wouldn't have wanted to deal with Nappi's displea-
sure at not doing his job. Jerry thought he could get
around me.

"Where have you looked for her?" I asked. From
the receiver to the room's landline, I heard Chief Raleigh's voice.

"Hold on. I've got another emergency. Meantime,
Jerry, go look for her. Get Sammy or Max to help."

"I don't know where to look," Jerry whined.

"Well, figure it out. You've been with her. You did
talk to each other, didn't you? Think. I'll get back to
you when I can." I disconnected and turned my attention to Chief Raleigh.

"I can't spend the day on the phone with you, Ms.
Appel. I wanted to let you know about Mrs. Falco be-

cause she admitted she was doing some snooping for you. It looks to me as if agreeing to help you got her in trouble with someone. Maybe you'd like to tell me all about it at the station. Now." The line went dead.

I called Mrs. Falco's house. She answered on the first ring.

"Chief Raleigh just called me. Are you all right?"

"I'm fine. A bit shook up, but unharmed. I'm certain they were after information about Eleanor. I think they connected the two of us. I heard them mention your name and Eleanor's as they were searching my house. The thieves tried to make it look like a simple robbery by taking a few pieces of antique jewelry."

"They're not fooling anyone. The chief wants me down at the station, and I'm heading there now. Did you tell him about the school records?"

"No, dear. I thought that should remain between the two of us. I think they may try to look for information on Eleanor by visiting you. This has got to be related to the hit-and-run. You're in danger, Eve."

I WAS THANKFUL the thieves had not tried to force Mrs. Falco to tell them what she knew about Eleanor. Grabbing the folder with the records in it, I called Nappi to meet me in the motel lobby, and the two of us headed for the police station. Although Mrs. Falco had withheld information about the records from Chief Raleigh, he was a smart cop, smart enough to know that it was no coincidence that a hit-and-run had been quickly followed by break-ins at the Montrose house and Mrs. Falco's. And they didn't add up to a vendetta against Nappi.

In the car, I told Nappi what had happened with Mrs.

Falco but decided to put off telling him about Jerry's call. One thing at a time. I did have to call Jerry back, but I'd do that later.

"I don't want to jeopardize Mrs. Falco's position at the school, so I didn't tell the chief about the papers she 'borrowed' on my behalf. Chief Raleigh knows something is up and that it has to do with Eleanor."

"Let's see what he knows. Let him talk before you say anything."

Chief Raleigh proved to be an even smarter cop than I figured. He showed Nappi and me into a small room with a one-way mirror on the wall, gestured to two uncomfortable chairs behind a rickety table, and sat down across from us. He crossed his arms and said nothing. Judging from his stony expression, he was prepared to wait us out for hours.

Nappi gave me a knowing look and nodded toward my handbag on the floor at my feet. *Damn.*

Reaching down, I pulled the folder out of my purse and slapped it on the table.

"I don't want to get Mrs. Falco in trouble with the school. These are 'borrowed' from the files, and she intended to put them back today."

The chief's expression never wavered. He didn't look down at the folder or reach for it.

"In trouble with the school? You could have gotten her killed," he said. "Someone is interested enough in Eleanor or her family and in your being here to try to run you down and break into two houses searching for something. What's going on? I suggest you tell me what you know and how you're involved."

I acknowledged the truth about the danger to Mrs. Falco, an unintended consequence. She'd seemed so eager to help and so concerned about Eleanor. I should have thought through her involvement. I had enough information with the hit-and-run, the house break-in, and especially Mr. Montrose already lying dead on a slab at the Sabal Bay Mortuary to know someone wasn't opposed to using deadly force in this case.

"We've been honest with you. Don't blame Nappi. I'm the one responsible. I asked Mrs. Falco to get those records for me. There's nothing more to tell you because we're just as in the dark as you are." That was the truth, just not all of it. I didn't think it was necessary to tell him the police in Sabal Bay had a suspect on the run and that I was working for the suspect's family. And there was the matter of how I might or might not be related to the Montroses—information irrelevant to the Tillahook police, I told myself. Nappi said nothing to contradict me.

"Have you looked at these?" asked Chief Raleigh. He pulled the folder across the table and opened it.

"Briefly. I thought finding out where the Montrose family lived before they moved here might provide information about Eleanor's mother. I heard she was once in a mental hospital."

"You thought you could track her down there?" Chief Raleigh raised a skeptical eyebrow. "As if the hospital would open their records to a private investigator? Not a chance."

This PI's license was proving to be less useful than I had thought. It wasn't the entrée I'd hoped for.

"How about this? You help me with the hospital administrators, and I'll track down the perpetrators of the break-ins here and my hit-and-run."

Chief Raleigh tilted his head to one side as if looking at Nappi and me from another angle would provide some insight into what we were up to.

The chief leaned back in his chair, and his body visibly relaxed. "I talked at length on the phone this morning with your friend Detective Martinez. She assured me that you are a real pain in the you-know-what, but that you've been right on a number of cases you've interfer—uh, involved yourself in. You're, according to her, 'tenacious, smart, and haven't a shred of humility' in you when it comes to solving cases. She seems to like and respect you. She also told me that your companion here," the chief nodded toward Nappi, "is an okay guy.' I find that hard to believe, but I'll go along for now."

I started to thank him, but he held up his hand to stop me. "I'll go along for now because I don't have the staff to track down these thieves who may also be involved in an attempted vehicular homicide—yours, Ms. Appel. So, since the crimes in Tillahook seem to be related to your detective work, it's only right you should finish up on the case here."

I interpreted "finish up on our case here" to mean "get out of town as soon as possible."

"To do that," I said, "I need more information, and that means I have to go to the town where the Montroses lived and find out more about them, especially Eleanor's mother. So you can see I need your help." I tried to sound humble, but since Frida had already convinced the chief I was anything but, I was unsure if I'd succeeded.

"My 'help.' What does that mean?" He sounded unconvinced he could help in any way other than directing Nappi and me to the main road out of town.

"You continue to work the robberies and hit-and-run from here because you can get more from sources in the town than we can. We go to…" I pulled the file toward me to read the name of the school Eleanor had attended before Tillahook, "Monroe, Connecticut." The name of the town hadn't registered when I scanned the files before, but I recognized it now. Monroe was a small town a few miles from Madison where my family spent the summers sailing on the sound. For a moment I felt lightheaded. Nappi reached for my hand under the table and squeezed it. He knew what I was feeling. So close to home for me, too close. I could almost smell the salt air blowing off the water and feel the sand between my toes as I walked down to the city docks where our boat was docked.

I pushed back my memories. "What about the files?" I asked, pointing toward the folder.

"I'll return them to Mrs. Falco, and she can replace them when she has the, uh, the opportunity," Chief Raleigh said.

"Mrs. Falco was the source who told us Mrs. Montrose spoke of being committed to a mental hospital. I don't know if I'll be able to track down the facility where she stayed, but if I do, I'll let you know if there's something you can do to help us access information."

"That will be tricky and require a court order, which might be difficult to obtain. Detective Martinez and I will help as much as seems reasonable." The chief showed us out of his office and added, "Try to keep your detecting within the law, will you?" He gave Nappi a hard look.

"She's the PI," said Nappi. "I'm just along for company and to see she doesn't get into any trouble."

"Good luck with that," said Chief Raleigh with a twinkle in his eye.

We thanked the chief, agreeing we'd be in touch by phone to update each other on developments.

"THAT WAS UNNECESSARY," I said as I slid into the passenger seat. "When am I ever any trouble?"

Nappi laughed and started the engine.

"I'm good at finding trouble, but I rarely cause it."

"You're serious?" Nappi headed toward the motel.

"All of you friends and family see me so differently from the way I am."

Nappi turned his head, and his mouth dropped open in a look of disbelief.

"Keep your eyes on the road." I crossed my arms over my chest and thought back to our conversation with Chief Raleigh. "I'm a little offended by Frida's comment that I'm not humble. Do you think that's true?"

"How would I know? As you just pointed out, none of us see you the way you are."

I saw a twitch at the corner of his mouth.

"Never mind about me. There's a car that's been following us ever since we pulled away from the station."

"I saw it. We're going to have to lose them or we'll have these guys on our tail all the way to the Connecticut shore."

"This town is too small to lose them in. What do you have in mind?"

"As the chief said, he needs help here, and he doesn't have the personnel to pursue the case. We'll lead them out of town tomorrow morning. That should take their attention off this town if they think they can simply follow us where they need to go. Unless...."

"What?" I asked.

"Unless they were just trying to confirm what they

already knew from the earlier house break-in. It's clear they've been on our tail for some time."

"You mean they got the information they needed when they tossed the Montrose house? Why enter Mrs. Falco's place then?"

Nappi shrugged. "Maybe to be certain they were on the right track and to determine where we were heading. That's just a hunch. We'll see what happens tomorrow. We have plans for tonight."

"We do?"

"I'm cooking. You like my cooking, don't you?"

Yes, I did, but I was finding it difficult to see Nappi cooking up some Sicilian delicacy on a hot plate in his motel room. I mean, the man was a whiz in the kitchen, but a hot plate is a hot plate, not a five-burner range.

As it turned out, he had managed to finagle an invite from Betsy Morelli to invade her kitchen and do his culinary magic. Mrs. Falco joined the three of us, and Chief Raleigh even stopped in for coffee and dessert. According to Mrs. Falco, Eleanor's folder had found its way back into the school file cabinet.

No one mentioned the Montrose family or talked about the hit-and-run or the robberies. The talk was light, the dessert dreamy, and everyone seemed to have a pleasant time, even Chief Raleigh. Still, when he left at the end of the evening, he stopped in the doorway and gave me a stern look. "I'll look forward to hearing from you, Ms. Appel," he said.

BACK AT THE motel room, I called Sammy and said goodnight to the boys, making kissy sounds over the phone.

"Any news about Eleanor's whereabouts?" I asked.

"She seems to have vanished into thin air. I can't imagine where she could be or why she left," he told me.

"I can think of several reasons, and they all begin with Jerry. I think he put the moves on her and she felt crowded by his attentions. From what I've learned, the Montrose family members are good at keeping a low profile. Eleanor and her mother may not be easy to locate."

"Maybe it's not Jerry at fault here. He told me Eleanor was preoccupied the last few days he was with her. He also said she seemed worried and jittery, as if she expected something unpleasant to happen."

It sounded as if Eleanor was on the run again. But maybe she had word of her mother and was following a lead.

I had just disconnected with Sammy when my cell rang. It was Grandy, hopping mad. "I thought you might call, but no, I have to find out through my contacts that you were almost run down by a car and that you fainted at the police station."

"I didn't want to worry you. And what contacts are you talking about? I didn't tell anyone about that."

"Humph. Wouldn't you like to know?"

"I would. And I'd love it if you wouldn't let on to Sammy about my, uh, accidents."

"I'll keep my lip buttoned, but only if you keep me posted on anything that happened. I mean *anything*. Don't be using your no-one's-business-but-Eve's filter."

"Fine. I'm sorry. I should have let you know what was happening."

Grandy sounded more than just angry I hadn't called

her to tell her about my "accidents." I might not have Grandfather Egret's sixth sense, but I knew Grandy well enough to realize there was something else on her mind.

"So tell me," I said.

She chose to intentionally misinterpret what I was asking. "I found out about all this from Frida. She stopped by the shop today."

So Chief Raleigh had again been in contact with Frida, who then blabbed to Grandy.

"I waited for you to call, certain that you would want me to know." Her voice was still frosty.

"How long are you going to stay mad at me?" I asked.

She gave me one of those lines parents like to use. "As long as it takes."

"What in the world does that mean?" I asked to a line that had gone dead.

Whatever was bothering Grandy, aside from feeling I was leaving her out of the loop, she chose to keep it to herself. She'd tell me when she was good and ready or when pigs fly, whichever came first.

WHEN WE LEFT the motel the next morning, the car that had been following us earlier pulled in behind, dogged us until we headed south toward the highway, then dropped out of sight.

"They know where we're going. Just as I thought," Nappi said. The tension in his shoulders dropped away, and he let one hand rest on his knee, steering expertly with the other.

"So much for taking those guys off Chief Raleigh's hands."

"If I'm right in my suspicion that they're confirming we're heading for Connecticut, they won't bother Tillahook. They're interested in us."

"Were you worried about the tail?" I asked.

"I can handle the situation, and if it comes to that, I will. It's just nice for now not to have to think about it. We can enjoy the ride through the Berkshires." He tuned to a jazz station on satellite radio and began to tap his fingers in time to the music.

Lack of sleep and a delayed sense of what could have happened with the hit-and-run caught up to me. The music lulled me into sleep.

"Okay, Eve. Here we are in Monroe. Wake up," I heard Nappi say.

"How long did I sleep?"

"Over three hours. I've never seen you so tired. Are you sure you're okay? Maybe we can find a walk-in clinic. You took quite a spill when that car came for you. I should have insisted you get looked at then."

I was as surprised as Nappi that I'd fallen into such a deep sleep and for so long. When I got involved in a murder investigation, I survived on little sleep, a lot of barbecue ribs, and a few Scotches. And thinking of ribs, I realized it was after one in the afternoon. Breakfast had been more than four hours ago.

"I'm starved," I said, sitting up and examining my face in the mirror on the visor.

"That's more like the Eve I know."

I ran my fingers through my hair to perk up the spikes that had been smooshed on one side from my nap. Smiling at Nappi, I said, "Look. There's a fast-food place ahead. I could use a burger and some fries. Maybe a chocolate shake too."

"Look. We've got a tail again," said Nappi as he turned into the restaurant.

"How long have they been back there?" I asked.

"Hard to say. They picked us up when we hit the edge of town, but they could have been behind us all the way, just not making it obvious."

Nappi parked the car, and we watched our tail pull into a parking spot several spaces down.

"You go on in and order, Eve. I'll be right with you." Nappi walked down the line of cars, and I watched him approach the black SUV that had been tailing us. Was a black SUV the official car used by the bad guys to tail the good guys? The driver's side window slid down, and Nappi and the driver talked for a while. Finally Nappi nodded and walked away. The car backed out of the parking space and left.

Nappi joined me in the order line inside, saying nothing. He feigned interest in the items on the menu overhead, examining the offerings as if he'd never been in a fast-food joint before. We got our food and chose a table by the front windows.

"So? Tell me."

He took a big bite of his burger and held up one finger as he chewed and swallowed. "Hmm. This is pretty tasty."

"Nappi. Get on with it."

"I thought I recognized the driver of the car that just took up the tail here. He used to work for Freddie the Bull."

At the name, I envisioned a huge man with black-as-midnight hair and no neck.

"I know what you're thinking, but you'd be wrong." He inserted several fries into his mouth, and I waited impatiently until he chewed and swallowed them.

"Freddie is a short guy, barely five feet, got the most delicate hands you've ever seen, long fingers. He could have been a concert pianist, I think."

"Okay, I'll bite. Where did he get the name?"

"I'm not sure, but I think it's because he's full of it—never tells the truth about anything, exaggerates every story he tells. Pretends to be a harmless kind of guy, but he's got contacts. The guys who tailed us in New York and this crew," he gestured over his shoulder with his thumb, "are contacts."

"Contacts with contracts?" I asked.

"They're the muscle Freddie provides when someone wants to scare someone."

"So what did you tell them to get them to leave?"

"I told them they were stepping all over my space, that this was my case, not Freddie's business. That's Freddie for you. Always invading someone else's territory. I keep telling him, 'Freddie, there are rules, you know.'"

"Did they tell you who Freddie is doing business with?"

"Nope, but I gave them a message for Freddie that I'd like to chat with him sometime soon."

A shadow crossed our table. I looked up into the palest eyes I'd ever encountered. Something about them reminded me of a reptile. Slight as this man was, he looked far from harmless. Slender hands reached out and grabbed one of my fries.

"I love fries." The man's voice was high and squeaky like Truman Capote's.

"See what I mean, Eve? The man just cannot keep his hands off other people's property," Nappi said.

Freddie the Bull had joined us for lunch.

ELEVEN

FREDDIE SEEMED NOT to take offense at Nappi's words, but pulled over a chair from a table nearby and sat down beside me.

"This must be Ms. Appel." He held out his hand. I hesitated a moment, then reached over and shook it.

"How do you know who I am?"

"Now that's a long story."

"Spare us one of your lengthy fabrications. There are any of a dozen ways you could have found out who she is." Nappi was doing a good job of looking bored, gazing around the restaurant and languidly nibbling on his food.

"Yes, but my story is a lot more interesting than any of those. And this time it's the truth."

Nappi put down his burger and sat back in his chair. "I'm guessing I'll have to listen to your story or I won't find out what I need to know."

Freddie smiled. It was not a nice smile, barely lifting the corners of his lips a fraction of an inch. His colorless eyes hardened, and their glacial hue made me want to reach for my sweater, which I'd left in the car.

"Okay, here's the thing. A very prominent family approached me through their lawyer and asked me to do some investigating for them."

"Pardon me, Mister, uh, Freddie, but why wouldn't they hire a private investigator rather than a...." I stopped myself, struggling for words to describe Freddie's work.

"Hit man? You think I'd do that kind of work? I'm hurt, terribly hurt to think you'd see me that way, but then you don't know me. We've just met. Unless, of course, my friend here," he gestured with his head toward Nappi, "has been talking about me." He leaned forward and tried a stare-down with Nappi. Nappi ignored him.

I gulped. The tension at the table seemed tight enough that I expected to hear a twang when it snapped.

Nappi set down his burger and brought his face within inches of Freddie's. "I told her you were a liar, and that this wasn't the first time you'd intruded on my turf. You remember how that came out, don't you?"

Freddie closed his eyes, and when he spoke, I had difficulty hearing him.

"What was that, Freddie?" Nappi asked. "Speak up."

Freddie's posture had changed from arrogant tough guy to reprimanded child. He slid down in his chair and fiddled with the salt and pepper packets on the table. "This is different. I got this case fair and square. How was I to know it was infringing on your interests?"

"Good point. You didn't know, but now you do. So back off. Or I'll do what I did the last time you interfered where you shouldn't."

"You've got it."

"And…?"

Freddie threw the packets onto the table and sighed. "I'm sorry."

"Good. Now, who are you working for?"

"I don't know. I'm working through their law firm."

I knew there were crooked lawyers. I'd met a few in

the past, one who worked for the mob and then went off on his own to kill someone. Why was I surprised to learn that a Connecticut law firm would do business with a mob guy?

"Freddie…" Nappi said with a warning tone in his voice.

"Teller, Markowitz, Sterns, Babcock, and Tranho," said Freddie. "And they're not gonna like it when I don't deliver."

"Deliver what?" I asked.

He looked around at the restaurant's patrons before continuing in a low voice, "Information. That's all." He wouldn't meet Nappi's eyes. He was lying.

Nappi laughed. "Ms. Appel said it before. You're not in the investigating business, Freddie. You're in the disappearing business. Don't lie to me."

Freddie again began to play with the salt and pepper packets. He kind of twisted his neck around as if he had a kink in it. "Information and other stuff," he said.

Nappi reached across the table and stilled Freddie's hands. "A name." He tapped one of Freddie's slender fingers.

I think Nappi and I already knew before Freddie could say, "The Montroses."

"But why?" I asked.

"I don't ask why. I just offer a service."

Nappi slammed his fist down on the table with a bang. The couple at the next table looked up. Nappi spoke through gritted teeth, his words coming out in a hiss. "That's why I hate having guys like you in the business. You'll do anything for money."

Okay, I knew Nappi had limits when it came to mob business. Now I knew he drew the line at murder. Did that make him more or less scary, more or less likeable, more or less mob-like, more or less likely to end up in jail?

BACK IN NAPPI'S CAR, after Freddie left us at the restaurant and after he stole another handful of my fries, I continued to think about the entire conversation. I had a few questions for my friend, and there was no time like the present to ask.

"Are you allowed to call yourself a mob boss if you don't engage in murder?"

"I do," he said.

"Engage in murder or call yourself a mob guy?"

"I'm pretty mob-like. You know that. You've seen the kind of connections I have. Should I be offended you asked that question?"

"I know you're connected, and I know you've been in scrapes with the law, but you've never been in jail, and I'm not aware of any really mobsterish things you've done."

"Now you're doubting my word? That's not like you, Eve."

"I'm not doubting you. I know you've never lied to me. So, now, I'm just asking you to say it. Say it. 'I'm a Mafia guy.'"

He gave me a questioning look, then laughed. "I'm a mob guy, Eve. I'm a smart mob guy. I don't get caught."

"You could be undercover for the Feds."

He was silent for a while, then said, "I could be. Would that make you feel better about me, Eve?"

Well, this was a dumb conversation. To be honest, I didn't care whether Nappi was mob or fed. He was my friend, had come through for me always, and most importantly, Grandy loved him. I trusted her, didn't I? This whole thing about my mother being alive couldn't shake that trust. Ever.

I leaned over in my seat and planted a kiss on his smooth-shaven cheek. "I don't care if you're an alien from another planet. I love you." So why did I ask? Maybe the issue with Eleanor made me want to be certain I knew who people were, and what they were to me.

He gave my hand a friendly pat. "There's a motel up ahead. Let's check in and get back to work."

"I'm worried about Eleanor. I'm going to call Grandy and see if they've found her."

"Freddie may have sent some of his guys to Florida."

"You think they're responsible for Mr. Montrose's death? We should let Frida know what you found out about Freddie."

"I'll let you make that call. You'll do better than I at persuading her of a mob connection in Mr. Montrose's death. She should be alerted that they could still be in the area looking for Eleanor and her mother."

I was relieved that he had an answer to Mr. Montrose's death. We didn't know why, but we knew who.

Nappi must have read the look of relief on my face. "Don't be so certain Freddie got to him. I didn't get the feeling from Freddie that he'd been successful yet in his task. He likes to brag and embellish his accomplishments."

"Accomplishments? You call murder an accomplishment?"

"I don't, but Freddie might. I'm not through with Freddie yet. He's got a lot more to tell me." He changed the subject. "I assume you'll want to continue your snooping here."

Yes I did, but where would I begin? At the school again? The records there on Eleanor were even older than the ones in New York. I'd been lucky to find Mrs. Falco in Tillahook, but I couldn't count on my luck holding. I'd set that aside for the moment. For now I was more interested in finding out about Eleanor's mother.

I needed to take a look at hospitals that were in operation at least thirty years ago, before Eleanor was born or when she was young. Many public institutions had closed, moving residents into out-patient clinics or into residential treatment programs. Other former patients fell between the cracks and found their way into the homeless populations. Eleanor's mother was not one of those because she met Henry and had Eleanor. It was a long shot, but there was a private hospital near Monroe. It was a place to begin, a place where the rich placed family members who were having difficulties adjusting to society—in other words, an old-fashioned institution for those with mental problems, a place for a family to hide children or other relatives who might embarrass them. Freddie said he was working for a well-to-do family. Maybe there was a connection between those wealthy clients and the institutionalization of Eleanor's mother. Could she be related to some Connecticut blue bloods? But why would they hire someone to kill the Montroses? Mr. Montrose was no catch for a woman from old money, but embarrassment at who your daughter or sister or cousin married wasn't motive enough to kill her and her family. And hiring a mob guy sounded desperate and vengeful, not like social humiliation. Nappi wasn't certain Freddie's contacts were responsible for Mr. Montrose's murder, and it didn't appear to be the usual bullet-to-the-head mob hit. It hit me how blind we had been. I was so obsessed with Eleanor's story about her mother, I had overlooked the obvious—Mr. Montrose. What about his family background, his associates?

I filed the questions about Eleanor's father in the back of my head for future consideration. Tracking down his background seemed more difficult than moving ahead with finding out about his common-law wife. And this mystery seemed to be all about her. For now, I decided to focus on determining if she had been in a mental facility. Maybe I was taking the easier path because I felt I had an "in" with the institution nearby. The legal leverage of a court order provided through either Chief Raleigh or Frida seemed problematic, as Raleigh had indicated. I decided to try a softer approach. Having lived in Connecticut for most of my life, I knew the blue bloods here. They would close ranks if they thought the authorities were trying to dig dirt on their private affairs. I'd try my contact at the institution first. Legal maneuvers might come later if I was unsuccessful.

The father of one of the women I attended college with many years ago was head of the Hopkins Institution, the private hospital on the Connecticut shore near Madison. Connecticut was a small state in geographical size and in people-to-people connections. Everyone seemed to know everyone else. It was many years since I had contact with Selma Sandhurst or her father. The chances were he wasn't even head of the place now, or he might not remember me. If Eleanor's mother hadn't landed in Hopkins, Dr. Sandhurst might know where she could have been a private patient. Would he tell me? Probably not, but maybe if I told him the circumstances surrounding Mr. Montrose's death, he might help me. I remembered Selma introducing me to him once. My impression was that he was an okay guy, pleasant and genuinely interested in others.

There was just one problem. Selma and I hadn't spoken since college and for a good reason. Jerry had been her boyfriend before he was mine. We hadn't parted on friendly terms. I thought I recalled her yelling, "You're a skinny, man-stealing bitch." Yeah, that was what she said. Maybe she'd forgotten all about it by now. Maybe she hadn't shared this episode with her dad.

Probably nothing would come of contacting her father, but I had to give it a try. I dialed the Hopkins Institute and asked to talk with the director, Dr. Sandhurst. There was a slight delay, then a female voice came on the line and informed me the doctor was in session and would call me back if I left my name and number. While I waited, I mulled over how much time I should let pass before I called again. Maybe Sandhurst would never return my call. What would I do then? I settled back into the pillows on the bed to consider my next move and was startled from sleep by my cell ringing.

"Well, hello, Eve. How is the man-stealing bitch?"

I recognized the voice even after all these years. She still sounded as enraged as she had the night Jerry and I hooked up. That was a plus. She hadn't forgotten me.

I decided to ignore her words, assuming they might have slipped out in her surprise to hear from an old school chum.

"Selma. Did your dad tell you I was in town?"

"No. My secretary told me you called. I'm the director of Hopkins now."

"So, how about dinner tonight, if you're not busy?"

"You're assuming I've got nothing to be busy about. No man in my life. Like I can't keep one. Is that what you're implying?"

"We could do it tomorrow night."

"No. Tonight is just dandy." She pronounced the words in a snappish tone, then added, "Meet me at the Wren's Roost. Seven." She disconnected.

The Wren's Roost is where the guys took dates when we were in college. It was the place she and Jerry frequented on weekends, and I'd seen them there, laughing, dancing, drinking. She seemed into the guy while he—in true Jerry form, I was to later learn—seemed interested in me. We'd exchanged stares across the dance floor, mine filled with romance, his with lust. At the time I couldn't tell the difference. I came in with my date that night. The four of us got real drunk, and I went home with Jerry while she left with my date. So why was she mad and I wasn't? Maybe it was because my date that night was her cousin. I went on to marry Jerry and she went on to medical school. Given the course of our marriage, I think she got the better deal. But, from the way she answered the phone, maybe she didn't see it that way.

To be honest, I'd never liked Selma. I know that's no excuse for stealing Jerry from her. I thought he was a hot item. I wanted him and figured a gal with her family connections could find other, more desirable men. I was right, of course, but Selma always had a temper and an attitude about what she thought was hers. She thought everything was hers. Like that cat book that says, "Everything I see here is mine." Selma was like that. She thought being *the* Selma Sandhurst entitled her to anything and anyone. Jerry was lucky to get away from her. And I was unlucky enough to marry the guy. Maybe I could convince Selma she was better off without Jerry. I know I was. Maybe she'd forgive me. Maybe.

I could bring Nappi along tonight and lead her to believe he was my boyfriend. Then she could steal him away from me, and the score would be settled. I didn't think Nappi would like being used that way, so I discarded that scenario and decided to meet Selma alone and hope for the best. How mad can a person stay for, what…over a decade, plus?

I told Nappi I was having dinner with an old college friend, someone I could get information from about Eleanor and her family. Nappi had his own plans for the evening. This was, after all, his home state, and he had many contacts here. I assumed he hadn't seen them for a while so I envisioned him sitting in a room filled with cigar smoke talking over old times—old times being when he and his pals divvyed up territory and decided who their friends were.

The Wren's Roost hadn't changed much since my college days. There was the same dark-wood paneling, red-velvet upholstered seats, and booths—now worn down to show grayish patches—the same dim light that made it easy to be friendly with your date without alerting everyone in the room. I found Selma sitting at the bar sipping a very pink drink—a cosmopolitan, I guessed. I slid onto the stool next to her and ordered a Scotch on the rocks from a bartender so bent with age that he could have been the same guy who served us the night I nabbed Jerry.

"So how's your cousin?" I asked. That was not the best of opening lines, but I wanted to keep her off-balance. I do not do apologetic. I am no wimp.

"Well, he's not still yearning for you, if that's what you think."

"Yeah, well, neither is Jerry. We're divorced."

She turned toward me. "Well. Here's to good-old Jerry." She held up her glass and took a sip.

"You didn't miss a thing, you know, by not marrying him."

"I heard he had zipper problems."

"He still does, but for now, he's interested in a young woman whose name you might recognize."

"Did you call me to try to pump me for information I shouldn't be giving you?"

"Yes."

"Okay, then let me tell you something up front before we get started. I was damn glad you left with Jerry that night. I was trying to figure out a way to get rid of him. He was such a leech. You came into the bar, and the plan fell into place. I'd pawn him off on you with a big scene about how you were stealing him from me. I knew Jerry would like that idea—so desirable that sassy Eve Appel wanted him as well as me. It worked." She held up her ring finger. "I married Frederick Banyon. We've got a house in the Hamptons, one on the shore, a ski chalet in Vermont, and a condo in Cabo. Life is good. What do you have, Eve?"

Now, you might think I'd want to put this snarky broad in her place, but I needed information, so I decided to play nice. For the time being.

"I have a secondhand shop in rural Florida and a shack in the swamps."

She had another drink at the bar, where she told me more. After college, she'd gone on to get her medical degree, then did a residency in psychiatry at Hopkins. When her father retired several years ago, she was appointed director. She kept her maiden name professionally, and that's why my call to Dr. Sandhurst went to her. I let her talk. Unlike her father, she seemed genuinely uninterested in others, but intensely interested in impressing others. She was the same Selma Sandhurst I remembered. I felt sorry for her patients. When she took a breath to finish off her drink, I suggested we nab a table and she agreed.

All that talking about herself must have put her in a better mood about me. Or maybe the booze warmed her up because we began to reminisce about our college days. I should say, *she* began to reminisce. I could hardly get in anything other than a "um-hum."

As if finally remembering her manners, she turned her attention to me.

"So tell me why you looked me up," she said after we had gotten our wine and put in our orders.

"I'm working a case. I'm a PI now."

"You won't get me to break confidentiality if you're trying to snoop into some poor individual's hospital records."

"I know. I know. I thought I'd run a name by you to see if you recognized it. All you have to do is nod, and I'll take care of the rest."

She poured herself another glass of wine. "Go ahead."

"Did you ever run into anyone with the last name of Montrose? Or hear that name among your colleagues?"

She rolled the name around on her tongue, then said, "Nope."

"I'm trying to track down family members because of the murder of a Mr. Montrose, and I have information that his wife was in an institution for some time."

"You think she might have killed him?"

"I need to know more about her. She's gone missing." I decided not to tell Selma about any mob connection or that my father-in-law was suspected of the murder. I wasn't surprised she couldn't provide any information. Montrose was the name Eleanor's mother had assumed when she and Henry met. I didn't know her maiden name.

The conversation lagged. Selma signaled for another bottle of wine when our entrées arrived. "I assume since you're working on a case you can declare this dinner a business expense and bill your client."

"Sure." Now that I knew she had nothing to tell me and we were finding it difficult to find other topics of conversation, I wanted to hurry her through dinner and end the evening. She poured herself another glass of wine from the bottle and held it up to me. I shook my head and indicated my still half-full glass. A Scotch and a glass and a half of wine were enough for me.

She sipped her wine and chased her food around the plate with her fork, then she gazed at me across the table and set down her glass. She appeared to have made some kind of decision. "You never talked about your parents back in college, only your grandmother. Didn't you say she raised you?"

I nodded. I never talked about the sailing accident

that took my parents. I saw no reason to say anything
to my college friends about it. I didn't need to see the
sympathetic looks on their faces or hear their mur-
murs of regret.

Selma's eyelids drooped with what I thought was
the impact of the booze, but then she opened her eyes
wide in a feigned look of innocence that came across
more as a sly grin. "Does the name Mary Appel mean
anything to you?"

It did. I held my breath for what came next.

"Dad mentioned the name to me before he retired.
He remembered meeting you years before when we
were in college. I told him your name was Eve, not
Mary. I then inquired why he brought you up, and he
said it was because your last name was so unusual.
He dropped the topic then, and so did I. I forgot all
about the conversation until you called. It seemed like
a good time for me to go through some old records.
And guess what I found?" She leaned forward and gig-
gled. "A Mary Appel came to Hopkins, admitted by
family, I believe. She claimed someone was trying to
kill her, but she was wildly paranoid about everything.
She stayed here for over six months, then left. Her family didn't know where she went. Could she have been
your mother, Eve?"

I sat very still and let her continue to talk.

"No wonder you didn't say anything about your
parents back then. And no wonder your grandmother
had to raise you. The file indicates Mary Appel was
a paranoid schizophrenic, Eve. A dangerous woman,
according to the records. Her family couldn't control
her. She went into wild rages and tried to stab a family member. You poor, poor dear."

Okay, I was wrong. Selma wasn't still mad at me for Jerry. She was just plain mad, crazy, insane. What kind of woman was she to wait all these years for such cruel payback?

I looked across at her as she rose from the table. "Thanks, Selma. You've been more helpful than you know."

She examined my face as if looking for some indication that her words had hit home. I wouldn't give her that. I glanced around the room, and spying the waiter, held up my hand for the check.

I waited until she left, then paid the bill and called for a cab. Back at the motel room, I shut off my phone and fell into bed for a good cry. That took more than half an hour, kind of a surprise for a gal like me, not given to tears, much less a downpour like that. I sloshed cold water on my face and turned my cellphone back on.

TWELVE

NAPPI ANSWERED AFTER one ring. "Eve? Is something wrong?"

"I booked a seat on a flight back to Sabal Bay to-morrow, early. I hate to bother you, but would you be willing to take me to the airport around six a.m.?"

"What's going on? Is someone ill?"

"No. I'll tell you on the way to the airport." I disconnected before he could probe, and again turned off my cell. I didn't want to talk with anyone back in Sabal Bay tonight. Tomorrow I would be there, and I would straighten everything out. Well, that wasn't quite true. It wasn't up to me to do anything. It was up to Grandy to tell me the truth this time. And for me to try to forgive her for not telling me the truth all these years.

My mother—my insane mother—had been in an institution, just as Eleanor's mother had. Coincidence? I knew better. Eleanor's crazy story that she and I had the same mother wasn't so crazy after all. Mary Appel had survived that boat accident, perhaps even caused it, and left her husband—my father—to die. But he didn't and came searching for her, was still searching it seemed after all these years. Was she responsible for the death of Mr. Montrose, her partner? Or had my father found the family and tracked them down, following each one to Florida? I was grateful for one thing: Selma Sandhurst didn't have all these pieces

of the Mary Appel puzzle at her fingertips to inflict
more harm.

I spent a sleepless night. Either the air conditioner
blew too much cold air on me or it was too warm in the
room. I suspected even a room with perfect tempera-
ture wouldn't have allowed me to sleep. In the morning,
I felt sick to my stomach and had a headache although I
had had one drink and a small amount of wine. Funny
how alcohol turned on you when you added emotional
distress to your mixed drinks. I called on Bacchus to
bring Selma the worst hangover ever. I had just finished
brushing my teeth for the third time after upchucking
yet again when Nappi knocked on the door.

He carried two coffees with him and a bag holding pastries.

"Thanks for the thought, but I don't think I can eat
anything."

He put the coffee and bag on the dresser and sat,
patting the bed next to him. "Can you tell me what
happened last night to make you decide to go back to
Sabal Bay? Talking might help. We have time before
your plane leaves."

I told him everything, and I didn't cry, but afterward
my stomach felt worse than before, and I ran back into
the bathroom for another round of vomiting.

"You're right to want to talk with Grandy in person.
This isn't something you should do over the phone,"
he said when I rejoined him.

I nodded.

"But," he held up a finger to stop me from interrupting, "do you want to take the word of a woman who

had issues with you and continues to hold them over your head? Talk about coincidences. Selma Sandhurst has reason to hate you for taking Jerry from her, or so she says at first, then changes her tune and says she's happy about it. In yet another about-face, she tells you a story about your mother, one meant to hurt you. She may be a psychiatrist, but she's not a healthy person. The other piece of the story you got from Eleanor. She's not the most grounded woman, is she? And where is she now? Your memories of your parents are loving ones, but this story is saying there was a lot of conflict, enough to make your mother try to kill your father and for him to try to hunt her down over several decades. Why didn't he tell the police she tried to kill him? Do you trust the stories of these two women over your own memories of your mother and father? Then there's this: what's the mob connection here? Freddie was hired to do a job, hired by a Connecticut family with money. How does that figure into this story?"

Nappi was right. Nothing fit just right. "Maybe my father changed his name after the boating incident. He could be wealthy now and trying to find my mother, uh, Eleanor's mother and kill her. Maybe Freddie's men got to Mr. Montrose and killed him."

"In a swamp in Florida? That's an unlikely place for a mob hit, and with your father-in-law's knife? That's not Freddie's usual style, but maybe it's evolving."

I held my head in my hands. Nappi's questions were not helping my physical symptoms, nor were they helping me think straight.

"I'm not trying to confuse you, Eve. All I'm saying

is don't go all accusatory on your grandmother before you let her tell her side."

"What side can she have? She must have known about my mother being alive. I have a crazy mother. No, correction, Eleanor and I have a crazy mother running around here. And a nutty father who is out there trying to find her so he can do her in for trying to kill him years ago. Who the hell am I?" My voice broke, and I broke down in tears again.

"Let's suppose your mother and Eleanor's are one in the same. Maybe Grandy didn't know about it."

"How could that be?" I wanted to believe him.

"Can you see Grandy keeping the truth from you all these years? And not wanting to find your mother, her daughter? You know she'd be looking for her."

Nappi was making sense, but his words didn't have much of an impact on my thinking. I was too upset, and I wanted too much for it to be true that my mother was alive. I'd take her back in my life, crazy or not, killer or not.

Nappi had to have seen my confusion, the push-pull of having my mother back versus having my life with Grandy as I knew it. He tried to provide comfort by putting his arms around me.

I held up both my hands to hold him back. I could not tolerate that much acceptance, that much love. "Please, please no more. I can't focus on this any longer. I need to know...." What did I need to know? I gave up trying to sort out my tangled thoughts, and I felt giddy from emotional and physical exhaustion.

I squared my shoulders, gulped and looked Nappi straight in the eye. "I need to know whatever Grandy can tell me."

Nappi's gaze examined my face as if he could read my intentions there. "Sure, Eve. I get it, but I'm going with you."

BEFORE WE TOOK OFF from Hartford, Nappi had called Sammy, saying I was feeling under the weather and was coming home for a few days to rest up. I don't think Sammy bought the excuse. He knew something was up, but he let it pass. While I was in the airport restroom throwing up again, Nappi also got in touch with Grandy and asked her to meet us at my house. He gave her the same story he had given Sammy. I was certain it met with the same skepticism. I was sick and needed rest—no doubt about that—but my anger at Grandy made me push fatigue and a pounding head and roiling stomach aside.

I was worried that flying would make me feel worse, but I had upchucked so often that there was nothing left in my stomach. Takeoff gave my stomach that funny lurching feeling like you get on the way down when you ride a Ferris wheel, but afterward it settled down. I began to feel better, perhaps because I would confront my grandmother and put an end to all my doubts. Selma's words came back to me and played in an endless loop in my head,

"…paranoid schizophrenic…"

"…wild rages…"

"…tried to stab a family member…"

"Her family didn't know where she went."

Could she have made this all up? I didn't think so. She was too thrilled to be telling me the story to have concocted it herself. Selma's comment about the family not being able to find her when she left made me wonder what family members had been responsible for placing her in the hospital. Someone must have visited her during her stay. I dropped off to sleep for a few minutes to awaken to another round of the loop and the thought that Grandy must have been responsible for committing her. And not a word to me about it. Did she visit her? How could she have hidden those visits? I groaned. Nappi stirred beside me and laid his hand on mine.

"I know there's not a word of truth in what others have told you about your mother. The truth is in what Grandy has told you and what she will tell you."

He was so certain. Why couldn't I feel the same?

We landed in West Palm at nine a.m. Nappi had made arrangements for a car to meet us at the airport. He was sensitive enough to know he shouldn't use Jerry as our chauffeur.

"I'm dropping you at your place to talk with Grandy alone. If Max is there, I'll get him out of the house with some excuse. Try not to judge too quickly, Eve. She loves you."

I gritted my teeth and said, "I know, but—"

"More importantly, you love her. Don't lose sight of that. I suspect you'll need her in your life more than ever now."

What did he mean by that? It was almost a Grandfather Egret mind-reading kind of thing to say.

On the ride to Sabal Bay, I felt the need to take some kind of action to exact control over a life that felt like it was being sucked into one of Florida's sinkholes. I called Jerry.

"Any news of Eleanor? Nappi and I have heard nothing from our end."

"She called me and told me not to tell anyone where she is. She's one flaky woman, you know? I think she's still worried someone is after her. She said she's had no word from her mother."

"Tell me where she is, Jerry," I said.

"I promised not to."

"Here, Nappi. You tell him what will happen if he doesn't tell me where Eleanor is." I handed the phone to Nappi.

"Tell her," Nappi said. Those two words did the trick.

"She went back to Tillahook," said Jerry and added, assuming we hadn't left New York, "so you might just run into her at the house. Everything is working out just fine. Right?"

I sighed and relayed Jerry's news to Nappi, who grabbed the cell out of my hand.

"Get on the first plane there and find her. Then bring her back down here. Don't you come back until you find her, and don't lose her again."

"You're back in Florida?" Jerry asked.

Nappi disconnected.

"Thanks for that, but do you think Jerry is the one who should go get her?"

"No, but do you know anyone better right now? He's built some kind of rapport with her."

"I'll talk with Grandy and then head back North. Eleanor and I are family, after all."

Nappi raised a skeptical eyebrow.

GRANDY MET ME at the door, and the look on her face said that while I was tossing up last night's dinner in the airport restroom, Nappi had been telling her more than I wanted him to.

"Max is out on the lake, fishing," she said. "We have the house to ourselves. I'll make you some toast."

"I'm more thirsty than hungry," I said.

"There's ginger ale in the cupboard. That will settle your stomach."

Toast and ginger ale—it was what Grandy gave me as a kid when I was sick.

"Nappi told you everything, didn't he?" I asked, following her into the kitchen.

She nodded. "He knows it's not true, so he thought I should be prepared for what you were struggling with, how upsetting this is for you."

I took a sip of the ginger ale she handed me, discovering I was more exhausted now than I was angry. I tried replaying the Selma tape in my head, to recover the sense of outrage I had at what Grandy had done to me, but Selma's words faded behind the need not to accuse Grandy. I wanted her to make things okay again. And I knew if anyone could right my world once more, it was Grandy. She proved it by moving toward me and putting her arms around me, hugging me into her roundness. Her words surprised me.

"I'm the grandmother to a private detective who is new to the profession. You'd think I could give her a little help, but I let the opportunity to do my own homework slip by. I should have talked with you when I first saw Eleanor."

"What do you mean?"

"When Eleanor walked into the shop looking so like you and telling her strange story about the two of you having the same mother, I thought of my sister Irene. I dismissed that idea because I was so sure that we would locate Eleanor's mother and this whole crazy thing would be resolved. I could have made one call and saved you a lot of pain." Grandy stepped out of the embrace and held me at arm's length. "You look exhausted. You'd better sit down. This story may take a while."

I sank onto one end of the couch while Grandy took the other end.

"I have one sister, as you know, Eve. She had a child around the same time I gave birth to your mother, but Irene was unmarried. The baby was born prematurely and had difficulties breathing and other issues common to preemies. Irene named the girl Brenda, and she grew into a beautiful child, happy and healthy. Brenda and your mother used to play together."

"I remember Mom talking about Aunt Brenda, but I don't remember much about her." My mind began to jump ahead in Grandy's story. "Aunt Brenda and Mom were the same age. Are you telling me Aunt Brenda was Eleanor's mother, and that she impersonated my mother?"

Grandy reached out and touched my arm. "I wish it was that simple, Eve, but there's more, much more to this story. We had lost touch during our daughters' high school and young-adult years. Then one day Irene called to tell me Brenda had died. She had gotten the flu and complications set in. The poor woman was dead in twenty-four hours. She was in her twenties. Tragic for Irene. Her only child."

"When my mother drowned, you lost your only child, too."

Grandy nodded and was silent for a time as grief

engulfed her once more. Then her face changed, and her soft lips tightened into a sharp line. "You'd think two sisters like us, sharing the tragedy of losing our daughters, would seek comfort in each other. But we didn't. I reached out to her and expected her to do the same, but she withdrew. She said she didn't want to talk about what had happened, and that I should never mention her daughter again. I had to abide by her wishes, but I missed her. We had been so close at one time. I wanted us to support each other through our tragedies. She didn't want my comfort, nor was she willing to give any to me."

"I'm sorry, Grandy. I wondered why we never saw my great-aunt except for that one time when she announced her engagement to Don. I was in high school then."

Grandy nodded. "I think Irene found some measure of happiness with him, even though they were too old to have children. I had hoped her joy in finding him might make a difference for us, but she and I were never close again."

"But, if Brenda is dead, why did you think of her when Eleanor came to visit?"

"It was a quirky thing. I was visiting your parents' grave one spring to put flowers on it. I think it was about ten years ago, right around the time Max and I married and moved down here. I wanted to pay what I was afraid might be my last visit to the gravesite because I wasn't certain I'd ever come back to Connecticut. While there, I decided to visit the plot Irene purchased, which was near your parents' resting place. I found the site easily because I had been there when Irene and I were younger. She decided to buy it because it had an old oak tree nearby and she loved the idea of being in its shade 'throughout eternity.' But the plot was empty. No grave, no marker, nothing. I called her and asked her about it. I asked why I didn't find Brenda's grave there."

"What did she say?"

"She told me Brenda wasn't buried there. She sounded kind of nervous over the phone. Her voice trembled, and I thought she was crying. But then, she kind of recovered herself and said that Brenda's father had her buried on his plot."

"Brenda's father? Who was that?"

"I don't know. Irene had never mentioned him. She hung up on me. I thought the whole story was odd. Why let your child be buried in a plot owned by a father whose name you never mentioned? And I don't think Brenda ever met the man."

"That's a very odd story."

"We haven't been in touch since then, and I'd written the whole thing off as another quirk of my sister's. I'd forgotten all about it. Until now."

"And now what are you thinking?"

"That my niece Brenda isn't dead."

THIRTEEN

PART OF THE story made sense to me. Brenda was Eleanor's mother. But what else did we know now?

"Grandy, you have to call your sister and talk with her—whether she wants to discuss her daughter or not. A man has been killed, and the authorities think my father-in-law is the murderer."

"He may still be the killer. Nothing about Irene's daughter suggests she's responsible for her husband's death. Why would she kill the man she trusted?"

"I don't know, but that's why you need to talk with your sister."

Grandy screwed up her face in disgust. "But a phone call, Eve? I think this is something that should be accomplished face-to-face, don't you?"

I did. I was about to recommend that I return to Connecticut with Grandy, but she must have read my mind. "You're sick, Eve, too sick to be traveling back and forth. You need a good night's sleep. I've got an idea. Let me work on it. Meanwhile, off to bed you go." She shoved me in the direction of my bedroom. Surprisingly, I didn't object. I had no gas left in the tank. My snoopy nature was failing me.

"I'll give Sammy a call. He's working at David's ranch today. I'll tell him you're back and resting this morning. And, you will be resting, Eve. Even if I have to call one of your cowboy pals to come here, lasso you, and tie you to the bed."

I chuckled, the first laugh I'd had in days, and flopped onto my bed. The next thing I knew, someone was planting kisses on my face.

"Sammy." I reached out to him and pulled him close. "Grandy said she'd call you and let you know I was sleeping. Does she know you're here? She threatened violence if I didn't nap. Now we're both in trouble."

"Eve, my love. It's five in the afternoon. You've been asleep all day."

I sat up in bed and looked at my bedside clock. He was right. The day was gone, purple shadows from the setting sun creeping across my bedroom floor.

"Grandy said you were sick. What's going on, Eve?" Sammy's dark eyes scrutinized my face.

"I don't know. I'm usually so full of pep, and I never throw up. I guess it's all the upset over this case."

"Then give it up, Eve. It's not worth your getting sick. We'll have Crusty McNabb take it over."

"No, no, no. I will not admit to failure with my first real PI case. I feel better now." Funny, but I did feel better. The nap must have been just what I needed. I was also hungry. That had to be a good sign.

"Are you sure?" Sammy asked.

"I'm my old self." I jumped out of bed to demonstrate how good I felt, and the world went black.

I AWOKE IN the back of an ambulance, Sammy holding my hand.

"You called an ambulance? I'm just hungry, that's all. I need food. A rack of ribs, and I'll be my old self.

Oh, damn. Hand me that barf bag over there, would you?"

"What? Where…" Sammy asked.

The EMT grabbed the bag and gave it to me. My stomach tried to turn over, but all I produced was some bile. God, I felt like hell.

In the emergency room, the doctor gave me the news. "Mrs. Egret, you are dehydrated and you need nourishment." He held up his hand to stem the flow of words he seemed to know was coming. "I do not mean ribs, slaw, and a few Scotches. I have seen you at the Biscuit eat a cowboy under the table. A balanced diet. Rest, plenty of liquids, and you should be fine. From what your grandmother and your husband told me, you've just been over-doing. Let your body make the necessary adjustments, and you'll be raring to go in a few days."

"Wait a minute. What adjustments will my body need to make? What are you saying?"

Grandy leaned close. "I think he's saying you're pregnant, Eve."

The doctor smiled and nodded. Grandy smiled and nodded. Sammy just looked terrified. He staggered backwards and fell into the only chair in the room.

After Grandy revived Sammy and brought him out of his dazed state of disbelief, she turned to me. I'd said not a word.

"Eve, are you okay?" asked Grandy.

"I think so, but boy am I stupid. How did this happen?"

Grandy laughed. "You don't know how babies are made? I thought we had that discussion years ago."

My stomach did a little flip, this one a leap of happiness. I was surprised at the news, but also overjoyed. I laughed at Grandy's joke, then turned my attention to Sammy, who had recovered sufficiently to hold my hand tight enough to cut off my circulation.

"You can let go, Sammy. It won't fall off."

"What? Oh, sorry, Eve." He dropped my hand, leaned over, and kissed me.

"I assume you're fine with this?" I asked.

"I'm better than fine. I'm gonna be a daddy. And the boys will have a brother. Or sister. Or… God, Eve, you're not going to have twins like Madeleine, are you?" For a moment, he had that pale, terrified look on his face again, then recovered and said, "That's fine, too. We could have triplets even."

I groaned. "No twins, no triplets. One healthy baby is what we're shooting for here."

I WAS IN the hospital for three days, IV fluids providing the medication and hydration I needed. I had plenty of visitors, and I was eager for news associated with the case. Thinking they would spare me any anxiety, no one would talk about it, changing the subject each time I brought it up. I was forced to use my cellphone to call Nappi. He'd had no word from Jerry, and when I called Jerry's number, it went to voicemail. Jerry. Always unreliable. I reveled in thinking about Sammy's and my baby, but I was also itching to get busy on the case again. The doctor was correct. My body seemed to be adjusting to the pregnancy. My appetite returned, and despite the blandness of the hospital food, I ate every bit of it while yearning for ribs and slaw. I bothered the doctor about it each time he visited my room. He finally gave in, and that afternoon Sammy entered my room carrying flowers as well as takeout boxes from the Biscuit. I gobbled the food down in record time and waited for it to settle. Would it stay down? It did, so I turned my concerns to getting back on my sassy, snoopy, stiletto-shod feet once more.

Where was I in the case now? I was almost certain Eleanor's mother was my Aunt Brenda and that Grandy could provide more information so we could be certain. Someone was after the Montroses and they were using Freddie the Bull as their "hit man." Why did they want the Montroses out of the way and how was this related to Mr. Montrose's death and my father-in-law's role in it? I had some of the answers I needed. I gritted my teeth in frustration. Time to get out of this hospital bed and back to work.

The day I returned home, Grandy shooed everyone out of my bedroom and said I needed rest. They bought her excuse, but I didn't. Neither of us had shared Grandy's speculation about her sister's daughter. Grandy insisted the story, if there was one, was Irene's to tell or not. Irene had kept her daughter's fate a secret all these years for reasons she hadn't revealed to Grandy. Speaking about her daughter would be painful, and there was no guarantee breaking silence about the past would help now. It might open old wounds. We had to trust that Irene was willing to speak about Benda because it was the right thing to do. Grandy thought that in order to make this decision, Irene would have to do some soul-searching. She'd have to weigh the value of telling the truth against the agony of revealing Brenda's past.

Alone in my room, I blew out an exasperated puff of air and said, "I do not need rest. And you know it.

I've been flat on my back for three days. Give me a break. This baby and I need exercise both physical and mental. I know something's up. So tell me." I patted the bed, and Grandy sat beside me.

"I had Max call Irene's house, and posing as a business acquaintance, he asked to talk with Don. I took over and let Don know my speculation about Irene's daughter and why Irene would need to come clean. He neither confirmed nor denied that Brenda was alive, but said he would find some way to convince Irene she should talk with me.

"He repeated what I'd told you, Eve. 'This is Irene's story. I think she has to tell it to you if she's willing.'"

Grandy continued, "I replied that I respected that, but that people's lives were in jeopardy, and one man was dead. They're flying down here. They should be arriving this evening."

"They're coming here?" I couldn't keep the excitement out of my voice. "What did Don tell her to change her mind about talking to you?"

"I don't know. I guess we'll find out later. Don't get your hopes up. She's kept this secret for decades. Meantime, Eve...."

"Meantime, could someone run out and get me a pepperoni, mushroom, black olive, and sausage pizza?"

Grandy shook her head and gave me a look of disgust.

I slapped myself in the forehead. "Duh. What is wrong with me? I'm sorry for being so selfish. Get something for yourselves too. It's on me."

She continued to shake her head as she backed out the door.

"I'm eating for two, you know."

She stuck her head back in. "That's not new. You always ate for two."

I rummaged through my closet for some clothes that said "private eye." I wanted Aunt Irene to believe she was talking with a professional, not simply one of her relatives. I thought an official look might persuade her of the gravity of the situation. It was more than the case of a disappearing daughter. It was a matter of murder. I chose black pants, a white cotton top, and silver faux-leather jacket and paired the ensemble with my best pair of red-leather pumps. I looked at myself in the mirror. *There. Eve Appel Egret. Sassy woman detective.*

Sammy, Nappi, Madeleine, and David greeted me when I walked out of the bedroom. My garb and the determined look on my face must have convinced them the old Eve was back.

Well, almost everyone except Madeleine.

"Do you think it's a good idea to wear so high a heel?" she asked.

"Hey, I'm pregnant, not handicapped," I shot back at her.

The doorbell rang and Nappi answered it. "Who ordered the loaded pizza, as if I didn't know?"

There were two pizzas and two liters of soda. Everyone stood back as I lunged for the box. Once I began stuffing the pie in my face, the others joined in. I ate more than anyone else. We cleaned up, and Grandy offered to make coffee. I eyed the last piece of pizza left in the box, but decided I was full enough to let it go.

Everyone turned down coffee and left to let Grandy and me have the house to ourselves for when Irene and her husband arrived. Sammy remained a few minutes longer to explain he was going to Grandfather's to spend the evening with the boys, then bring them back here later.

"I'll call first to make certain we're not interrupting, and if we are, we'll stay overnight with Grandfather," he said.

"I wish I could say I believed this conversation will go well, but it could be a short one if Irene decides not to talk about her daughter."

"Then what?" asked Sammy.

"I may have to return to Connecticut to find Eleanor and perhaps have another chat with Selma. I wish Jerry would get in touch. He must know something about Eleanor by now." No one had mentioned it, but more important than locating Eleanor was finding her mother. She hadn't been seen since she fled Connecticut to come here, and according to Eleanor and her father, to find me. She hadn't made contact with me or anyone around here, and that made me worry that Freddie and his guys had found her first.

Sammy's brow wrinkled in concern.

"Don't worry about me, Sammy. I know how to look after myself. And the bump here." I patted my small tummy.

"If you go, I'm insisting Nappi accompany you, although he didn't do a very good job of taking care of you the first trip."

I knew Nappi had taken the very best care of me. I was the one at fault for not listening to what my body had been screaming at me. I hadn't told Sammy about Freddie and his guys and how Nappi had run them off. I wasn't going to do that now and take the chance of alarming him. He wouldn't forbid me to go—he wasn't that kind of a husband—but he would worry and worry and worry.

"WHAT TIME IS IT, GRANDY?" I asked.

"Ten minutes later than the last time you asked me."

I wanted to be certain that Eleanor's mother wasn't my mother. Her mother had to be Brenda, my aunt, and I expected Irene would confirm this, but I knew nothing else. How had she gotten into the hospital and why had she used the name Mary Appel? Was she hiding from someone real or fleeing some imaginary boogeyman? What was Freddie the Bull's role in all this? How did this relate to the death of Eleanor's father? I had a lot of questions for my great-aunt. I had one piece of the puzzle and none of the others, and I was counting on Irene to help me put everything together. Foremost in my mind as I paced back and forth in front of the window that looked out onto the street was this unsettling thought: what if Irene didn't know the answers to these questions? Grandy had cautioned me to let Irene take the lead tonight and not pressure her or say too much until she was done speaking.

A car slowed as it passed my house, then sped up again.

"That looked like a rental. Do you think she chickened out?" I asked Grandy.

I watched the car drive to the end of the street, then turn around and come back. It pulled up in front of my house. A man and a woman got out. It had been years since I'd seen my Great-Aunt Irene, but I would have recognized her anywhere. She was the doppelganger of my Grandy, right down to the mass of curly white hair that shone almost blue in the glow of the streetlamp.

I opened the door without letting them knock first.

Irene hesitated a moment, then stepped into the living room. There was no attempt to hug me or Grandy, but Grandy was not having any of that. She grabbed her sister and enveloped her in a Grandy-sized hug. Irene stiffened as if itching to push her sister away, but Grandy pulled her closer. I could see Irene's body relax, and the two sisters, separated for so long, gave themselves up to an embrace so close an elf's eyelash couldn't have come between them. Tears ran down their cheeks. I dashed to the kitchen for a box of tissues.

When they stepped back from each other, each dabbing at their cheeks, I hugged Irene. Grandy included Don in her embrace. I gave him a kiss on the cheek and whispered, "What did you say to convince her to come here?"

"That it was overdue for her and her sister to get together again."

"That's it? She doesn't know anything else?"

He shook his head.

Once Don and Irene settled on the sofa across from Grandy and me—we sat in chairs across the coffee table from them—Irene couldn't seem to stem the tsunami of tears that kept spilling from her eyes. She grabbed Don's hand and tried to speak, but her voice cracked with emotion and she shook her head.

"I wasn't expecting Eve to be here."

"Is that a problem for you? I can leave, and you and Grandy and Don can talk without me if that would make you feel better." I hoped she would ask me to stay. I wanted her to answer all my questions. I didn't want that information filtered through another party.

"No, no. It's fine, Eve. I need to talk with you and

Grandy, my family. We've been estranged too long, and it's my fault."

"Tell us about Brenda," said Grandy.

"Grandy," I hissed in disapproval, "you told me to take it easy and not push her. And now what have you done?"

Irene gave me a soft smile. "Your grandmother always had a way of getting right to the point. It appears her granddaughter is just like her. Besides, I didn't fly all this way to shy away from talking about Brenda. What do you want to know?"

"Where is she? I know she's not buried in her father's plot. Why would she be? She never knew the man. No one did."

Irene paled. Despite her claim that she understood Grandy's forward nature, it was clear Grandy's words hit home and hard.

She seemed to gather courage from Don's arm around her shoulders. She looked up at him, and he nodded, signaling her to talk despite the pain it was causing her.

She blew her nose on a tissue and settled herself deeper into the couch. "I guess I'd better go back to when Brenda was small." She gave her nose another blow and cleared her throat. "Could I have a glass of water?"

"Sure." I jumped up from the couch to get it for her.

"Would anyone like coffee? Or something stronger?" asked Grandy.

I could have used about a barrel of Scotch, but that was out of the question.

Don said yes to coffee, and we waited while Grandy got it together for him.

Are we all cozy and settled now or do we have to exchange pleasantries about the weather? I ground my teeth and suppressed a growl. If this took any longer, I would be due to go into labor.

Irene cleared her throat again and resumed speaking, her voice stronger than I expected. "Brenda was a difficult child." Turning her gaze on Grandy, she added, "You must have noticed it when we got together. And don't you remember that time when Brenda and Eve's mother were playing together? Brenda bit her and then tried to hit her with the paddle from a canoe? We chalked it up to over-exuberant play, but Brenda grew more and more aggressive in her interactions with classmates. I knew something wasn't right, though I tried to deny it. I was contacted by the school and asked to remove her because of her disruptive behavior. The teachers couldn't control her. For a time I tried to home-school her, then I hired someone to come in and give her lessons. She hit the person I hired with a wrench, knocked her unconscious, then tried to set the house on fire. Brenda had been in and out of therapy with several psychiatrists and psychologists before this, but nothing seemed to help."

"So you committed her to a mental institution?"

Irene smiled at my question.

"My dear Eve, you just don't know. I committed her to many such facilities off and on through most of her teen years and into adulthood. She'd stay for a time, get better we thought, then come home to relapse again. She became convinced that someone was after her. Instead of coming home, she sneaked away from the institution, and I never heard from her again. I tried to find her. I hired several private detectives, but no one could find a trace of her. Finally, I gave her up for dead, although sometimes I felt as if she might just walk back into the house again. One occasion I thought I could feel her presence just outside the door or in the woods. But she never returned."

"So you made up that story about her dying of influenza," Grandy said.

"Most of the time I wished it was true. She was so unhappy, so frightened, so delusional. It would be better if she was dead." Irene broke down in tears once more.

This was not an easy story for her to tell, and my news that Brenda might still be alive might not be of any comfort to her.

"Did you receive a diagnosis for her condition?" I asked.

Irene gave a snicker and a half smile. "Many. You know how that goes. Each diagnosis necessitated yet another round of medications, and she was placed on so many, I can't tell you the names of all of them."

"Why did you use my mother's name when you admitted her to Hopkins?" I asked.

Irene paled and hesitated before answering. "I never admitted her to Hopkins. And why would I use your mother's name?"

FOURTEEN

IRENE LOOKED PUZZLED, her brow knit, her head tipped to one side as if trying to understand why I would ask such an odd question.

All my hopes for resolving the mystery of my mother came to a sudden end, but not in the way I wanted. Grandy reached across and patted my hand.

"Hopkins is very expensive, Eve," Irene said. "There's no way I could afford to place Brenda there. Is there something you're not telling me?"

I seemed to have gone mute. I wanted to explain, but the words would not come, so Grandy jumped in and told Irene most of the story about Brenda and Eleanor, editing here and there, especially with respect to my mother, and avoiding any mention of why I'd asked the question I had.

Irene seemed unable to take in what Grandy had said. She sat frozen on the couch, staring across the room.

"Maybe something stronger than water?" I suggested, grabbing a snifter from the liquor cabinet and splashing brandy into it. I handed it to her and she took a small sip. Her voice when she spoke was almost too soft to hear. "So, Brenda is still alive? And I have a granddaughter?" She turned her attention to Don. "Did you know this when she suggested I come here?"

"Some of it," he replied.

Irene's face brightened as if she had dropped ten years. "That's wonderful. I want to see them. Where are they?"

"We don't know right now," I managed to mutter.

Irene's look of joy turned to one of anger and despair, her eyes narrowing. "Is this some kind of a cruel joke? You extract a painful story about my daughter from me, one I've kept secret all these years to protect her, and now you say you can't find her or her daughter?" Irene's face was mottled with rage.

"It's very complicated, and a man is dead. Murdered. He was your daughter's common-law husband," Grandy said.

Irene mouth twisted in a look of suspicion. "You think my daughter killed him, don't you?"

"The police think my father-in-law killed him, although there doesn't seem to be a motive."

"And you think Brenda had a motive," Irene snapped. "What would that be?"

Don, noting how anguished Irene had become, took both her hands in his and said, "It won't do any good for us to become angry. You can understand why your sister and Eve might think Brenda was responsible for Henry Montrose's death. Brenda was often violent and out of control. Be honest, Irene. You were scared of her. I was too."

Irene nodded and covered her face with her hands. "Oh, God. I find her and it begins all over again."

My thoughts exactly. *It begins all over again.* If it wasn't Brenda using my mother's name, then who was it? Not my mother. Not that again. I shook my head, trying to prevent my thoughts from returning to the question: was my mother alive?

Grandy shook her head. "No, Eve. It had to be someone else."

"Is there any reason you can think of why Brenda might claim that she was my daughter and come here looking for Eve?"

"She did that?" Irene said.

"She was pretty convinced she was Mary Appel," I said, "and she'd also convinced her husband and her daughter. She's been living with that persona for over twenty years." I decided I had to go with the most obvious explanation for what Selma told me. "It appeared she used my mother's name to seek treatment at Hopkins. What reason would she have for doing that?"

I caught a flicker of something in her eyes before Irene blinked and said, "No reason at all."

Irene appeared to be either lying or hiding something. With a shrug of her shoulders, she looked me in the eye and said, "I can't imagine, but Brenda was mentally ill, and she was close to your mother when they were children."

That made sense, and yet I felt Irene was avoiding telling us something, something very important.

We talked for several more hours, catching up on our own lives. Finally, the subject turned to Brenda, her daughter, Eleanor, and Eleanor's father.

"The entire family seemed to feel someone was after them. Does that make any sense to you?" I asked.

"Brenda always expressed a fear of someone coming after her. It was one of her delusions, so I'm not surprised it has followed her all these years," Irene said.

"Could it have been more than a delusion? Could somebody have been after her?" I asked.

"Don't be silly," said Irene with a look of wide-eyed

innocence, then changed the subject. "We have to find her and my granddaughter."

"We're working on it, and maybe you can help," I said.

"Of course. Anything I can do to get her back."

Grandy pointed out what I had neglected to mention: Irene needed to talk with the authorities. Unable to find any living relative for Mr. Montrose, Frida would want to find out as much as possible about Brenda.

I could understand how bittersweet this visit was becoming for Irene. She now had reason to believe her daughter was alive, but she had to be overwhelmed with worry that Brenda could be a person of interest in the death of the man she called her husband.

As for me, I still had work to do and no certainty that I could put aside the possibility that my mother was alive. If my mother hadn't entered Hopkins and Brenda hadn't used her name, then who was the woman whose records in Hopkins held my mother's name? All my options seemed to point in one direction. I had to return to Connecticut to find Eleanor and Jerry and to question Selma again. I needed more information from my old frenemy, information I was certain she would not be willing to provide. I needed to strong-arm her in a way Nappi would respect. No, not with threats of physical harm or blackmail. Something more powerful.

IT WAS LATE when Irene and Don drove off to their motel.

"All that time talking, and we managed to avoid one of the most important questions about Irene and Brenda's plight," I said, stifling a yawn with my hand.

Grandy knew what I was saying. "I think Irene had

enough difficulty telling us about Brenda and then adjusting to finding out her daughter was alive and mentally no better now than she had been years ago. We'll leave the other for another time."

The "other" to which Grandy was referring was the matter of the identity of Brenda's father. Did he know about Brenda? I decided the answers to these questions had to be related to Freddie the Bull's contractual interest in locating the Montrose family. I assumed Freddie's tail on us up North had everything to do with the Montroses and was unrelated to my family. A tiny voice that would not stop nagging at me said I could be wrong. Shoving that doubt to the back of my mind for consideration when I was less tired, I called Sammy and told him not to wake the boys, but to come on over if he wanted to. He wanted to.

When he arrived, we sat in my backyard and I caught him up on the evening's events. He said nothing when I was finished, but put his arms around me and squeezed me close. Then he kissed my hair and gazed into my eyes.

"We should tell the boys," he said, moving his hand to my stomach and touching it gently, "before you leave for Connecticut."

"Will they be happy, do you think?" I asked.

"They will."

"Sammy!" I said. "I haven't told Grandfather. Have you? Everything has happened so fast around here that—"

"He knows."

Of course he knew. He'd also know whether it would be a girl or a boy. I could save the expense of an ultrasound and just ask him.

Sammy chuckled.

"What?" I asked.

"Miccosukee medical technology," he said.

Now how did he know what I was thinking about Grandfather? I sighed. Would I be the only one in this family who didn't have the ability to read thoughts? I felt a tiny tug in my belly. Was that a yes or a no?

THE NEXT MORNING, Nappi and I talked over croissants and coffee, decaf for me, at my house.

"What do you have up your sleeve?" asked Nappi.

"What do you mean?" I asked, trying for a look of innocence, something I'm not much good at.

"You've got that look in your eye, the one that says 'don't get in my way.'"

"I'm going to visit Selma for another chat."

"She won't be willing to talk to you, you know."

"I'm going to take a chapter from your book, Nappi, and try a little 'family persuasion.'"

His eyes widened in shock.

"Oh, don't worry. I don't intend to get physical. If this doesn't work, I'll turn her over to you." I chuckled. "But it's gonna work."

"I thought I'd visit a law firm in Hartford while you're persuading Selma."

"Oh, come on. I want to go, too."

Nappi waggled a finger at me. "Private detectives have to know when to delegate, and you just delegated finding out about the law firm to me."

I agreed, but the issue bothered me the entire day while Grandy and I worked the shop.

"I can hear your brain grumping about something, Eve."

"That's my stomach growling."

"Don't lie to me. You're chewing on something. I want to know what it is."

"Delegating stuff. I hate to delegate, but Nappi says it's something any good detective does."

"He's right, and it's kind of him to call it 'delegating.' You're just so snoopy you can't let go of anything. You think no one else can do it as well as you. You're a control freak."

"A what?"

"A control freak. Like me. Now what's up?"

I shared with her our run-in with Freddie, leaving out, of course, the incident of the hit-and-run and the break-ins so she wouldn't worry or not worry as much.

"I want to know the name of the family Freddie was working for, but Nappi insists upon visiting the law firm alone. I think he has some kind of a contact there."

"Let Nappi do his work and you do yours. I know you're going to be looking into Brenda's past, but I'm not certain how you intend to go about that."

"I'm going to pay Selma a visit."

"That will get you nowhere."

I smiled and shrugged. "You never know." I hung a silver cocktail dress on the rack, considered it for myself, then decided there was no room in that dress for both me and the little one.

NAPPI AND I were to leave for Connecticut the next morning. This evening Sammy and I chose to tell the boys about their new sibling. We were seated around the table at Grandfather's, finishing our bowls of chicken stew. The boys were excited about the upcoming rodeo, and I was worried my trip would mean I couldn't see them compete.

"I'm going to try calf roping this year. My cousin Max has been teaching me, and he's loaning me one of his horses," said Jason, his smile wide with pride. "Of course," he added, a serious look overtaking the smile, "I don't expect to take first place. Next year."

The other boys pitched in excitedly with their stories of riding horses at their cousins' and also taking part in the calf roping.

"You guys don't have a chance of even placing. You'll be lucky to stay on your horses," Jason announced in that way older brothers can...with an adolescent sense of know-it-all.

At this jibe, the youngest burst into tears. Sammy reprimanded Jason for his unkind words and comforted the other boys by reminding them that participating was what this was all about. Not winning.

"Who knows? You all might surprise yourselves and us," Sammy added.

"Speaking of surprises," I piped up, grabbing hold of a good segue, "this family is going to have another member."

The three boys faces lit up and they looked at me. Jason asked, "Are we adopting another boy? I hope he's as old as me so he can help take care of these two." He gestured with his fork at his younger brothers.

"No, we're not adopting anyone. I'm going to have a baby." I pointed at my stomach.

The boys looked surprised, but smiled.

"You'll all get to look after the baby," Sammy said. The smiles faded a bit, but returned as they agreed among themselves that it might be fun to have someone younger than any of them to boss around.

"As long as it's not a girl," said Jason, making a face.

"Yeah," the others chimed in. "No girls allowed in this family."

"I'm a girl," I pointed out to them.

The boys considered this for a moment.

"If she's like you, then it's okay," he said. The others nodded their heads.

AFTER DINNER, WHEN the boys had snuggled into their sleeping bags in front of the fire in the main living space, Sammy, Grandfather, and I sat on the porch. Grandfather sat in his rocker puffing on his pipe while Sammy and I sat on the steps and gazed out over the canal to the dark swamp beyond.

"No sign of your father?" I asked.

"None," said Sammy.

Grandfather extracted the pipe from his mouth and said, "He's out there. I can feel him. He's waiting."

"Waiting for what?" I asked.

"For you to solve the murder." Grandfather tapped his pipe on the porch rail. "I'm going in." He bent and touched my shoulder. "Don't forget to wear the amulet I gave you when you go North tomorrow."

"I never go anywhere without it," I assured him. "When you're in there, tell the boys to quit talking and go to sleep. Tomorrow is a school day."

"I wish it weren't so late. We could take a ride in the canoe and go to our place in the swamp," Sammy said.

I wondered if he was more interested in being alone with me or if he thought being out in the swamps would bring him closer to his father, but I said nothing.

We sat for a while longer, listening to the music of the swamp, the croaking of frogs, the call of a bull alligator, and the soft walk of a shore bird through the reeds and cattails at the edge of the water.

Sammy got up and held his hand out to me. "You've got a long journey ahead of you. You need the sleep. Both of you need the sleep," he added.

He was right. I should get to sleep, but I was disappointed that we couldn't spend this night at our special swamp place. I took his hand and we went in.

I AWOKE HOURS LATER, restless and wide awake. So much depended upon what I could find out up North, both the fate of Sammy's father, the safety of Eleanor and her mother, and my own unfinished story. I got up, grabbed a sweater against the damp air, and went out to be by the water, to walk in the moonlight and think.

As I stood at the canal's edge, I heard a footfall behind me and turned, expecting that Sammy had also been wakeful and had joined me.

Mr. Egret stood behind me, unsmiling, a huge Bowie knife in a scabbard on his belt.

"I thought…" I began, my mouth dry with fear.

"You thought I left my knife in that man's gut, didn't you?"

FIFTEEN

"I HAVE MORE than one knife," he explained, pointing to the Bowie.

Why was I so afraid? I was only a scream away from the house. I couldn't let him see my fear.

"You know the police are looking for you," I said, standing my ground, although I wanted to turn and run.

He nodded.

"I also know you didn't kill that man, but you might know who did. You should give yourself up and tell the authorities what you know. It might help heal a lot of wounds from the past, mine included."

He was silent, then he held out his hand to me. "Come, I want to show you something."

A canoe was beached alongside the one Sammy and I used. This one was more crudely made, older. The wear on it indicated it had been used for many years. He gestured for me to get in.

"This must be the canoe you used all those years you spent in the swamp. You left it there, hidden, as if you planned to return. Were you not planning to remain here with your family? Was this always your intention? To come back and tease them with your presence and then disappear again? I guess Mr. Montrose's death gave you a good reason to go back into hiding."

I knew I was taunting him, perhaps an unwise move on my part. Maybe I did have the sight of Grandfather.

I could read this man's animosity toward me. The rage written in the lines on his face was revealed in the moonlight. He raised his arm, and I thought he would strike me, but instead he moved it toward the water, and again said, "Come."

Dared I go with him? Or would I be risking my life and that of my baby?

He made a grunting sound and the sides of his mouth curved upward. Was that a smile of some sort?

"I know of the baby. I would not hurt him."

"Well, now you've gone and spoiled it. We didn't know it was a boy."

He gave another grunt, this one filled with satisfaction. "The Egrets always have boys."

"I respect your Indian ways, but could we dispense with the intrigue for a moment? Why do you want me to come with you? And where?"

His whole person seemed to relax, and this time, he laughed out loud for just a moment. Then he looked back at the house as if worried he might wake someone.

"You are as everyone described you. More than curious. Nosey. You took on this case to prove me innocent, and I know you do not like me. I, too, am curious. I wonder why you would do that."

"I'm not doing it for you, you selfish old man. I'm doing it for Grandfather, for Sammy, and for our children."

"For your child."

"No, for all our children."

"If Sammy knew I was here," he said, "he would want me to do as you say: turn myself in. I have no intention of doing that. I will help you find what you're looking for." Again he held out his hand to me and gestured toward the canoe.

What the hell. I believed he wouldn't hurt Sammy's child, and that meant I was safe. Maybe he could help.

"Did you see who used your knife to kill Montrose?"

Before he could answer, a sound erupted, followed by another. Bullets. Someone was shooting at us.

Mr. Egret fastened his gaze on me. "You evil woman. You tried to trap me." Without another word, he ran for the cover of the palms and disappeared.

"What the hell were you thinking?" said a voice I recognized. It was Frida and she sounded angrier than I'd ever heard her.

She and a tall, thin man stepped from behind the chickee hut. "You jerk, you total jerk." She continued to spit words of derision toward the man at her side. "We want to take him into custody, not kill him."

"He's an Indian, and he's wanted for murder. What difference does it make whether we take him alive or not?"

I stood frozen, staring at the palms into which Mr. Egret had run. I could not forget the look of black hatred on his face. He hadn't liked me before this happened, and now he thought I had betrayed him.

Frida continued to berate the man as they walked up to me.

"You absolute idiot," I said. "I almost had him convinced he should cooperate with authorities. Who the hell is this man anyway? And what are you doing here? Are you spying on my family?"

"I'm sorry, Eve. We've had Grandfather Egret's house under surveillance since the murder. We thought his son might return here and I, er, my boss thought it might provide an opportunity to talk to him."

"You mean arrest him, don't you?"

The idiot who shot at my father-in-law found his tongue as well as his weapon. "I'm Reginald Butler. Miss Martinez is my partner."

Frida made a growling sound and poked her finger in his chest. "That's *Detective* Martinez to you, buddy, and you are *my* partner—for now, at least. I hope you didn't kill the man, and until we know for certain his fate, I need your weapon." She held out her hand.

"What the hell? No way. I'll give it to the captain, but no way am I allowing some backwoods detective to disarm me. We need to pursue our suspect, and that's what I'm going to do. I'll get him." Before she could stop him, Butler ran into the palm trees after Mr. Egret.

"You know he doesn't have any chance of finding him, don't you?" I asked Frida.

"Yeah, but the chase might settle him down a bit. That is, if he can find his way back here." She stepped over to the spot where Egret had stood and shined her flashlight on the ground. "I don't think he was hit. No blood. I'm not surprised. Butler is a notoriously bad shot at the range."

"What's going on here?" called Sammy from the porch. "Eve? I thought I heard a shot. Are you all right?" Grandfather was silhouetted in the porch light behind Sammy.

"It's just Frida."

"Frida? What's she doing out here at this time of night?" Sammy asked as he approached the two of us.

"I was trying to talk with your father," said Frida.

"He was here?" Sammy said.

"My partner drove him off." Frida explained what had happened and assured Sammy that his father was not hit.

Sammy shook his head in disbelief.

"There won't be another chance to talk with my father-in-law."

"Was he willing to cooperate?" Frida sounded surprised.

"Well, kind of. He wanted me to come with him. He had something to show me. Now we'll never know what he intended. Any trust he might have begun to develop in me is blown. Thanks a lot, Frida."

"I didn't shoot at him." There was a sharp edge to her voice.

"It was your gun-happy partner, I know, but Mr. Egret isn't stupid. Even if he hadn't been shot at, he would know from your appearance that you've been sitting on the house."

"He's our main suspect. It was his knife that killed Montrose, you know."

"Anyone could have used that knife. You said there were other prints on it."

"Oh right. There are hundreds of people wandering around in that swamp just looking for an opportunity to steal a knife and kill someone."

"Ladies," interrupted Grandfather Egret, "you're going to wake the boys with all your shouting. Angry will accomplish nothing. Where is your partner now?" he asked Frida.

"Off somewhere." Frida sounded discouraged. "Eve's right. We messed up. I should go look for him. He's a city boy. He'll be running in circles by now if he hasn't already been eaten by a gator."

"Leave him there then," I suggested with only a hint of humor.

"I'll make some tea and we can wait until the sun comes up in an hour. There's no sense in trying to find him in the dark." Sammy put his arm around my shoulders and pulled me toward the house. No one mentioned going after Lionel Egret. We all knew we wouldn't find him, even with the light of the coming day. The man was gone, perhaps this time for good.

By now I was so tired, I took a few sips of tea and then excused myself and fell into bed. I was awakened later by the sounds of laughter coming from the other room. It was late morning, and I had slept through the boys getting up to go to school and another event I wished I hadn't missed. At first light, Frida, accompanied by Grandfather Egret, set out to find Detective Butler. After several hours of searching, they found him tied to a palm tree with his handkerchief stuffed in his mouth. He was too terrified by having spent the night in the swamp to be anything other than grateful when Frida untied him. She took him back to the police car and left. According to Grandfather, he spoke not a word on the walk back. Grandfather was just relating the story to Sammy as I came into the room.

"I guess Frida won't have to talk to the captain about letting him go. I bet he resigned first thing this morning," I said, pouring myself a coffee.

I didn't want to leave without saying goodbye to the boys, so Nappi and I rescheduled our departure for the next morning. Frida called me as I was finishing my orange juice and confirmed my speculation that Reginald Butler would no longer be one of Sabal Bay's finest.

"Now what?" I asked.

"I'm hoping Linc will hate life in the city and be eager to return here. As incentive, the captain is offering him a raise."

"What were you offered to stay?" I asked. "And to work short-handed until Linc returns or they find someone else?"

She chuckled. "More of a raise."

"Good. I wonder, did Grandy's sister and her husband pay you a visit yesterday?"

"They stopped by, but I was called away on another case. I never got to talk to them. What's up?"

"A story you're going to find interesting. It might put the Montrose murder in another light."

"So tell me."

"Nope. As Grandy has pointed out to me many times, some stories are not mine to tell. This one is Irene's. I'm sure she'll be very cooperative."

I was more than a little certain Irene would tell her story to Frida, because I would be paying a visit to her this morning to ask a few more questions about her daughter, questions we had let slip by the other night. I wasn't trying to be unkind to Irene, but she hadn't told us the entire story. I understood she wanted to protect her daughter, but the daughter needed more from her mother than Irene could provide.

"HOW NICE OF YOU to stop by, Eve," said Irene when she opened the motel room door to me later that morning. She tried a welcoming smile, but it barely lifted the corners of her mouth. She knew my visit wasn't social, and the stiffening of her shoulders told me she was bracing herself for what was to come.

There was no sense in making the woman suffer any

longer. She had been through so much. It was time to bring out the whole story. I was just the one to get at it, so I asked the question that should have been asked the other night.

"Who was Brenda's father?"

Irene and Don both gaped at me, astonished.

"Why do you ask?" said Irene, recovering enough to gesture toward the sofa. I shook my head and continued standing.

"You know why I'm asking. Here's another question that you should answer: did Brenda know about her father? Did she know who he was?"

"No! I would never have told her about him. He wasn't a part of our lives."

"Well, no, at least not until someone paid you a visit and began asking you questions about her. You should have told us."

"And I told them what I had told everyone—that she was dead." The words seemed to slip out, and when she realized what she'd said, her hand flew to her mouth as if she could shove them back in.

My question about someone visiting her was a shot in the dark, one that paid off.

"Tell me about them. Who were they and what did they want?"

Irene looked at Don for encouragement.

"It was a few weeks ago. They said they were from Bay Ridge Hospital. That was the last facility where I placed Brenda before she disappeared. They showed me some official identification indicating they were from the accounting office at the hospital. They said they were tying up loose ends and trying to bring some closure on patients they had lost track of. Brenda was one. They wanted to know where she was, and when I told them she had died, they wanted to know the circumstances. They seemed satisfied with the story about her death and were about to leave when one of them told me it would help if I could show them a copy of her death certificate. I was terrified. I have no death certificate, you know."

"What did you do?"

"What could I do? I told them the truth, that she had disappeared many years ago. They assured me that they would enter 'unknown' in the files. I haven't heard from them since."

"You didn't think their visit was important enough to tell us about it the other night?"

"What difference does it make now? She's alive." Irene wrung her hands and her eyes darted around the room in anxiety.

"Let's get back to my original question. Who was Brenda's father?"

"I'd rather not say. What does it matter after all these years? He never took an interest in her. In fact, I never saw him, once he found out I was pregnant. That was a pretty clear message he wasn't interested."

"Maybe he is now."

Irene smiled. "I don't think so. I read his obituary in the Hartford papers. His chance to know his daughter is long past."

Irene assured me she and Don would return to Frida's office today to tell the detective what they knew about Brenda. Even now, it was clear the story of Brenda's birth and her disappearance made Irene uncomfortable, bringing up memories that were unpleasant. She blamed herself for Brenda's difficulties, and no amount of reassurance that she had done all a mother could do would dissuade her from that guilt. She believed finding her daughter alive would give her a second chance to be a good mother. Irene felt the death of Brenda's father made his identity all the more irrelevant. Something told me it wasn't, but the closed look on her face said she didn't want to pursue the subject.

Like Irene, who blamed herself for being a bad mother to Brenda and yearned for a chance to redo the relationship, I had my own guilt to deal with. I knew it wasn't my fault that Frida and her partner showed up just when my father-in-law decided he could trust me, but I kept replaying the incident again and again in my mind, hoping for a different outcome. It all came out the same way: my chance to find out what he knew had come and gone.

I WAS LOST in thought as Nappi and I sped down the Beeline Highway toward the airport in West Palm the next morning.

"You're quiet, Eve," he said. "Is everything all right? You're not feeling sick, are you?"

"Physically, I feel fine. In fact, I can't think of when I felt better." It was true. My appetite was back, the nausea gone, fatigue settling in only when I didn't get at least eight hours of sleep at night. Of course, a nap in the afternoon could make up the difference.

I recounted my conversation with Irene. "I know she thinks the identity of Brenda's father is irrelevant, and I can't push her into revealing his name without telling her why I think it is important. This whole thing has made her both frantic and hopeful. I don't think she needs any more aggravation right now."

"Are you thinking what I'm thinking?" asked Nappi.

"I'd bet a pair of my stiletto heels that Brenda's father is from a prominent Connecticut family. Why else has Irene kept a lid on his identity for so long? If he's just some average dude, why the big secret, but if he's someone important, from a family with influence and an image to maintain, that's another matter."

"He could be from the very family with connections to the law firm named by my friend Freddie," Nappi said. "Maybe I was too quick to scare Freddie off. Now who will the firm hire to find Brenda?"

"You think the family is that interested in Brenda?"

He snorted. "You know as well as I do that Freddie wasn't hired to find her, but to eliminate her."

"Did she see something that made her a threat to the family?" I asked.

"I think it might be simpler than that. She *is* someone—her father's heir, as is her daughter Eleanor. Someone in that family isn't keen on sharing the wealth with either of them."

We had veered onto the turnpike at Jog Road. I watched the scenery go by, expensive houses and condos protected by high walls from the world of ordinary folks.

"Isn't it interesting," I said, "that Brenda's so-called delusions of someone stalking her were probably correct? Maybe the woman isn't as crazy as everyone has made her out to be. You might have difficulty shaking the truth out of the law firm. Lawyer-client privilege and all that."

"Privilege between a mob guy and this hoity-toity law firm? Are we talking about the same client here?

Freddie the Bull? I can be very persuasive, you know," Nappi said, a smile in his voice.

"Hmm, but you'll be taking on a law firm. They know the law and can use it against you."

"I know a lot of lawyers, most of them better at what they do than the firm that hired Freddie."

We pulled into the long-term parking garage and dropped off the car. As we made our way into the terminal, Nappi put his hand on my arm. I stopped walking and faced him. "You're going to tell me something I don't want to hear."

"Hear me out before you say anything." He looked around at the people scurrying past with their luggage, parents trying to restrain children cranky from lack of sleep, while passengers hurried toward the gates, worried they would be delayed in a security line and miss their flight. He pointed toward a nearby restaurant. "In there."

We took a seat in the corner where the noise was less deafening than out near the concourse.

Nappi signaled to the waiter and ordered two iced teas.

"It's never a good thing to obtain your money by hiring the likes of Freddie. That says to me these people are desperate. They don't want anyone to get in their way. By taking on this case, you're getting in their way, Eve. I can't let you take point on this one. I'll find out the name," he held up his hand to stop me from interrupting, "and follow up on it."

"What do you want me to do? Go to a matinee while you use your powers of persuasion to find out who is trying to kill Eleanor and her mother? This is my case, you know."

"I think you're defining 'case' too narrowly. Don't you want to talk with Dr. Sandhurst again? Isn't that part of the case?"

"It looks as if that is about me and Selma, not about Brenda."

"You don't know that for certain, do you?"

He was right. Mary Appel as a patient in Hopkins Hospital was something I wanted to know more about, whether it concerned my mother or Eleanor's. Or both.

SIXTEEN

THERE WAS SOMETHING to be said for delegating parts of the investigation to others, as Grandy had urged me to do, or dividing the case in half, as Nappi liked to define it. The case, however, was much more complex than Nappi determining the name of Brenda's father and finding out who was trying to find her and my following up on the Hopkins Hospital connection. There was still the matter of who killed Mr. Montrose and why, and what bothered me most of all: where were Eleanor and her mother? My concern about Eleanor brought to mind Jerry. Neither Nappi nor I had been able to get in touch with him for days. His phone went to voicemail and later to a message saying the mailbox was full. What trouble had he gotten himself into now? Did he drag Eleanor into it with him? This was the question I asked Nappi as we deplaned in Hartford.

He shook his head and said, "Later."

True to the pact we had established with Chief Raleigh in Tillahook, I called the chief and updated him on what we were doing.

"Tell Mr. Napolitani thanks for ridding the town of those goons. No sign of them since you left," said Chief Raleigh.

"Nappi had a chat with them and warned them off looking for the Montrose family. He and I had to fly back to Florida, but we're back in Connecticut now. We have some leads here to follow.

"I'll keep you posted on what we find here, and you'll do the same. I'd like to think that Eleanor's mother might want to get in touch with her daughter, but that doesn't seem to be the case. No one has set eyes on her since she left for Florida." I decided he didn't need to know that Eleanor had dropped out of sight and we were looking for her. It made us look too much like rank amateurs if we couldn't keep track of an important witness.

We disconnected.

Nappi took the car we'd left at the airport, and I rented a compact. While waiting for the bus to take me to the car-rental place located off terminal, I made a call I wasn't happy to make. The person I contacted, however, seemed to understand my request and didn't seem surprised to hear from me. We arranged a meeting at Hopkins after lunch.

On the way to Hopkins, I stopped for lunch at a restaurant I remembered my parents and I often visited. It overlooked Long Island Sound, today shrouded in low-lying clouds. The view was gray, visibility limited to the rocky shore nearby, but the Reuben sandwiches were as gigantic as I remembered. I gave the serving my best and left only a small remnant of crust on the plate.

I arrived at Hopkins several minutes before one in the afternoon. Selma's secretary told me she was in, but when she buzzed Selma, she was told she didn't have time to see me.

"Tell her I will let the hospital administrative board know she talked about patient files with me."

The secretary relayed the information. Selma opened the door to her office, her face like a Nor'easter. She beckoned to me to come in.

"I guess my threat scared you, huh?"

"Don't be silly. It's your word against mine." She didn't ask me to sit, and she didn't either. She wanted this to be a brief meeting.

"There is the question of how I knew about those files if you didn't tell me."

"A shot in the dark from a daughter who knew how crazy her mother was. That's all." She tilted her head back and to one side and crossed her arms over her chest, a posture of smug certainty. "Now, I suggest you leave or I'll be forced to call security and—"

"And they'll slap me in a strait jacket and throw me in a padded cell?"

She laughed. "You don't know much about facilities for mentally ill people, do you?"

"Well," I said, standing my ground, "if the administrative board won't move you, then how about someone else?"

"The only person who could sway me into releasing those files would be your mother, Eve, and I understand she's dead."

"No, there's someone else, Selma." Dr. Sandhurst, Selma's father, appeared in the doorway, a scowl on his face. "You seem to have crossed some ethical lines here, my dear," he said. "You told Eve about patient files, violating patient confidentiality, and you compromised me at the same time."

Selma reached behind her and steadied herself by grabbing her office chair. "I never implicated you, Dad. I never would do that."

"No? Well, the files have been compromised, and Eve is willing to go to the board to tell them that. If they find out what you said, it will be your job here, and you'll never work anywhere else."

I thought Selma might break down in tears. Her hands shook and her face was pale. Her glance moved from her father to me. "Eve," she begged, "please don't do this to me. I'm sorry I said what I did. Can't we just forget about it?"

"No, we cannot forget about it. That file is important to me, not just because it has my mother's name on it, but because there are lives at stake, lives that are intertwined with that of the woman in that file. I could get a court order to have it released, but if I do that, I won't keep my mouth shut about how I came to hear about it."

"What do you want?" she asked, her mouth drawn in an ugly, tight line.

"I'll give the two of you some time together to talk about it. I expect to hear from you tomorrow."

I could have convinced Selma to show me the file, but she would have done so grudgingly. The knowledge that she had failed in her father's eyes would work far better. Selma would fall all over herself to be helpful if her father told her to cooperate. I patted myself on the back for calling him this morning before I approached her.

What did I think I would find in that file? I wasn't certain, but I needed to know how old the woman named Mary Appel was when admitted to Hopkins, what year she had entered treatment, and how long she had stayed. I was taking a chance, hoping that I wouldn't find *the* Mary Appel, the woman who was my mother.

THE CALL CAME the next morning. I was awake and feeling perky, satisfied that things would go my way with respect to the file. Man, was I wrong.

"It's Selma," she said in a sulky voice. "I can't let you see the file."

"What?"

"It's gone."

What was she trying to pull? "It was there just the other day. You were snooping into it before we met for dinner. Remember?"

"I know, but when Dad and I went to retrieve it yesterday, it was gone."

"It took you almost a day to get back to me and tell me this."

"You gave us twenty-four hours."

"I gave you twenty-four hours, but not to lose the file. Are you at the hospital now?" I asked.

"Yes. Dad's here with me. What are you going to do?" She sounded frightened.

"I'll be right over."

I called Nappi in his room. He had contacted me when he got in late last night, and we were planning to meet this morning over breakfast to compare notes.

"Are you awake?" I asked him. "I'm sorry to disturb you so early, but—"

"I'm having my second cup of coffee. I had room service send up coffee and pastries. Come on over. We can talk."

"Oh, you're not going to believe what happened to me just now," I said, but the line had gone dead.

I grabbed a quick shower and was at Nappi's door in less than ten minutes. Let Selma stew over the lost file. It wasn't likely it would reappear on its own. I was certain she and her father were working hard on determining how they would handle this. I couldn't imagine any story with an ending that let Selma or the institution off the hook. The file was gone.

When I told Nappi about the missing file, he said, "I'm not surprised. This case is turning out to be uglier than I thought, but let's set aside what I know and focus on that file. Someone had to have taken it, but why?"

"And who?"

I chugged a cup of decaf and grabbed a croissant. "I want you with me when I talk to the Doctors Sandhurst." If they were lying about anything to do with that file, Nappi could use his persuasive personality to extract the truth from them.

I COULD TELL by the drawn expressions on their faces that they weren't lying. Both of them looked as if they hadn't slept at all. They'd discovered last night the file was gone, but waited until this morning to tell me. Selma seemed to have figured out when the file went missing and how it happened, or so she said.

"We had our yearly audit last week. The auditors were in and out of my office for several days."

"They wouldn't have reason to look at confidential patient files, would they?" I asked.

"No, but the files are all here, and the auditors were in my office for the day. The patient records were locked." Selma gestured at the file cabinets that lined one side of the room.

"Were they broken into?" asked Nappi. "I don't see any evidence of forced entry." His gaze traveled over the cabinets, and he stepped across the room to get a closer look at them.

"No, but I suppose someone could have gotten a key…" began Selma.

"How? Who?" I spit out the questions.

"I don't know. One of the auditors."

"Who are your auditors?" asked Nappi.

"We used a new firm this year," Selma said. "Our old firm informed us they couldn't handle the job because one of their accountants left and they were short-handed."

"Where did you find the new auditors?" asked Nappi.

"The old firm recommended them to us. They have great references. In fact, they do a lot work for prestigious law firms," said Selma's father.

"Firms like Teller, Markowitz, Sterns, Babcock, and Tranho?" asked Nappi.

That was the firm Freddie the Bull said he was working for before Nappi shooed him off. Nappi and I exchanged knowing looks.

"You know who took the file?" said Selma. "Can we get it back before the board finds out it's missing?"

"You think you're off the hook because the file is gone. I assume it's the only file missing?"

"We think so," said Selma. She sounded relieved there was only the one file stolen, but she was wrong.

"We don't know what else is gone from the files, Selma," her father said. "The board needs to know about this situation. We'll need to go through all our patient records now. The board will want to know the details about the theft, too."

Selma fell back into her office chair. "I am so screwed."

I pointed at her. "It's not just about you, Selma. I

have a stake in this too. You read that file earlier. You need to tell me everything you remember from it."

"I'm not going to tell you anything. This is all your fault."

"*My* fault?" I grabbed her arm and pulled her out of the chair and shook her like a dog with his favorite chew toy. "How is this my fault?"

The door to Selma's office opened.

"Hi, everyone," came a voice from the doorway. It was Jerry, and behind him was Eleanor.

"What are you doing here?" I asked.

"I found Eleanor. Aren't you glad?" Jerry sounded disappointed, as if he expected me to offer him some kind of a reward for his work.

"I was going to tell you this morning, Eve," Nappi said, "but the news about the missing file got in the way. I asked Jerry to meet us here."

"Did you find her?" asked Eleanor. "Did you find our mother?"

Selma and her father looked confused at Eleanor's words. It was an issue I wasn't keen on delving into right now, so I hustled Eleanor and Jerry out of Selma's office and closed the door behind me.

"We'll deal with this later," I told them. "Sit." I pointed to some chairs in the waiting area. "I'll be back as soon as I finish in there. I may have some news for you then, Eleanor."

Nappi was patiently explaining what Selma needed to do about the stolen files. Jerry's appearance seemed to give her some kind of hope that the theft could be kept from the authorities and the board. Selma was grasping at straws.

Her father took her arm and shook her gently. "This

will not go away, my dear. You made a mistake and now you need to own up to it. We must let the authorities know there has been a break-in, and we'll need to do a more thorough search of all our patient records to determine what all was taken." The firmness in his voice signaled he would brook no argument from her. He picked up her desk phone and held it out to her.

Her father looked at me and shook his head while she made the call. The lines on his face seemed to deepen in sadness. His daughter had disappointed him.

"The police are sending someone right out," said Selma.

"Good," I said. "You have time to review with me what you know about that file. Perhaps your father can help, since he was the director here at that time."

"I'm not certain if I can remember much about the woman. She was your mother, is that right?" asked Dr. Sandhurst.

"I don't think so. I think she was posing as my mother. My mother died when I was a child. Her stay here seems to have been after, but perhaps you can corroborate that by telling me the dates she was here."

"I can't give you the exact year, but Dad and I had our discussion about your unusual last name when both of us were in college, so it had to have been shortly before that."

I remembered from our conversation over dinner a few weeks ago that Selma had mentioned her father had asked about my name when Selma and I were college friends.

"How can you not remember the year at least? You just read that file a short time ago, or did you skim it for just enough details to throw in my face and make me squirm?" I felt the heat rise in my chest. I wanted to put my hands around her throat and squeeze.

Selma almost made me act on that impulse when she said, "I did make you squirm, didn't I?" She gave me a smug little smile of triumph. She might lose her job for her ethical lapse, but she would make me pay by withholding information about the file.

"Selma…" her father said with warning in his voice.

"Oh, all right. Let's see. I do remember we changed our filing system about the time I did my residency here. Your mother's file," she shot me another smirk, "was in one of the older folders—folders that went back fifteen or twenty years."

Dr. Sandhurst nodded. "That would be about right. I remember the name was fresh in my memory when Selma introduced you to me. That had to have been when the two of you were freshmen in college."

That would have made me around eighteen and Eleanor, at least ten years my junior, about eight.

I must have spoken out loud without realizing it.

"You told me when we were in college that your mother was dead. Now we find that not only was she alive but that you have a younger sister," Selma said. Her tone was haughty, as if I had betrayed her trust by withholding family secrets.

"That's not the case." At least I didn't think it was.

Both Sandhursts seemed to prick up their ears.

"You see…" I began and told them everything I knew about the Montroses.

Both of them were silent after I finished.

"Now you understand why that file is so important," said Nappi.

Dr. Sandhurst nodded. "Shouldn't Eleanor be here when we discuss the file then?"

I shook my head. "That's not the way she should learn about her mother's identity. She's still convinced we share the same mother."

"Isn't that possible?" Dr. Sandhurst said. "What if your mother didn't die in that boating accident? Surviving an accident like that might have resulted in amnesia and what we now call post-traumatic shock syndrome."

I tried to dismiss his words. I didn't want to circle back through what I had believed and now didn't want to believe.

Selma broke in before I could say anything, "I remember when I read through the file that Mary Appel repeatedly said someone was trying to find her—her husband, I think."

"But did she say it was her husband?" I asked.

Selma was silent for a moment. "I can't remember. I didn't read the file for details."

"So it could have been one of her delusions that her husband was trying to harm her?" I said.

"Some of the details about her are coming back to me," said Dr. Sandhurst. "She had a lot of delusions, and she felt someone was after her, but I can't say whether it was her husband." Dr. Sandhurst fell silent, his lips moving as if he was working through some memory, trying to bring it to the surface.

I let him think and turned the conversation in another direction. "Hopkins is an expensive place. Did the file indicate how she paid for her therapy here?"

"That wouldn't be in her patient file, but in the business file," Selma said.

"Can we look at that?" I asked.

"It's gone also," Selma said.

"Whoever wanted to find Mary Appel's files did a thorough job of removing her from our records. It's as if she was never here," said Dr. Sandhurst.

"I think that's what they wanted to accomplish. Mary Appel or the woman posing as her never existed," said Nappi.

"Except we know she did," said Selma.

"That may not be to your advantage," said Nappi, a note of warning in his voice.

Dr. Sandhurst seemed to understand what Nappi was suggesting. "We might be in danger then."

"Let's not overdramatize this. Someone took some files 'That's it," said Selma, flipping her hand in dismissal.

Selma's secretary knocked and opened the door. "The police are here," she said.

"Look," said Selma, "since there are no records to say Mary Appel was ever a patient here, can't we just tell the police I made a mistake and there are no files missing? Who's to know and who will get hurt by not admitting the break-in?"

My God. Selma was still trying to save her ass.

Dr. Sandhurst heaved a deep sigh of disappointment in his daughter.

"Oh, all right, then. I'll talk to them." Selma straightened her shoulders and tried to look professional, but her hand shook when she ran it through her hair to smooth it back.

"No, Selma. We'll talk to them together. I should never have mentioned Eve's mother's name. It was what began this whole thing."

Dr. Sandhurst was an honorable man, but I wanted

to tell him he wasn't doing his daughter any favors by sharing the blame with her. I wondered if this was how he had raised her, sharing responsibility for deeds that were hers alone.

"Dr. Sandhurst," I said to him before he followed his daughter out of the office, "did you raise Selma by yourself?"

His brow wrinkled, but he didn't seem altogether surprised by my question.

"Selma's mother died when she was beginning kindergarten. Breast cancer. You think I did a bad job with her, don't you?"

"I'm sure you did what you thought was right. It can't be easy being a single parent."

"That's kind of you to say, but when I see what Selma has become, I think I failed as a father." As he spoke the last words, his eyes lit up. "That's it. Now I remember. Mary Appel was committed here by her father."

SEVENTEEN

I WAS ALMOST shocked into silence, but I blurted out, "Her father? She was admitted here by her father? Are you sure?"

"I can't believe I forgot about our conversation. He told me he hadn't been involved in Mary's upbringing, but he was trying to do better. That's what he said, 'I'm trying to do better for her now.'"

"What was his name?"

"I don't remember that. I assumed it was Appel. I don't recall any other name being used."

"But she was in a relationship with Henry Montrose, Eleanor's father. The name couldn't have been Appel," I insisted.

"I'm sorry. It was so long ago, and we have so many patients. I wouldn't have remembered him if it hadn't been for our shared circumstances, our feelings about our daughters."

I followed him out of the office as his daughter was showing the police into a conference room next door.

"I think we'll just leave you to explain the situation to the police," I said to Dr. Sandhurst. "Don't let Selma put the blame on you for this one. She can stand on her own two feet."

I signaled to Jerry and Eleanor, who followed Nappi and me down the hallway toward the exit.

"The cops may want to talk with us also," said Nappi.

"Later is soon enough. It will just muddy the waters to have us around here now. I think we all could use a coffee break. Somebody has a lot of explaining to do," I said.

"Me? I found her, didn't I?" Jerry said.

"For once you're off the hook. No, I mean Eleanor."

Eleanor's mouth opened in an expression of surprise. "I didn't—"

"You can ride with me, and we'll talk." I grabbed her arm and steered her toward my rental car. "There's a diner down the road. We can meet up there," I called to Jerry and Nappi.

"I don't know why you want to talk with me. I didn't do anything wrong," said Eleanor. Tears filled her eyes.

"Your father was murdered, and you could be in danger also. Your mother has her issues, as you well know, but she's right. Someone is trying to harm her, trying to harm the entire family. You were in a safe place in the apartment in Sabal Bay. You knew that. Why did you leave there?"

"Mother got in touch with me and told me to go back to New York. She said it was safe now, that she would meet me there. The reason she went to Florida was to find you, to protect you from your violent father, to warn you he might be after you too."

It was a crazy story, but one Eleanor and her father had lived with for years—Eleanor's belief and Brenda's delusion that I was her daughter, that her name was Mary Appel. Her feeling of being pursued might have been dead on, but the identity of her stalker was not what her delusional mind told her it was.

After talking to Eleanor, I had two important tasks to accomplish: I needed to make a phone call to my

Great-Aunt Irene, who was still keeping family secrets she needed to let go of, and I had to find Eleanor's mother, who held the key to this whole mystery. I hoped I was right to believe she might now be capable of differentiating between delusions and reality.

"She didn't show up at the house in Tillahook, did she?" I asked Eleanor.

"No." Eleanor cried quietly, wiped away her tears, and then asked, "Was she ever a patient at Hopkins?"

"Yes, she was. You would have been around eight when she was admitted there. You don't remember it?"

She shook her head. "She was in and out of places, but when I was in second or third grade, she came home after a hospital stay and said she was never going to any institution again. Dad said she could stay home. She said something strange: 'They won't find me, will they?' And Dad said, 'No, he promised me they wouldn't find you.'"

He. Who was that?

"He who?" I asked.

She shrugged her shoulders. "I don't know. Maybe the doctor."

"Do you remember anything else your dad said?"

She shook her head. "I was glad Mom was back with us, but then her bad dreams and her hallucinations began again. As I got older, she got meaner to me. She wanted you back. I don't know why she let you go. I guess for your own safety, because she claimed your father was a bully. I didn't know your identity until she told me who you were and that she was going to find you and warn you."

I pounded on the steering wheel. "Enough!" I shouted. Eleanor jumped.

"Sorry, sorry, sorry, but I can't let you go on like this. We don't share a mother, Eleanor. You mother assumed my mother's identity. My mother was dead, and your mother used my mother's name."

Eleanor shook her head. "No. No, Eve. Why would she do that? Why would she use a dead woman's name and identity?"

"Because the real Mary Appel was dead. It protected your mother. She was delusional, but some of what she believed was true."

Eleanor continued to stare at me, but the look of shock and disbelief on her face was soon replaced by another expression—pity.

"Oh, poor Eve. You don't want to believe your mother is still alive because it means people you loved betrayed you. What can I do to make you understand?"

I had just the answer for that. "I need to talk with your mother face-to-face. So, where is she?"

Eleanor's face changed again. This time it took on a sly look. "You're trying to make me tell you where she's hiding so you can inform your friend Frida, that detective. Then she'll arrest my mother for the murder of my father and your father-in-law will be able to leave his place of hiding. I'm not telling you a thing, even if you are my sister." She sat back in her seat, crossing her arms over her chest in defiance.

WELL, AT LEAST she had revealed her mother's location when she said Frida would arrest her. That meant she had to be near Sabal Bay and not in Connecticut or New York. I smiled to myself.

"How about one more little thing?" I said as I pulled into the diner parking lot.

She drew her lower lip under her top one and thought for a moment. "I'm not saying yes or no until I know what you want."

"I want you to get in touch with your mother and ask her to meet with me. We're going back to Florida this afternoon."

No one had spotted Brenda since this whole saga began. I wasn't even certain she was still alive. We had only Henry and Eleanor's word that she had come to Florida looking for me. Maybe they'd lied. Sure, Eleanor said her mother had told her to return to New York, but maybe Eleanor was lying about that conversation also. Or she was having her own set of delusions. Given how the poor woman was raised, it wouldn't surprise me if she had emotional issues. This detecting business was making me skeptical of almost everyone I knew.

I parked and got out of the car. Eleanor remained in the passenger seat. Rolling down the window, she said, "I don't want to talk anymore with anyone. I'll wait here."

I opened the door and pulled her out of the car. "No you won't. You led us on a merry chase trying to find you, and that's not going to happen again. I also don't want you in touch with your mother without my hearing what you're saying." I grabbed her purse and tried to extract her cellphone, but she snatched the purse back and held it behind her back.

"Leave me alone or I'll scream," she warned.

"No, you won't, because if you do, it will draw attention to us. You don't want that. The police will get involved, and you'll have a lot of explaining to do when I tell them I'm a PI and responsible for bringing you back to Florida as a witness in a murder."

"I'm not a witness!"

"Who do you think the authorities will believe?" I gave her a minute to think about that, but I needn't have bothered. Jerry came over to us and put his arm around Eleanor.

"What's wrong, Pookie?" he asked, rubbing her shoulder in a comforting manner.

Pookie?

She leaned into his caress. "Eve is threatening me."

"Evie, how can you do that? Eleanor is very fragile right now with her father murdered and her mother missing."

Okay. So now I was the bad guy, and Jerry was her knight in shining armor, here to rescue her. I didn't care. I wanted to ensure she didn't bolt again, both for her own safety and because she was our ticket to finding her mother.

Jerry and Eleanor walked arm and arm into the diner, Jerry turning to give me a dirty look—eyebrows drawn together, eyes dark with disapproval. And then he winked. Good old Jerry. Maybe this time he'd be an asset.

"So you see, Eleanor," Nappi explained to her as he patted her hand in a fatherly way, "it's unlikely that the woman who was in Hopkins when you were a kid was Eve's mother, even though she used Eve's mother's name."

We had chosen a booth by the window. Eleanor sat across from Nappi and me, Jerry at her side. He had an arm draped over her shoulders.

Eleanor looked into Nappi's face as if she could determine from his expression whether he was telling her the truth. She seemed to want to believe him, but that meant she would have to accept that her mother had lied to her. Eleanor was having none of that.

"I know that's what you think, but my mother knew everything about Eve's childhood, down to details about Eve's birthday parties when she was little." She turned to me with a frown on her face. "Not that you'll believe me on this, but she told me you had a teddy bear named Teddy."

So did almost every kid my age, I thought, but since I had given up trying to convince Eleanor that we didn't share a mother, I let it go and played with a sugar packet. Finally I ripped it open and dumped it into my tea, along with the three I'd already added. This pregnancy seemed to be giving me a sweet tooth. No cole slaw and ribs for this gal. I wanted to devour an entire chocolate cake and follow it with a lemon meringue pie.

The expression on Nappi's face said he was about to give up convincing her the woman in Hopkins wasn't Mary Appel.

"I don't get it," said Jerry. "Why would Eleanor's mother use the name Mary Appel if she wasn't Mary Appel?"

I wanted to jump across the table and shake him for taking Eleanor's side, but then it occurred to me that maybe he was just playing dumb, something Jerry was good at. His question opened the door to further explanation, one Eleanor might just buy. If not, she needed to hear it.

Okay, I'd give it yet another try. I explained what I had worked out when in Selma's office. "It was to protect her. Your grandfather, whom you've never met, paid for her stay there. I think he knew she was in danger from someone, perhaps—"

Nappi didn't let me finish. "Perhaps from his family. They can't have been happy that he had a child out of wedlock. I think the poor man rethought how he had treated his daughter and decided to help her by having her stay at a private, well-respected facility."

"What I don't understand is how he found her," I said. "Irene thought she was dead, so he didn't learn about her through Irene." I gave the container holding the pies and cakes a longing look.

Eleanor had listened without commenting, but now she said, "Who's Irene?"

"Well, that's the good part of our not having the same mother. You have a grandmother who I know will be thrilled to meet you."

"But I already have Grandy," she said.

I gritted my teeth in frustration, trying to control myself, but I couldn't help saying, "Grandy is mine. You get Irene, and that's that." It was a mean thing to say to someone who was grieving the loss of a father to murder and suffering from confusion over her mother's past.

Jerry, Nappi, and Eleanor gave me startled looks, then Nappi came to my defense. "Eve's right. You'll still have Grandy. You're related. You're just not her granddaughter."

"So, is Irene as nice as Grandy?" asked Eleanor.

"Nicer," I rushed to assure her. What I didn't share with her was my suspicion that as nice as she was, she hadn't come clean about her daughter's past. When I got a free moment alone, I thought I should call her so we could have a heart-to-heart, but then I nixed that idea. Heart-to-hearts when it came to the secrets Irene was keeping to herself were meant to happen face-to-face.

"So, when do I meet her?" asked Eleanor.

At long last we had broken through her stubborn insistence that we were sisters.

"Not that I believe she's my grandmother, but she is a relative, I guess." Eleanor raised her chin in triumph.

"Fine, then. Let's go back to the hotel and pack. We need to make the evening flight to West Palm."

NAPPI STOPPED BY my room before we left for the airport.

"We haven't had a chance for a moment alone to talk," he said. "But first, sit down and let me take a look at you. I promised Grandy and Sammy I'd take good care of you. You look exhausted."

I sank onto the bed. "I am, but it's more the emotional ups and downs that are tiring me. I've pretty much resolved my own doubts about my mother, but then there's Eleanor and her insistence that we share the same mother. It's so aggravating dealing with her, but I try to remind myself that she's without a father now and her mother's location is at best in flux."

"You see now that Eleanor's story about your mother is total fabrication, right?"

I nodded. "At this moment that's what I believe, but then the doubts come flooding back. I know it's because I want to believe my parents are not gone, but...." I sighed and rubbed my hand across my forehead.

"If they are not dead, then what are you left with? A deceiving grandmother, a crazy mother, and an abusive father. You can see what having a mother with emotional problems has done to Eleanor."

Nappi's putting it that way swept the doubts from my mind. My loving parents were gone. Grandy had raised me. I'd turned out just fine except for my relentless need to snoop into criminal matters.

"Nappi, everyone feels sorry for Eleanor. I do, too, most of the time, but she can be stubborn, can't she?"

"What are you saying?"

"All our information says her mother abused her emotionally, maybe even physically. Maybe her need for us to share the same mother is a way for her to convince herself that although her mother was a bad mother, she was also my bad mother—not that Eleanor deserved to be abused by her."

Nappi looked down at the floor, considering what I had said.

"That's possible, but we were told her mother often compared the two of you, saying what a wonderful daughter you were and how awful Eleanor was. That's not two abused children sharing the abusive mother, is it?"

"No, but maybe Eleanor doesn't see it quite that way. She's just focusing on pleasing her mother, helping her find me, the lost daughter. Eleanor might think that would make her mother love her more."

Nappi began to pace the room, then stopped abruptly. "It's more likely that finding you means less love for Eleanor. Bringing the two of you together might not get Eleanor the love she wants. Unless you continue to behave as you have."

"What do you mean?"

"You don't believe Eleanor and her mother's story. If you meet up with Eleanor's mother and still deny she's your mother, then aren't you the bad daughter in both their eyes?"

"I suppose so. So what?"

"You'd need to be punished for not recognizing your own mother."

"Punished? How? By whom?"

"Maybe by Eleanor. Or perhaps by her mother. That she is Mary Appel is Brenda's delusion, one she convinced Henry and her daughter to believe. We know the woman has had mental problems most of her life. If the diagnosis of paranoid schizophrenic given her at Hopkins is correct, then the woman is capable of violence."

"As in killing her husband?" I asked.

EIGHTEEN

NAPPI SAT DOWN beside me on the bed and took my hand in his. "I know you're going to try for a meeting with Eleanor's mother, but I think it would be best that you not see her alone."

"I'm sure Eleanor will want to be with me."

"I don't think that's safe either. We've never met the mother, but we know her history, and I'm not certain Eleanor doesn't share some of her mother's paranoid tendencies."

I nodded. "She thinks I want to tell Frida where 'our' mother is hiding."

"There's something else."

"What?"

"I met with that law firm that hired my buddy Freddie to help locate Eleanor's mother."

"Good. So now we have a name."

"No name. My powers of persuasion failed me. My contact at the firm has been let go. I think Freddie let the firm know I would be paying them a visit, so they cleaned house and removed my snitch."

"We still have ways of finding out the identity of the family. I'm sure the police will put pressure on the accounting firm that did the Hopkins audit. That should give us a lead."

Nappi smiled. "Why not give your friend Selma a

call before we go to the airport? It might be nice to hear how she fared with the authorities."

I considered his suggestion and decided Selma wouldn't want to hear from me again, not ever again. So I called her father.

Dr. Sandhurst's voice dragged with fatigue on the phone, but he understood my need to know what had happened. "The police contacted the accountants, who informed him that one of their employees involved in the Hopkins audit was new to the position. They gave the authorities his name and said he had not showed up for work after the Hopkins job. Further investigation revealed that he doesn't exist; his references are phony, as are his education and his home address. I'm sorry I can't give you more, Eve."

"I understand. How did things go with the Hopkins board?"

"We meet with them this evening. I assume Selma will be fired."

"How do you feel about that?"

I heard his deep sigh. "She brought it on herself. I could try to intervene with some of my friends on the board, but I think I'll let her be the grownup on this one."

"She'll do just fine." I didn't have any reason to believe that, but I felt sorry for the man.

"By the way, the police would like to talk with you at some point. They asked where you could be found, and I said I didn't know your whereabouts. I assume you'd like to follow through on what you have about Mary Appel and not be bothered tying up loose ends just for the sake of Selma and me."

"I'll give them a call from Florida."

"Oh, is that where you are now? Fast trip home, then."

I left it at that and wished him well.

"Another dead end." I shared with Nappi what I had found out about the auditing firm. "Let's get going. I'm eager to get back to Florida and have a talk with my Great-Aunt Irene."

I wanted to go home for other reasons, more important ones. I missed the boys, I missed Sammy, Grandfather, Grandy, Max, Madeleine, David, their twins, and my friends. I missed my family. There was nothing I would miss about Connecticut, which had been my home for so many years, yet I needed to make one more stop before we went to the airport.

IT TOOK ME more than fifteen minutes to locate the family gravesite at the cemetery. I hadn't visited here for years, and I assumed I would not visit again for a long time. Sabal Bay was now my home. My parents' bodies were not buried in this cemetery. No bodies had been found to be buried—something I knew would, despite everything that is rational, haunt me forever. Even if they were, it was more important to hold my memories of them close and not the location of their remains. The site was at the crest of a hill close to an old oak tree. The marker read, "Mary and Josh Appel, together in Love," and gave the years of their births and the date of their drowning. I had nothing to place on the grave, so I touched the marker and said goodbye, thanking them for being the wonderful parents they were to me and for handing me over to the care of Grandy. I thought in passing that Eleanor had the opportunity to be reunited with her mother and to be introduced to her grandmother, and I hoped that might turn out well for her.

Nappi, as if reading my thoughts, said, "Making good out of that mother-daughter bond might prove difficult."

"But worth a try," I said. "Psychiatry has come a long way in recent years. There's hope for both of them." Perhaps the help they needed would be found outside of a prison's walls and in the arms of what family Irene could provide.

I understood truth was not a psychiatric cure, but it might serve as light for the dark corners of the human psyche and warmth for a family in deep pain. It was a necessary start for healing. Could I convince Irene of that? Family secrets began with Irene, and she handed them down to her daughter, who turned them over to Eleanor. Delusions from a twisted mind or convenient stories to escape the consequences of bad choices, secrets, and lies could no longer stand if anyone had a chance at happiness. I would begin with Irene. After I'd hugged my family members.

ONE OF NAPPI'S MEN had delivered an SUV to the airport in West Palm, leaving the keys to it at one of the car rental desks. Eleanor and Jerry sat in back, while Nappi and I took the front seats, Nappi driving. No one had much to say on the way up the Beeline Highway to Sabal Bay. I noticed the highway had been widened to four lanes all the way from West Palm through Indiantown. I guess that's progress, but I missed the reeds, water lilies, water hyacinth, and water lettuce that dotted the surface of the standing water and small canal, and the wading birds—herons, egrets, and ibis—as well as turtles and a few small alligators that called the waters home. Now the canal had been widened and straightened, and organized plantings of fancy palms— not the wild-growing sabal palms—and other plants from the large nurseries in the area adorned the water's edge and the roadside. Neat rows of sod had replaced the unruly weeds along the road. It looked so organized, so groomed, and so uninteresting. Wild was becoming passé.

Nappi dropped me off at my house, where Sammy awaited me, having taken the afternoon off from his job at the hunting reserve.

"Grandy is at the store and said she'd mind it the rest of the afternoon. She also offered to make dinner tonight for all of us," Sammy told me as he held me in his arms. Eating was high on my agenda of things to do, and even more so since I was eating for two, but Sammy's news about dinner hardly moved my "oh goodie" meter. I was more interested in how good his body felt close to mine. I snuggled my head into his neck and nipped at his ear.

"I guess you're hungry now," he said, missing my intention in the way so many smart but naive men did around women.

"Oh, Sammy. Forget the food." I grabbed him by his belt buckle and pulled him into the bedroom. His eyes opened wide and then darkened in that sexy way they did when we made love. Yep. He got it.

EVERYONE CROWDED INTO my living room to give Grandy command of the kitchen, where she fried up a mess of speck and potatoes for dinner. With the accompanying cole slaw, it was just what I wanted following my afternoon of "exercise" with Sammy. Two of my sons tugged at me to get my attention and be the first to tell me about the upcoming rodeo. They were thrilled I was back to see them perform.

Jason told me he had roped his calf and taken it to the ground each time during practice today.

"And what about you, Jeremy?" I asked my youngest.

"He missed all five times," said Jason before Jeremy could reply.

Jason loved to tease his younger brothers. Jerome usually ignored him, but Jeremy was most often hurt at not being able to keep up with the older two. This time, however, he smiled and said, "Yeah, but you fell off your horse the second time out."

Jason stuck out his tongue at his brother.

"What's going on with Jerome?" I asked the boys. Jerome sat on the couch with Grandfather, watching something on television. By the way his eyes darted around the room, it was obvious he wasn't paying much attention to the program. I also was surprised he didn't rush forward with his brothers to tell me about rodeo practice.

Jason shrugged and joined Grandy in the kitchen. He was avoiding answering my question, so I turned my attention to Jeremy, who wouldn't meet my gaze.

"Okay. What's up?" I insisted.

Jeremy screwed up his face as if he was going to cry. I shook my head. "Tell me. I'm not going to punish you for the truth."

"Jerome didn't come to rodeo practice today."

I shot a quick look at Jerome. His gaze caught mine, and he slid off the couch and came over.

"You didn't go to practice today. Weren't you feeling well?" I asked.

"Uh, I had a stomachache."

I knew he was lying.

"He had the same stomachache the other day. He missed practice then too," said Jeremy.

Jerome's face reddened, and he shot his brother an angry look. Something was wrong. I was about to take him to one side to get to the bottom of it when Grandfather intervened.

"Jerome has had something on his mind, I think," said Grandfather, "but he wants to tell me all about it after dinner tonight."

Jerome gave Grandfather a relieved look.

"Is that right?" I asked. "Will you talk to Grandfather? We don't want you to carry whatever is going on by yourself. We'll help."

"I'm not sure anyone can help, but I'll try to talk about it."

"If you're not feeling well, we can take care of that, and if it's something that's worrying you, Grandfather is the best at helping with that."

He gave me a tiny smile, then he and Grandfather returned to their seats on the couch, where Grandfather turned off the television and the two of them began talking. I caught a few words and realized Grandfather was discussing fishing with Jerome. Max, hearing the word "fishing," joined them.

I wondered what was bothering Jerome. I was certain it was not an upset stomach. He was so keen on participating in the rodeo that he would have tried to rope a calf even if he was suffering from appendicitis. It wasn't a physical ailment. It was something else.

Grandfather would know how to deal with this, and he would let Sammy and me know how we could help. I wondered if Sammy had noticed anything while I was gone.

Grandy wiped her hands on her apron and signaled me she wanted a word. She and I stepped out the back door and into the yard.

"Glad to be back?" she asked.

"You mean am I glad to be home?"

She scanned the far horizon, where cattle grazed grassy fields, broken by stands of scrub pines and palms. "It's beginning to feel like home to me, too. Max and I may not want to operate fishing charters much beyond this year."

I was pleased to hear that, knowing that it had taken some time before Max didn't yearn for the ocean and began to feel at home on the Big Lake.

As if in response to my thoughts, Grandy said, "He'll never want to leave the ocean completely. We're thinking of buying a place in an RV park down there and renting someplace up here until he feels more settled."

"You can rent this place or buy it, if you like. You know Sammy and I are going to build a bigger house next to Grandfather's."

Grandy slid me a twinkle-eyed look. "I was hoping you'd say that."

That was settled.

"So what's up?" I asked.

"I know you want to talk with Irene, because you think she didn't tell you the entire truth about her daughter."

"Do you think she did?"

Grandy paused for a moment to think. "No. There's more to that story, but will you promise me you'll go easy on her? She's had a lot to handle, thinking her daughter was gone forever, dead probably, then learning she's alive, but can't be located."

"You know my strong suit is not diplomacy, but I'll try to remember how it feels to lose someone you love and know they are never coming back to you."

Grandy gave me a quick squeeze. "I've got the best cooks in the county in there helping, but I'd better make certain he's got everything under control."

"Grandfather? I'm sure he'll do fine."

"No, I meant Jason and Sammy. I didn't know Sammy could cook. Did you?"

No. I did not. I laughed and started to follow Grandy back in when she turned to me. "What I wanted to tell you is that I invited Irene and Don to join us tonight."

Irene was family, so of course she should be here, but what about Eleanor, who was also family?

"Irene and Eleanor got together this afternoon at the shop," added Grandy. "I didn't think you'd mind. You were busy." She gave me a goofy grin, as if she knew what Sammy and I had been busy doing.

I didn't mind any of this except that it meant I'd have to put off talking with Irene until we could have some time alone. That wasn't likely to be tonight. The doorbell rang just as I stepped back into the house. Sammy opened the door to Madeleine and David, twins in their arms. I looked around the room, and made a mental note to myself to talk with Sammy about making certain the house we were building would accommodate all our friends and a family growing beyond what anyone had anticipated. I felt a slight tug in my abdomen, and smiled. Sammy caught the look on my face and came over.

"What's up?" he asked.

"Our boy is letting his presence known."

Sammy's face paled. "Oh, no."

"No, no. I'm fine. It's normal and a sign that I'm hungry."

He pulled me close. "I told you earlier today that I thought you were hungry."

"You were wrong, remember?" I said, punching him in the shoulder.

"I must have gotten my meals mixed up," he said.

Irene, Don, Jerry, Nappi, and Eleanor arrived right after Madeleine and family. It was lucky the rain predicted to arrive this evening had held off and the clouds, which had begun to build up, thought better of their appearance and fled, gobbled up by a pink and coral sun. The backyard had been given over to a picnic table and an assortment of other tables and chairs. If the mosquitoes held off, we could finish the meal without *becoming* the meal.

Irene and Eleanor did not leave each other's side the entire night. I couldn't have taken Irene off for a private conversation if I had wanted. It was as if she had found something she had lost in her granddaughter, and the granddaughter had found a kind of maternal love never provided by her mother.

After dinner, that loving connection changed following an intense exchange between grandmother and granddaughter as they helped clean up in the kitchen.

"Tell me!" shouted Irene, grabbing Eleanor's arm and shaking her. "You have to tell me where she is."

Don pulled her away from Eleanor, who rubbed the place on her arm where she had been grabbed.

"You hurt me," she said, "just like my mother used to do." Eleanor bolted for the front door, pulled it open with a jerk, and fled into the night. Nappi signaled to Jerry, who ran after her.

Irene sobbed and cried, "Come back! I'm sorry. I'm so, so sorry."

"What happened?" I asked.

"I couldn't stand it anymore. I want to know where she is. I want to see my daughter. Eleanor must know where she's hiding. They've talked. Why won't she tell me?" Irene continued to sob. Grandy handed her a tissue and led her to the couch.

"Will you get us some water, Eve?" Grandy asked.

Again with the water. I don't know why people want others to drink water when they are upset. It never made any sense to me. I walked over to my liquor cabinet and poured Irene a snifter of brandy, then handed it to her. "Here. Drink this. It'll do you better than water."

Irene gave me a wan smile and took a sip of the liquor. "Wow. That is strong."

"Puts hair on bald guys' heads and exfoliates the legs of women," I said.

Grandy gave me a dirty look, but Irene seemed to like my recommendation. She gulped down the liquor and kind of shook herself in a shudder that went from head to toes. "I'm better now. Thanks, Eve."

"I'm not certain Eleanor knows just where her mother is. We're convinced she's in the area, but you've seen what's out there: miles and miles of grass, trees, and swamp. She could be hiding anywhere."

"How can that be?" asked Irene. "She wouldn't know how to take care of herself."

"Irene is right," said Nappi. "She must have help, and I'm certain it's not from her daughter."

Who, then? I wondered. Who knew this wild place? I came up with one name, the most unlikely person to be giving Brenda Montrose help. I shook that name out of my brain. Mr. Egret didn't even know Brenda. Why would he help her?

I had my work cut out for me tomorrow. First, I would question Irene to find out what she was holding back, then I wanted to talk with Eleanor's mother, if I could convince the woman to meet with me. If she was hiding out, I knew Mr. Egret could find her, but I didn't think there was much chance of his trusting me enough to talk to me ever again. I was on my own.

Don took Irene back to their motel room, everyone left, and our dinner party, which had begun with so much joy, ended on a subdued and unhappy note. Grandfather took the boys home with him, reassuring me he would get to the bottom of what was bothering Jerome. When Sammy asked me what was going on, I filled him in on Jerome's "stomachache."

"He's been kind of quiet of late," he reassured me, "but I didn't know he wasn't practicing with the other boys. I trust Grandfather to find out what's wrong." He kissed me goodnight and rolled over onto his side. The sound of his steady breathing told me he was asleep.

I was exhausted, but sleep eluded me. Instead, my mind raced with thoughts of Jerome, Irene, Eleanor—somewhere out there in the night—and Eleanor's mother, Brenda, who no one around here except for Eleanor had ever seen. I hoped for Irene and Eleanor's sake that

Brenda was safe, and I cursed the stupidity of Frida's new partner at having chased the one man who could find her back into the swamps.

I heard a noise at the bedroom slider and sat up in bed, peering into the darkness of the night. Maybe Sammy's father was just outside. I jumped out of bed and went to the door. A raccoon dashed off the patio and into the bushes, and then all was quiet again.

NINETEEN

DESPITE LITTLE SLEEP, I was up early preparing coffee, toast, and eggs, surprising everyone because I didn't cook often and never in the morning. To be honest, I was starved, and I could hardly make breakfast for myself alone. That would be selfish, and I was working on being less selfish.

Grandy offered to clean up after breakfast, while Sammy and I decided to drop by Grandfather's and help him send the boys off to school. At the house, the boys greeted us at the door, backpacks in hand, gave us a cheery "hi," and rushed down the stairs into the yard. I gave Grandfather a questioning look and pointed at Jerome's retreating back as the three boys ran across the yard to wait for the bus. Grandfather shook his head and said in a low voice, so the boys wouldn't hear, "He wasn't ready to tell me anything," referring to Jerome's silence. "Don't worry, Eve. He's a good boy, and he's working out for himself what he should say and when he should say it."

"Did he give you any idea what this is about?" I asked. Sammy stood by my side in the doorway, watching the school bus pick up our sons.

"Maybe I should talk with him tonight," Sammy suggested.

"No," Grandfather said. "Let him work this one out. He'll come around soon."

Sammy and I were acting so impatient about Jerome that I wondered what we would be like with yet another boy to worry over. Maybe the two of us should consider meditation or tai chi to help us bring a bit of Zen to our parenting.

In his usual manner, Grandfather shook his head and gave my arm a reassuring pat. "You'll do fine," he said, as if reading my thoughts.

Grandy and Madeleine were covering the store this morning, giving me the opportunity to have my talk with Irene. Before I could call her on my cell to make certain she was up, Nappi's black Escalade pulled up to Grandfather's house.

He hopped out of the car and approached the house with a spring in his step. I hoped that meant that his news was good. We sat around the kitchen table, the men drinking Grandfather's excellent coffee while I had a glass of orange juice.

"Jerry found Eleanor last night, but it was so late I didn't want to call and wake you," he told us.

"No danger of that. It felt as if I was awake the entire night. Where did he catch up with her?"

"Where would you go if you didn't know the town well? She showed good sense and returned to her rental," Nappi said.

"So, why did it take Jerry so long to find her?" Sammy asked.

"It didn't take him long. According to Jerry, it took half the night for him to calm her down. She wanted to go to the motel to speak with Irene, but Jerry talked her out of that. She's pretty upset about last night. I'll bet she made Jerry drive her to Irene's motel this morning, and that's where she is now."

Well, that made me cranky. Would I never get a chance to talk with Irene alone? It was time to get pushy. I needed answers and right away.

"I'm going over there now. I'll inform Eleanor that this investigation takes precedence over her need to make things right with her grandmother."

"Hold on, Eve. Maybe letting the two of them work things out between them might make it easier for you to get the information you need," suggested Nappi.

I thought about that for a minute. He was right. There's pushy, and then there's Eve-pushy, which is too, too pushy.

"Okay, let's give the two of them some time together this morning. Afterward, I'd like Jerry to take Eleanor back to her rental. I'll promise to bring her grandmother there as soon as we've finished our talk."

"Aren't you forgetting something?" Nappi asked me.

I raised one eyebrow and said, "Huh?"

"Your friend Frida might like to know the same things you'd like to know. Despite the authorities believing they know the identity of Mr. Montrose's killer, Frida isn't convinced. I assume one of the questions you'll ask Irene is the name of Brenda's father. He has to be involved in some way. He could be a member of the family who hired Freddie to 'find' the Montroses."

"Irene told me Brenda's father is deceased, and didn't we discover he paid for her stay at Hopkins? Revenge against Brenda from the grave? Why?" My thoughts raced ahead. "It does appear there's a powerful family behind the theft of her file from Hopkins," I said. Until I knew the identity of Brenda's father, I couldn't be certain it was his family. "You're right. Frida needs to know what I find out from Irene. That is, if Irene will tell me. I can't blame her for being impatient with everyone once she found her daughter was alive. Believe me, I can relate." Sammy and Nappi gave me knowing looks of agreement. "She's desperate to find her." I paused, then added, "Don't you wonder why Brenda isn't trying to see Irene? Eleanor told me she informed her mother that Irene was here. Brenda knows she's just out of reach. Is there something going on between the two of them that we don't know about? Something from the past?"

What I didn't say was what all of us had to be thinking: how crazy was Brenda? According to Selma, the records at Hopkins indicated a serious mental disorder. Was that the case, or had Selma incorrectly reported what was in the file? Selma. The thought of her made me grind my teeth. I wouldn't put it past her to make up things that she thought might aggravate me. I comforted myself with the thought that Selma couldn't make up too many lies, because her father might remember the case differently.

Brenda Montrose was a ghost: her file had disappeared, and no one around here had seen her. Even Eleanor seemed only to have phone contact with her mother. Maybe she *was* a ghost. Maybe she *was* dead, and Eleanor, following in her mother's footsteps, had lied about or hallucinated the calls with her.

"Nappi," I said, "Eleanor has a cellphone. She insists that's how she gets in touch with her mother. I need that phone. I want to see what numbers she's calling. I'll bet Frida would love to take a look at it too. She wouldn't be able to get a search warrant for it, but if I had it and shared it with her...." I let my thought go unfinished.

"You think I'm a pickpocket?" asked Nappi, pretending to be offended.

"Of course not, but I'm sure you can find a way of taking it without her knowing."

I wanted to be sensitive to Eleanor's needs, those of her elusive mother and Irene's, but two issues stood in my way, and they had nothing to do with my impulsive nature. These women could be in danger, especially if someone had hired people like Freddie to make certain they disappeared. I also felt in my bones that my father-in-law wasn't responsible for Mr. Montrose's murder. I'm not saying he knew nothing about the circumstances surrounding the murder, but I knew he didn't kill him. I'd been hired to find out who was responsible and clear him. I was just tired of what felt like chasing my tail from the Florida swamps back and forth to the mountains of Upstate New York and the Connecticut shore. My gut told me I'd find all the answers right in my own backyard: rural Florida.

SAMMY LEFT FOR the game ranch and his job, while Grandfather and one of Sammy's cousins opened the airboat business. After a few phone calls to ensure that I would have Irene to myself, Nappi drove me to her motel and told me he'd come back to pick me up whenever I liked. I told him I'd call.

Irene opened the door after my first knock.

"I guess it's time we talked, Eve," she said.

"This time I want the whole story."

She gestured for me to take one of the chairs at the small dining table. We sat across from each other. Irene drummed her fingers on the table top and glanced out the window, refusing to meet my gaze. I knew this would not be easy for her, but I shoved that concern to one side. I needed the truth.

"There's not much more to tell you that you don't already know, except for—"

"Except for the name of Brenda's father."

"I don't understand how that changes anything," Irene said.

"Brenda has insisted for many years that someone was after her, you know."

Irene gave me a sad smile. "Brenda always thought someone was after her, even when she was little. She was terrified that people were following her, hiding outside the house, waiting for her when she got off the school bus. At first I thought she had a vivid imagination, but she was terrified, enough so that she refused to go to school. Brenda was delusional. You know that."

"Oh, I suppose she was, but not all her fears were unfounded. Some of them were real. I think someone was after her. At one point I think they meant to find out about her, a kind of shadow. But lately, something has changed. Some not very nice men have been hired to make her disappear, and along with her, your granddaughter. They might want you out of the picture also. Nappi scared them away, but others will come, if they haven't already."

I could tell Irene didn't want to believe me. She got up and walked away, dismissing me with a swipe of her hand.

"You told me you and her father never were in touch about Brenda, that he was never a part of her life. Wasn't that hard? You worked as Grandy did, as a housekeeper for wealthy families. That wasn't a lot of money. And you were a woman raising a child with no father. Didn't he offer you any support, financial or otherwise? What kind of a man was he?"

Irene seemed to deflate from within. She sank onto the bed and looked at me with hollow eyes. "He was a coward, weak. He was too terrified to tell his family. He was afraid they would cut him off without a cent. And he was right. They would have. Isn't it interesting that Grandy and I both fell victim to the charms of men with too much money and too little backbone?"

I knew what she was saying, but she was wrong about much of it. Grandy had fallen in love with the son of a prominent family in Connecticut—there was no baby— but unlike Irene's man, Grandy's would have given up everything to marry her. Grandy insisted he not do that because she feared he'd come to resent her in the future, and that his resentment would destroy their love. Grandy made the sacrifice, and I reminded Irene now of the difference between them.

"You're right, Eve. I don't think the man Grandy cared for was spineless. He loved her enough to see how right she was about what might happen, and he let her go. I was tossed away with a huge sigh of relief that all I wanted was support for my child."

"So he did give you financial support?"

Irene nodded. "Money every month, cash, delivered by a trusted servant. He rang my doorbell and handed me an envelope the first day of the month. The money continued until Brenda was eighteen. Untraceable, unless the servant told someone. I don't think he did. Brenda's father did the least he could do for her in a way that never compromised his position as one of Hartford's richest men and most eligible bachelors."

"Did you love him?" I asked.

"I thought so at one time. When I got pregnant, we talked about marriage, but I said no. I stopped loving him when I saw the relief written on his face when I turned him down." She gave a derisive snort. "You're right, Eve. It wasn't easy raising a child alone, and Brenda required special care."

"You didn't tell him about her problems?"

"Would you have told him, knowing how little he wanted to be involved?"

"No, but I think there's more to the story than you know. Brenda was admitted to Hopkins, and she used the name 'Mary Appel' as a patient there. That's how Eleanor and Henry Montrose knew her. As my mother."

"Eleanor told me about Mary Appel," Irene said. "I think she still believes in some way that your mother is her mother. Eleanor thinks her mother is Mary Appel, and she's more than a little resentful that you were the preferred child."

"I can't shake her from that."

"She told me you believe it too."

I shook my head. "For a time I wanted to believe my mother was alive, but now I know that the name 'Mary Appel' was a cover identity, part of her delusions, and what better way to hide than by assuming a dead woman's identity? Your daughter may be mentally ill, but she's not stupid. Her father had the resources to keep an eye on his daughter without your knowing. She knew, or she thought she knew, that someone shadowed her—her paranoia helping her to form that delusion. Friend or foe? Brenda couldn't decide. Her father decided at one point to rescue her by placing her in Hopkins in hopes that the facility could help her through her troubles, but it only served to convince her that she was her cover identity. Her father then helped her to disappear into the life she'd begun with Henry Montrose and her daughter. Unfortunately, it was a life filled with Brenda's continued problems, which resulted in her mistreatment of Eleanor."

Irene dropped her head into her hands and sobbed, coming up for air when dismissive laughter replaced her crying. "Wasn't that just like Robert Farley? He walked back into her life thinking he could enact some kind of miracle cure for her at Hopkins. When that didn't work, he walked away. Again."

When Irene spoke the name of Robert Farley, a shockwave went through me. I expected the father had belonged to a wealthy Connecticut family, but I didn't expect him to be part of the Farley family, rich beyond belief.

Leaving the story there was sad, but what I had to add would increase Irene's distress.

"Irene, I think the Farley family has gotten hold of your story, and I believe one of them wants to do harm to her, to you, to Eleanor, and to anyone who knows about Brenda's birthright."

"What do you mean?" Irene blew her nose and looked puzzled by my comment.

"The father of your daughter was one of the wealthiest men in the Northeast. Don't you think his family would want to protect any claims she might make on his estate?"

"You're right, of course." She paused and looked away from me again, as if there was something she knew she should say but didn't want to. "I think I know why everything is coming to a head now. I should have told you this earlier, but I was still trying avoid using Robert Farley's name."

I waited. She heaved a deep sigh, straightened her shoulders, and met my gaze.

"Those men who came from the hospital to visit me about Brenda's records…you remember I told you about them?"

I nodded. When she told me about the visit it seemed plausible that a hospital was trying to close files that had been open for a long time. Irene's mentioning them now made me wonder.

"Something about them made me uncomfortable. Don said he thought one of them was armed."

I felt a humming up and down my spine. "Can you describe the men?" I asked.

"One of them didn't say much. He was average height like Don, with sandy, thinning hair. The one who did most of the talking was short, not more than five feet tall. The odd thing about him was his hands. They didn't seem to go with the rest of him. His fingers were long and slender, the hands of a concert pianist almost. He had a high-pitched voice. When he spoke, it sounded like he was whining."

Well, well. Freddie the Bull and one of his goons had visited Irene in the guise of hospital personnel. I didn't tell Irene she had been visited by men probably hired by the Farley's law firm to find out about her daughter.

Irene continued speaking, her words breaking into my thoughts. "You see, I remember the timing well. It was right after I read Robert's obituary in the Connecticut papers. He's been dead to me for many years, but he died about six weeks ago."

So that was what started this whole thing: Brenda

coming to Florida to find me, followed by Henry and her daughter, and then the murder of Mr. Montrose. It couldn't be a coincidence that Brenda took flight soon after her father died. She had her mental issues, but she wasn't wrong in thinking someone was after her. The Farley family didn't want her existence known. In fact, they wanted her and her daughter wiped off the face of the earth.

"I think we need to find your daughter, not just for your sake, Irene, but because I think she and your granddaughter are in real danger."

She nodded. "His family is after them."

"Robert Farley's known heirs are trying to protect what they have. They aren't willing to share. You'd be in danger also if you decided to come forward on behalf of your daughter and granddaughter and claimed part of his estate."

A red flush spread upward from her neck onto her face. "I'd never do that. I read the obituary, and my one thought was that he was gone for good. It was a kind of relief to know he'd never intrude in my life again. I would never claim any part of his estate."

"I'm not so certain you shouldn't. Brenda is his daughter. You told me he never acted like a father to her, only providing you monthly stipends, which ended when she turned eighteen. He tried to keep you a secret from his family, but it appears he wasn't successful. Given Brenda's mental issues, you and she deserved more than a monthly allowance. The family money could buy her a lot of therapy now. She also has a daughter who needs a mother who is sound and happy. Brenda and you are all Eleanor has now."

"Are you saying I should come forward and make a claim on their behalf?"

I nodded. "Yes, but first we need to make certain all of you are safe."

Help for Brenda, if Brenda was still alive. I didn't say that to Irene, nor did I share my concern that Brenda's uncertain mental state might have led her to kill Henry. Why, I reasoned, would the men sent to silence Brenda and her daughter have any interest in murdering Mr. Montrose, who believed Brenda was Mary Appel and knew nothing about her connection to the Farley fortune? If the authorities knew about the Farley family connection and Freddie the Bull's role in all this, they might have doubled their efforts to find my father-in-law.

Not as a suspect, but as a witness to the murder.

TWENTY

I wasn't certain when I left her room that Irene believed what I was saying about the danger to her and her daughter and granddaughter, but she insisted it was time to see her daughter. I told her I agreed. In fact, it was past time for the authorities and any family to meet with Brenda. Family included me. I wondered what this woman who had called herself Mary Appel for such a long time would think of me. I still wasn't clear why she had come to Florida or how she knew where to find me.

As difficult as it was for me to deal with Irene's disbelief about everything that had happened surrounding her daughter, Eleanor posed a greater problem. Irene might listen to reason as she had this morning, but Eleanor was flighty, naive, stubborn, and sidestepped questions so well I figured she'd be a natural at the Electric Slide.

When Nappi picked me up at the motel, I filled him in on what I had told Irene. He agreed that she could use protection, which we both knew the police would not provide. Nappi made a call and took care of that. As we pulled away from the motel, another black SUV pulled into the parking lot. Nappi nodded at the driver, who nodded back. I sat back in the passenger seat and relaxed. For a moment, anyway.

"Where to?" asked Nappi. "I already stopped to see how Jerry was doing with Eleanor."

"Do you think she's safe with Jerry looking after her?"

He gave me a wink. "No, but she said Irene was joining them for lunch at the Biscuit. It's a favorite restaurant for several of my, uh, associates."

Why did I worry? Nappi's so-called associates would babysit everyone at the Biscuit. Nappi, my dear friend, had everything and everyone covered, even me.

I wiggled around in my seat so that I was facing him. "You know, I've managed to involve you in a lot of my, uh, adventures over the years, and…" I began.

Nappi held up a hand to stop me. "This is where you thank me and say how you cannot repay me, blah, blah, blah. Shut up, Eve. I don't want to hear this from a friend."

He was right. I was insulting him.

"Where to?" he asked.

"To the shop. I need to check to see if Grandy and Madeleine can use some help."

"I already checked while you were talking to Irene. Business is slow today, and Shelley is in, working on some dresses, so she'll provide backup if things start jumping."

"Then it's time to check in with my boss, Crusty. I owe him an update on how I'm doing with my case. I'm supposed to be working on the Montrose murder, not warning my relatives about mob guys looking for them."

"It's all related," Nappi said.

"Yes, but I should be providing him with written

reports he can forward to his clients, Grandfather and Sammy."

Nappi dismissed my concerns with a flap of his hand. "I think they know what you're doing, don't you? Besides, do you want to hear McNabb natter on about how you shouldn't be working this case in your condition?"

"He knew my condition when he took me on. I'm nosey, impulsive, and intrusive. That was why he took me on."

"That wasn't what I meant," Nappi said.

"I know what you meant and forget it."

"Oh, I almost forgot." Nappi reached over, opened the glove box, and extracted a cellphone. "Compliments of your friendly pickpocket."

"I thought you said you didn't do that kind of work. You implied it was not on your mob-guy list of acceptable jobs."

He handed the phone to me.

"I didn't take it. It was Jerry's doing."

I raised both eyebrows in surprise. "Hmm. So Jerry does have some marketable skills after all."

"Are you drooling over what you'll find in there? You look like a coyote about to take down a rabbit."

I swallowed. It was a correct observation. I was drooling, but not over what the phone records would provide. I had opened the phone to Eleanor's contacts.

"Look at this," I said, showing the screen to Nappi.

He glanced at it out of the corner of his eye.

"Most of her contacts are restaurants and food places around here," I said, scrolling down the page.

"And you're hungry," he said with complete certainty.

AT THE LOCAL DINER in the middle of town, Nappi ordered one of their famous giant burgers with a side of fries, but I, aware that I shouldn't be feeding my little one greasy foods, opted for protein and vegetables—a giant burger with extra tomato and lettuce, no fries. I bit into the burger and wiped the ketchup and mayonnaise that oozed from it off my lower lip.

"I was so proud of you when you didn't ask for fries, but now I'm not so sure," Nappi said as I picked yet another crispy potato off his plate.

"It's like smokers when they're trying to quit—they bum cigarettes so they can maintain the illusion they're no longer smoking." I picked at my burger and Nappi's fries as I scrolled through Eleanor's call list again.

"Find anything?" Nappi asked.

"Mmm." I nodded with a mouthful of fries. "Aside from food places—getting her a place with a kitchen was unnecessary because it's clear she does not cook and I know Jerry doesn't—there's one number she calls several times each day. That has to be her mother because it's a cell with a New York area code."

We finished our food and talked about our next move. Should I turn over the telephone to Frida and let her use the GPS to track Brenda's location or should I call it myself and try to get Brenda to meet with me and her mother and daughter? Or, third choice, use Eleanor to intercede with her mother and set up a meeting?

"I veto the last option," I said to Nappi as we headed toward the car. "Eleanor has been anything but cooperative. I can understand she's trying to protect her mother, but I'm finding her attitude as annoying as crab grass in my lawn."

Nappi smiled. "Eve, you still haven't learned the

fine art of patience, have you?" He reached out and patted me on my shoulder, then pulled back his arm and said, "I must be losing my touch. Look at that, would you? I've got ketchup on my sleeve." He moved his wrist and leaned toward me so I could get a look at the offending stain. I heard a loud *bang* and the ketchup stain spread over his chest and drops spurted onto me. He sank to his knees and pulled me down with him.

"Get behind the car!" he yelled as he collapsed on the pavement.

There was so much blood—on the pavement beneath his body, on me, and all over his expensive designer jacket. I crawled over to him. His eyes were closed, but his chest heaved with each breath. He was still alive.

"Nappi, Nappi. Can you hear me?"

He opened his eyes. "I hear you. Are you okay? Were you hit?"

I shook my head.

"Freddie," he said, then lost consciousness. I looked around at the crowd that had gathered. Up the street I spotted the taillights of a black SUV driving away from the crowd. If it was one of Nappi's men, it would have been heading this way.

"I'll make him pay," I whispered in Nappi's ear. There was no response, and his chest was no longer heaving.

THE AMBULANCE ARRIVED in minutes. The EMTs moved me to one side, one of them ascertaining I was not injured, the other two checking Nappi's vitals and beginning an IV. Thank God he was not dead, but could they get him to the hospital in time to save him? They loaded him in the ambulance, and it sped away, sirens blaring.

Frida's cruiser pulled up at almost the same time. She looked at the blood on me and asked, "Are you okay?"

"I'm not hurt, if that's what you're asking, but I'm not okay. They wouldn't let me go to the hospital with him." I pointed with a shaking finger at the retreating ambulance.

"He's being taken care of, but I need you to tell me what happened," Frida said, walking me to her car and putting me in the passenger seat. She gave a curt nod to her partner, who began securing the scene.

"I need to make certain he'll be okay," I insisted.

"You can do that by helping catch the person who did this."

"Oh, I know who did this," I said with certainty.

Frida sighed. "Okay. Tell me everything. My partner can handle interviewing witnesses and taping off the scene." She took out her notebook.

I told her everything I knew about my investigation of the Montrose murder in New York and Connecticut and about my Great-Aunt Irene's daughter and granddaughter. I finished with a description of Nappi's and my lunch. "We had just left the diner and...you know how neat he is?"

She nodded.

"For once he wasn't. If he hadn't spilled on his jacket and leaned toward me to show me the stain, he wouldn't be alive."

In an attempt at humor, Frida said, "Well, good for you, Eve. You taught him how to eat like you do."

At first I looked at her in horror at the callousness

of her statement, then I got it. I tried a small smile, but my lower lip quivered.

"Here's Grandy," she said. "I called her to give you a ride to the hospital. You can check on your friend."

I got out of the car, but Frida called to me.

"He may not be my favorite person, but I know how much he means to you. I hope he'll be okay."

I retold my story to Grandy. We parked and ran up to the emergency room entrance.

"He's in surgery right now," said the attendant behind the counter. "Are you family?"

"Yes, I'm his daughter and this is his…" I could have said "mother," but instead I said, "sister."

"His younger sister," explained Grandy.

The attendant didn't blink an eye at Grandy's white curls, but pointed to the corridor leading to the surgical area waiting room.

"I've got to call Jerry," I said.

Jerry, Eleanor, Irene, and Don were still at the restaurant, finishing lunch. I told him what happened and ended with, "He warned off Freddie once, but I'd wager my best pair of ostrich leather boots that this is the work of Freddie the Bull. He thinks if he takes out Nappi, the men he assigned to guard Irene and her granddaughter will back down."

"He's wrong about that. Don't worry, Eve. I'm on it. If you talk with Nappi before I get there, tell him everything will be taken care of. By me." He disconnected.

"I think Jerry has found himself," I said to Grandy.

"He was never lost, my dear, just a little confused. Sometimes a person can step up when things get tough."

"You mean when the going gets tough—"

"The confused find their way," she said.

After another hour, a doctor in scrubs came through.

"I'm Dr. Hernandez. He's being moved to ICU, and you can see him in an hour or so. The bullet came close to his heart, but he's doing fine. He won't be doing any line dancing in the immediate future, but he'll recover. He's a tough man."

I laughed, imagining Nappi on the floor at the Biscuit, line dancing with Grandy. Well, maybe I was wrong about that. He could still surprise me. He might like a little country two-step and some boot-scootin' line dancing.

Jerry rushed through the doors to the waiting room, followed by Grandfather Egret, Sammy, and Madeleine and David.

"Family," I said by way of explanation.

"Big family," said the surgeon.

"You don't know the half of it," I said.

The doctor smiled, then signaled he wanted a private moment with me.

"Before we put him under, he asked me to give you a message. He was very insistent."

I leaned in closer to hear what he was saying.

"He said to take his jacket to Prestige Cleaners in West Palm. He said they could get the ketchup out."

I smiled and nodded. "Will do."

SEVERAL HOURS LATER, all of us exited the hospital, having visited Nappi in ICU in pairs. For a man who had come within a half inch of death, he looked pretty good. Maybe it was the pain medication, but he appeared happy and expressed his certainty that Jerry had things in hand.

"Did the medication they're giving him make him goofy?" Sammy asked. "He seems to think Jerry can take over his operation."

"For once, I think Jerry will step up," I said.

Frida came up behind us. "Who's stepping up to what?"

"Can I get the jacket Nappi was wearing, or is that evidence?" I asked, ignoring her question. There was no need to tell Frida Jerry was taking over for Nappi.

"The crime lab has it for now. Why?"

"Nappi wants it cleaned."

"I doubt the blood stains will come out, and there's a bullet hole in it also," Frida said.

"I'll need it to buy him a new one just like it."

Frida shrugged.

The cell in my purse rang, and I knew from the unfamiliar ring tone that it was Eleanor's, not mine.

"Sorry. I've got to take this." I stepped to one side, under the palm tree that stood next to the hospital's emergency entrance.

"Why haven't you called me?" The voice belonged to a woman, an irritated one. "I told you I want to leave here, but that big Indian is guarding the place. He or one of his buddies or relatives or whatever follow me everywhere. I told you how awful the food is. It reminds me of some of the hospitals I was in." Then the demanding tone changed to pleading. "Please, please get me out of here."

"Brenda?" I asked.

"No. this is Mary. Who is this? You aren't Eleanor."

"This is Eve. I need to see you. Your mother wants to see you. She's close by. Tell us where you are."

"Oh, Eve. My Eve. My darling. I miss you so."

The sound of sobbing came through the phone, then stopped. "Your sister is responsible for all this. She put me here, and now I'm being held prisoner. I think they may kill me. You've got to get me out of here." Irritation had turned to desperation.

"Of course, we'll get you out of there."

"You be careful. I came down here to warn you. Somebody is after us, all of us. Henry didn't believe me when I told him that, so...." She stopped talking and I heard her take in quick breaths. "He's dead, you know."

"How did you know where to find me?" I asked.

"You can't hide from your mother. I read a story about you in a local newspaper. It said you had moved to Sabal Bay, Florida, to set up some business there. I came looking." The voice turned weepy and pleading again. "Why did you stay away all these years? I needed you. *I needed you.*"

"Tell me where you are, and I'll come get you."

There was silence for a moment, then I heard noise in the background as if someone was talking with her. The voice was that of a man, and I recognized it.

"Eve? Can I trust you this time?" It was Lionel Egret.

"Lionel? You can trust me. The reason you were shot at and pursued was because the cops were sitting on Grandfather's house, waiting for you to make contact. You need to turn yourself in."

"The reason I was shot at is because I'm an Indian, the authorities' favorite suspect when it comes to crime."

"That was a mistake. It was Frida's clueless new partner. You know her well enough that you can't believe she'd want to kill you."

He made no reply to this.

"Are you still there?"

There was no reply.

I was about to end the call when he said, "We'll meet. Just you and me. No one else must know. Not my father and not Sammy. And not Frida or her trigger-happy partner. You and me. We'll settle this. I'll let you know where."

Before I could reply, he disconnected.

Frida still stood near the parked cars in the hospital lot, eyeing me with suspicion. I knew what I should do, what I had to do. I had to trust Frida, trust her not to tell her boss or other police, trust she would not betray my confidence.

I walked over and handed her Eleanor's phone.

"You'll know what to do with this," I said, "and you'll know not to tell anyone about it."

SAMMY, GRANDFATHER, AND I drove home together in Sammy's truck. Although I was dead-tired after this difficult day, I filled them in about the circumstances surrounding Nappi's shooting.

"We'll need to be vigilant," I said. "Freddie thinks he's put Nappi out of business, assuming that like him, the loyalty of Nappi's people comes from money and fear. It doesn't. Jerry might be able to find men to guard us, but I know you don't want that and neither do I. Having a couple of black SUVs with men in suits sitting in front of our house, your business and mine, would drive away our customers and confuse and upset the authorities. They couldn't tell the difference between the good guys and the bad guys."

"We have family who will help us," said Grandfather.

"About that," I said, "would your family help Lionel? Would they help him kidnap someone?"

Sammy's and Grandfather's faces showed some surprise, but not enough that I believed them when they shook their heads. I did not tell them Lionel wanted to meet with me. The baby gave a tiny kick or burp in my stomach, as if reminding me of the risk of agreeing to a solo meeting with a man who might have killed another and was now holding a woman against her will.

"I know this has been a tough day for you, Eve, but the boys are home. Their cousin Serena is staying with them until we get back. Jerome told me he wants to talk with us, all of us. He told me he's responsible for the death of Mr. Montrose."

TWENTY-ONE

JEROME? RESPONSIBLE FOR Mr. Montrose's death? That was absurd, and that's what I told Grandfather. Sammy nodded in agreement.

"That may well be," Grandfather said, "but we need to hear what he has to say. Whatever happened out there when my son took the boys camping is eating Jerome alive."

But not the others? I wondered what it was, and my anger grew at Lionel Egret for allowing my son to get into trouble. Moreover, Lionel knew Brenda's location and had known since her husband's murder. Why would he kidnap her? It didn't make any sense. First things first. And that was Jerome.

We drove home in silence. I couldn't read the others' thoughts, but added to my worry about Jerome was concern about Nappi's condition and my certainty that I had to locate Lionel Egret in order to find Brenda. To make myself feel as if I wasn't useless, I used my cell to connect with Frida.

"Can you find Brenda's location from Eleanor's cell?" I asked when Frida answered.

"I'm kind of busy looking for Nappi's assailant right now, Eve. I'll get to it," she snapped at me.

I had told her at the scene of the shooting that I saw a black SUV speeding away and the direction it headed.

How easy would it be for some goons from up North to hide out in rural Florida?

"You didn't happen to see the license plate on that car, did you?" she asked.

"No, but I'll bet they drove down here from up North. Look for Connecticut or New York plates first."

"That's not a lot to go on, but we'll give it a try." She disconnected.

We pulled into the parking lot at the airboat business and took the dirt driveway leading to Grandfather's house. Serena stepped out onto the porch.

"Jeremy and Jason are in the bedroom playing a board game. Jerome is out back, tossing sticks into the canal. I sure hope you can get to the bottom of what's bothering him. He's so upset."

She called goodnight to the boys, got into her car, and pulled away.

I checked on the other two boys, then Grandfather, Sammy, and I went out to the canal. Jerome sat on an old log and stared out over the water.

"Hi," I said and leaned down to kiss him. He wasn't yet old enough to reject a mother's public displays of affection. He leaned into me. Grandfather and Sammy took up seats on the log on either side of him while I sat in an old lawn chair across from them.

Knowing it would be hard for him to speak, we waited until he worked up his courage.

"I think I'm to blame for that man's death," he stammered, and a tear ran down his round cheek.

"Sometimes we blame ourselves for things that aren't our fault even though we think they are. We can be hard on ourselves," said Grandfather.

"That's what you said earlier, but if I hadn't left that knife there, he wouldn't have been killed."

"Why don't you just tell us what happened?" Sammy said, rubbing Jerome's shoulder.

"Okay." He swallowed hard. "Grandfather Lionel took us out to the swamps. We camped one night near the lock, but we wanted to get away from the noise of the boats entering and leaving. Grandfather said it wasn't a real swamp experience anyway, so we moved our camp the next day to a hammock of trees not far from the old fishing pier. Grandfather was cutting down branches with his knife to build the campfire while Jeremy and Jason set up the tent. There wasn't anything for me to do, so I asked if I could go down to the fishing pier. I wanted to carve one of those boats like the ones Grandfather Egret made for your wedding. Remember?"

We nodded. Grandfather Egret had carved boats for the three boys at our wedding party, and they had sailed them off down the canal, then chased after them as far down the canal as they could until the tiny boats were lost in the current and swept away.

"I had my jackknife and thought I could find some dead wood and make one, but my knife was too small. It would have taken me half the day to carve the boat. I came back to the campsite, and there was Grandfather Lionel's big knife lying near the fire where he'd left it. I called out to ask him if I could borrow the knife, but he must have been too far away to hear me. So I took it." Jerome stopped talking and burst into tears. "I know I was wrong to take it without asking, but...." He swiped at his tears with the back of his hand.

"I went back to where I'd left the wood I was trying to carve. I was right. The knife worked great. I finished my boat and was about to sail if off when I heard Grandfather Lionel call me to lunch. I was starved. Carving is hard work. I grabbed my boat and ran off."

"And the knife?" I asked.

"I left it lying on the ground near the pier. But I remembered it after we ate and told Grandfather where I'd left it. He was pretty mad I'd taken it without his permission. He went to look for it, came back, and told us we'd have to go home."

"You didn't see anyone other than Grandfather Lionel out there?" asked Sammy.

"No, but I heard voices after we'd eaten. I hoped we wouldn't have to move the camp again to get away from them."

"Voices," I said. "Were they men's voices or women's?"

"I think there were a couple of men's voices. And...." He stopped and squeezed his eyes closed as if trying to visualize the scene again. "I think I heard someone crying. I can't remember."

"Maybe your brothers can," I suggested.

"I don't think so. After lunch they went upstream to look for corn snakes."

"Why didn't you go with them?" I asked.

Jerome gave me a guilty look from under lowered eyelids. "'Cuz my punishment for taking the knife was to do all the dishes after we ate."

We sat in silence for a while, then Grandfather spoke. "What you did that was wrong, Jerome, was to take the knife without asking. You weren't responsible for that man's death. Do you understand?"

Sammy and I nodded in agreement.

Jerome continued to stare at the ground. "Okay. I

understand, but Grandfather Lionel must still be mad at me."

"Why do you think that?" I asked.

"Because he went back out into the swamp after I took the knife, and he left without taking it with him. I know because I heard you talking. The knife was still in that man."

"That's true, son," said Sammy, "but your grandfather didn't leave because he was mad at you. He left because he was afraid he would be blamed for killing the man."

Jerome looked up and met Sammy's eyes. "I don't think he killed the man."

"We don't either," said Sammy. "That's why your mother is investigating the case."

Jerome wrinkled his forehead in confusion. "I thought the police were supposed to do that."

Oh, God. How could I explain prejudice to him? How could I teach him to trust authority when it was clear the police took one look at the Miccosukee knife and knew they had the murderer without looking beyond his brown face? Not all cops. Not Frida, and I needed to tell him that.

Grandfather stepped in before I could say anything. "Sometimes the police work in different ways than private investigators like your mom."

"Oh, I like Mom's way of doing things." He gave me a tiny smile.

"We do too," said Sammy. "That's why we hired her to take this on—just like you and your brothers hired her to find out who killed your father in that hit-and-run. Remember?"

The boys had hired me to find the person responsible for killing their father. I had told them I couldn't work for them because I didn't have my license then, but they had insisted on emptying the jar of money they had been saving from odd jobs to pay me in what they called "an Indian contract." I'd found the man responsible. As for the pay?

"Hey. I don't think I got all my money for that work," I said.

Jerome's smile got wider. "Too bad, 'cuz we spent it at the carnival. Are you gonna arrest us for not paying you?"

"No, but I'll send you a bill with 'overdue' stamped on it."

The smile fled from his lips and he paled.

"I'm kidding. Go join your brothers. It's time you all headed for bed."

Jerome got up from the log, lowered his head, and dragged his feet through the dirt as he walked to the house. Now what was wrong, I wondered, then I heard him say, "Dang. Bedtime. I didn't get to play even one game."

I knew then he'd be just fine.

"WE'VE GOT TO find my father," said Sammy, "and find out what happened out there. It's not just a matter of the murder, but the issue of our traumatized boy. I don't care how worried Father is about being arrested for the murder. He owes it to Jerome and to us to tell what he knows, what he saw." Sammy was angrier than I'd ever seen him. His eyes were black as the darkest night and his jaw twitched. Though his father's innocence was still a concern, it paled compared to our son's wellbeing.

"That's how he's always dealt with the world," Grandfather Egret said, "and it's my doing. I let him run wild as a kid. I thought his love of the swamps was true Miccosukee, and I believed being out there would heal him. It didn't, or he would have come back to us a more responsible man. My son is a coward." He hung his head, seeming to shrink under the burden of responsibility for the man his son had become.

I wanted to put my arms around Grandfather, to tell him that his son was now a man and the responsibility for his behavior was his; his misdeeds couldn't be blamed on anyone else. Grandfather shook his head.

"I know what you're going to say, Eve, but I must shoulder part of the blame. Every parent sees that when children err, it's because they haven't been taught well enough."

I was beginning to understand what he meant. I had seen it in my Great-Aunt Irene, who was still berating herself for failing to heal her child, now a grown woman with a daughter of her own. How would Irene feel if she found her daughter had killed the man she loved, a real possibility? And if this child I carried grew up to be as impulsive, as impatient as I was, would I see it as my fault? Probably. Grandy and I joked about how like her I was, but I could see the very real fear in her eyes that my snoopy nature would lead me or someone I loved into danger. Some of that fear reflected her concern that she hadn't cautioned me enough when I was a child, that she had let my wild nature flourish, unrestrained.

Grandfather, Sammy, and I talked for a few more minutes. Sammy yawned and said goodnight, as did Grandfather. They walked arm in arm into the house,

Grandfather to sleep on the small cot located on the far side of the fireplace while Sammy joined our sons on the bedroom floor in sleeping bags. We would have been more comfortable at my place, but I didn't want to disturb the boys by rousting them from their sleep, and I thought our presence might provide some comfort to Grandfather as he wrestled with his feelings of failure about his son.

Back inside, I poked my head into the bedroom to say goodnight to Sammy and check on the boys. I knew I would not easily fall asleep. Sammy knew it too.

"Don't stay up too late," he said when I indicated I'd come back to the bedroom after straightening things up in the kitchen.

I looked at my watch. It had been a long day. Why wasn't I more tired? *Because, dummy*, I said to myself, *you are anxious to get moving on finding Henry Montrose's killer.* I'd had enough of traveling back and forth between here and up North, when I knew the answers to who killed him and the location of Brenda and her role in his death could be found here. By shooting Nappi, Freddie had made his presence in the area known. The next move was mine, not his. Eleanor and Irene were safe because Jerry had taken over from Nappi and positioned men to look after them. Nappi was in the hospital, guarded by one of Frida's men. The person most at risk was Brenda. Or so I told myself.

Another look at my watch convinced me that it was late, but not too late to give Frida a call. I was wrong about that, too.

She answered her cell on the first ring. "It's been a

hell of a day. Don't you ever sleep, Eve? Or better yet, don't you like it when others sleep?"

"Sorry, but I was wondering if you've made any progress locating Brenda through her daughter's cell."

Frida's tone changed from sleepy to sharp and alert. "We're working on it. I tried to call the number a few hours ago, but got a message the phone had been turned off. I'm going to have some techs look at it tomorrow. Is that soon enough for you?"

Well, no, it wasn't, but it would have to do.

"I don't know if this will help, but I think Lionel Egret may know where she is."

"Big, big help," she said. I could hear the sarcasm in her voice. "We don't know where he is, so now we know we don't know where either of them is."

"I think he may be helping her, but I can't see him trying to hide her out in the swamps."

"Oh?" Now she sounded interested.

"I'm wondering if another member of the tribe is helping to hide her."

"An intriguing idea, but why should he care about her?"

"I think he knows what happened out there—and I don't mean he was responsible for Montrose's death. He knows who is."

"Brenda?"

"Maybe."

"So he'd want to hide the person responsible for killing someone we think he killed? Have you lost your mind?"

"I know it sounds crazy, but I think he's seen how fragile she is and is trying to help her."

"Now he's a therapist?" Frida said, sarcastic again.

"No. But he might seek help from one of the tribe's healers."

She was silent for a long moment.

"Can you come to the office bright and early tomorrow, Eve? The tech will be in by then, and he may have something for me."

"Why so willing to let me participate?"

"I'm just tired, Eve. I know if I leave you out of this one, you'll be calling me every night, and I'll never get any sleep." There was a click, and she was gone.

Frida often said that about me. "Let Eve in on this one or she'll make things worse," was her usual reason for sharing police business.

I WASN'T CERTAIN what she meant by bright and early, so I dragged Sammy out of his sleeping bag at dawn and insisted he take me home so I could get my car and drive to the police station. I told him what was up with Frida and gently probed him for what he thought about my idea that his father might have taken Brenda to a tribe elder for help.

"Maybe," he acknowledged. "If he did, that's a good sign. It means he's willing to trust someone."

I nodded my agreement.

"I wonder if he knows what he's dealing with," Sammy said. "Brenda does not sound rational. If she killed Henry, the only person she seemed to trust, she might do the same to people she doesn't know. She has a long history of not cooperating with mental health people. She might see a tribal elder as another therapist, just dressed differently."

"That's why we need to find her as soon as possible."

Sammy and I hugged. I jumped out of the truck and ran into the house to grab my car keys.

Grandy was just getting up and had made a pot of coffee. I told her where I was headed.

"You're not going out dressed like that," she said, pointing at my clothes.

I looked down at my rumpled shirt and jeans. At Grandfather's last night, I'd changed out of the outfit I'd worn yesterday, which had been covered in Nappi's blood. The only clothes I had there were a pair of old jeans and one of Sammy's T-shirts, many sizes too large for me. I chuckled.

"What's so funny?" asked Grandy.

"The shirt is huge on me now, but soon I'll grow into it."

"Until then, hop in the shower and change. I'll make you some toast and juice."

"I'm not..." I began.

"Maybe you're not hungry, but the little one may be," she said, pointing a spatula at my belly.

"Darn," I said to myself as I pulled into the police station parking lot. Eating breakfast had made me late. Frida's car was already in the lot. I rushed into the station and was ushered into the office area by the officer on duty.

"You're late," said Frida.

"Grandy, shower, eggs, juice," I managed, out of breath.

"Well, can you imagine? We've got a fix on the phone, and it's in the oddest place."

I wouldn't have to wait on Lionel Egret's call after all.

THE TRIBE'S CASINO was located several miles outside of Sabal Bay. I hadn't been here since Sammy had been taken from the casino by a carload of bad guys and dumped off days later, fortunately still alive. The only good memory I had of the place was meeting inside with a group of gambling grannies who had taken Jerry for a Texas hold'em ride when he'd anted up his car and lost it to them. That was one lesson Jerry was not soon to forget—beaten at poker by a foursome of blue-haired ladies.

Frida and I pulled up in front of the casino and left the police SUV in the parking lot, almost empty at this hour of the morning. Two police cars followed us into the lot, backup in case my hunch was right and both Brenda and Lionel Egret were here.

Inside the casino, a few die-hards hung onto the one-armed bandits, pulling the levers in an indifferent manner, their eyes staring into space, their faces expressing little hope their luck would change. The cleaners were present, vacuuming the rugs, dusting, wiping down the machines, and emptying the waste bins. One roulette wheel was open for takers, its operator leaning against the table but coming to attention as we passed. When he saw we weren't interested, he took up his slumped position once more. The vacuums stopped, and the slot players gave up, taking their almost empty buckets of tokens off to the windows to exchange for paper cash. The casino was eerily quiet. Frida took Eleanor's cell out of her pocket and searched the contacts for the number. She punched it in.

"I hear something coming from over there." I pointed toward the door to the bar and restaurant area. We walked away from the roulette wheels, craps tables, and one-armed bandits and into the restaurant. Three people sat at a far table. The big Indian looked up and our eyes met. He didn't seem surprised to see me, and a flickering scowl crossed his face when he caught sight of Frida. Another tribe member sat across from him, her gray hair plaited in long braids that hung down over her shoulders. If it wasn't for her traditional hairstyle, I would not have taken her for a tribal member. She was dressed in a blue suit and white blouse and wore sensible black heels on her tiny feet. She held the hand of the woman next to her, who raised her head and looked at me. A smile came to her lips. "Eve. Where have you been all these years?"

I was startled by her appearance. She looked exactly as I would have visualized my mother at this age.

TWENTY-TWO

"THIS IS MY DAUGHTER, EVE," she said, introducing me to the others. "Now, if I could find my other daughter, we could go home." She started to rise from the table, but the woman next to her gently pulled her back into her chair.

I could feel the tension coming off Frida's body. I was certain her cop instincts told her she should arrest Lionel, but she played it cool and hung back, letting the scene unfold. The officers who had accompanied her here moved forward, but she directed them back with a wave of her hand.

The Indian woman patted Brenda on the shoulder, whispered something in her ear, then rose and held out her hand to me.

"I'm Dr. Birdie Rainfall. I've heard a lot about you." I shook her hand, and she indicated we should move away from the table to talk. Lionel remained seated, his lips drawn together in a grim smile. I knew if Frida made any movement, Lionel might bolt. She seemed to know it too, so the two of them continued to eye each other warily.

"You must be wondering what this is all about. I'm a psychiatrist. Mr. Egret called me several weeks ago and told me he had a patient for me. When he revealed the circumstances, I was skeptical, but he made it clear that the woman was in danger as was he, so I volunteered to help. I'm sorry this has taken so long, but she was in no shape to see anyone. She witnessed a man she called her husband being killed, and she only avoided the same fate because your father-in-law grabbed her and hid her in the swamps until he could come back to find her and bring her to me. Given time, she will heal. What she needs now is her family. I'll leave that to you."

Frida heard what Dr. Rainfall had said. "Why couldn't you have told us what happened that day, Mr. Egret? Instead you lead us on a merry chase among the gators and snakes."

"Would you have believed me when my sole witness was a woman whose emotional health is shaky? What kind of witness would she have been and why would I put her through that?"

Frida said nothing.

"I don't quite understand," I said to Dr. Rainfall as we returned to the table. "How did my father-in-law find you? We thought he'd returned to the swamps. We had no idea until a few weeks ago that he knew of Brenda Montrose. Sammy and I speculated that he might bring her to a tribal healer, but…" I left my question unfinished.

She smiled. "I am a tribal healer, of the new sort. Lionel knew me because we went to high school together."

Dr. Rainfall patted Brenda's hand. "Good luck to you, my dear." She then turned to me. "If there's anything I can do to help, Lionel has my number." She appeared to have been just what Brenda needed all these years. I watched her walk out the back door of the restaurant.

My cell rang. I pulled it from my pocket and checked the caller ID. It was a Connecticut area code. Odd.

"Hello?" I said.

"It's Sammy." His voice sounded funny, choked as if he was having difficulty swallowing. "Where are you?"

"I'm at the casino. We've found Brenda. And your father. You sound funny, and whose phone are you using? What's going on, Sammy?"

"Is Frida with you?" he asked.

"Yes, but—"

"Don't say anything. Just listen. Some men came to the house this morning, and well, there was a scuffle. Don't worry. We're all fine, but they took all of us out into the swamps."

"All?"

"Yes. The boys, Grandfather, and me."

I heard some noise in the background and a voice came on the phone, a voice I had heard once before.

"I have your husband, his father, and your sons, Ms. Appel. If you want to see them in one piece again, you will do as I say."

The voice belonged to Freddie the Bull. I gulped, terror rising in my throat. I turned to hide my face from the others and again walked away from the table so that I couldn't be overheard. As I did, the fear turned to anger.

"You slimy little bastard. It wasn't enough to shoot Nappi, but now you kidnap my family. You're not going to get away with this, you know."

"Oh, I think I will. I just need a little help from you."

"What do you want?"

"I want Brenda Montrose. Bring her to the shack where you and your husband go. Come alone without the law, or I'll see to it that I extend my services to your family. You have one hour."

His *services*, as he called them, entailed making people disappear.

I decided to bluff, hoping it would earn me more time. "Are you crazy? Even if I wanted to do it, that's not enough time. I don't even know where to find Brenda."

"I trust you will find her. One hour."

"You have to listen to reason," I began, but it was clear I was talking to dead air.

Lionel Egret had been watching me the entire time I was on the phone. Frida was watching him, so she didn't see the effect the phone call had on my body. I was shaking all over. I tried to gather myself together, but Lionel must have spotted my trembling.

"I think it's time we left," he said.

"Fine with me," Frida replied, pulling her cuffs off her belt.

"But not with you," he replied.

She signaled to her men. If she thought taking him in would worry him, she was wrong. Lionel smiled and nodded. Several tribal members stepped out of the shadows of the room.

"I wouldn't recommend a showdown, Lionel," Frida said. "You're coming with me."

He shook his head. "This is tribal land. You have no jurisdiction here. Make any trouble, and I'll have the tribal police take you and your men to visit our new jail facilities."

Frida's mouth dropped open in shock. "What? You'd arrest me?"

"*I* wouldn't, but these tribal officers might object

to you and your men interfering in tribal affairs and on our land."

Lionel, seeing he had game point, came over to me and whispered, "I can see something's wrong. What?"

I told him.

His dark eyes turned to the color of obsidian and his jaw tightened. "We need to move. I don't know the whole story, but he wants to destroy the entire Montrose family. He's doing this for money. Am I right?"

I nodded. How did Lionel know so much? Then I remembered. He was from the Egret clan, and they seemed to know everything.

Something else bothered me about Freddie's demands. "What about Irene and Eleanor? And you—you saw him or one of his men kill Henry Montrose. He has reason to want you dead too."

"I think Freddie is like other white folks. He doesn't think the word of an Indian counts for anything. Or he assumes I'm in the wind."

That still left the question of Eleanor and Irene. Why didn't Freddie want me to bring them along with Brenda? Ice crawled up my spine. I ignored it for now. I'd call Jerry later to reassure myself they were still safe with him.

"You can't come with me. He said I should come alone and no cops. We're making the exchange at Sammy's and my shack."

My knees were shaking with fear.

"I'm coming with you." His tone brooked no argument. "We can come up with a plan on the way."

"Now you sound like me."

He cocked his head, waiting for me to explain.

"Everybody says I'm impulsive, that I never plan things out, that I go off like the Lone Ranger."

"So now I'm your Tonto, it would appear."

I glanced at his face to see if he'd spoken in anger, but his jaw twitched a bit as if the irony in the remark was intentional.

Frida watched the two of us as we conferred. "Is there something going on, something I should know about, Eve?"

I shook my head and continued to whisper to Lionel, "He's given us so little time that I can't think clearly." The germ of an idea began to take shape. I shared it with him, and he agreed it was stupid and wouldn't work, but he also said it was the only thing we had going for us. I put my cell back in my pocket and walked over to Frida.

"There is something, but I can't tell you much. Will you trust me?" My half-formed plan depended upon my relationship with Frida. Annoying as I had been over the years, I was counting on her to see me as a friend. She squeezed her eyes partly closed and tipped her head forward, trying to read my intentions. I held my breath.

"Okay."

"I can't let you know where I'm going now or why, but I need you to find me, just not too soon. Or too late."

"You have something in mind, so I guess I'll have to trust you." That was not a smile on her face.

"Don't worry. I'll give you a call when I need you. Just wait here until I do." I grabbed Brenda's hand. "Come on, Brenda. We're going to visit family."

Brenda looked at me and smiled. "We're going for a ride?"

Lionel, Brenda, and I headed out of the casino. The two cars left in the lot belonged to Frida and her men and the tribal police.

"This isn't going to work. We don't have a vehicle," I said.

Lionel jangled a set of keys in his fingers and pointed to the tribal police cruiser.

"I thought you didn't trust or like anyone, and now I find you're pals with the tribal police?"

Lionel fixed angry eyes on me. "Just because you're white doesn't mean you know everything."

"Just because you're an Indian doesn't mean you do, either," I shot back.

The anger faded and was replaced by something close to respect or admiration. Gosh, if I'd know it was that easy to get the guy to back down, I'd have sassed him instead of trying to be nice to him. As if reading my mind, he gave a quick nod and gestured toward the car. We all got in.

"Where to?" he asked, pulling out of the parking lot.

"I'm calling Jerry now to let him know we're on the way to Eleanor's apartment. I need to make certain Eleanor and Irene are okay, and I need his help."

"Hey, Eve," said Jerry when the call connected. "What's up?"

He sounded so cheery I thought my concerns about Eleanor and Irene were unfounded. I'd worried that Freddie had taken them too.

"Irene and Eleanor are okay?"

"Sure. I'm watching a game on television, and they're out in the backyard having some private time."

"Humor me, Jerry. Go check on them."

"I've got Big Randy, one of Nappi's men, out there keeping an eye on them. They're fine."

"Just do it," I said, yelling into the phone.

"What a grump." I heard the back slider open and then silence, followed by Jerry's voice again. "Oh, no."

"What?" I demanded.

There were background noises of someone moving, then silence.

"Jerry?"

A minute passed. I could tell from the sounds coming through the line that we were still connected.

Finally, I heard Jerry's voice again, no longer cheery but shaky.

"They're gone, and Big Randy is out cold."

"Freddie took them, and right under your nose while you were watching television. Jerry, Jerry, Jerry."

"Don't start on me, Eve. I feel awful."

"Well, good then. Maybe you'll be inclined to be more willing to help me save your girlfriend."

"Of course I will. Tell me how."

"We'll be there soon. See how badly hurt Randy is and do what you can for him until we arrive."

"Gone?" asked Lionel.

I nodded.

Lionel stomped on the accelerator. I watched the speedometer hit sixty in a thirty mph zone and said, "Do you have a driver's license?" I grabbed onto the armrest to stabilize myself as we rounded a corner.

"Who's going to stop a tribal police car?"

We swung into the driveway next to Eleanor's rental house. Jerry ran out to meet us.

"Randy's coming around. He should be checked

out by a doctor at some point, but it's not critical right now."

"Hop in. We're off to the shop to pick up some items. I just called Grandy and asked her to meet us there."

Jerry gave Lionel Egret an uneasy smile and jumped into the backseat with Brenda.

"I know your daughter," he said.

"Which one?" she asked. He gave me a questioning look.

Grandy opened the shop door to greet us. She hugged Brenda, who seemed to remember her or thought she did. I was just happy that Brenda acted content to be in Grandy's care. I raced through the shop, pulling items of clothing off the rounds and racks and tossing them over my shoulder at Jerry while I explained what was happening.

Grandy looked at me in horror. "That horrible man," she said, referring to Freddie. She glanced at Brenda and mouthed the words, "Does she know about Eleanor and Irene?"

I shook my head.

"Well, I'll tell you one thing, my dear. You are not going out there without me," Grandy announced.

"You need to stay here and take care of Brenda. There are enough lives at risk. No sense in adding to the count."

"What are you going to do?" she asked.

"I'm going to do just as Freddie said except that Jerry will be playing the part of Brenda. He does women very well, don't you, Jerry?"

Jerry dropped the clothing he was holding and his mouth dropped open in surprise. "Wait a minute. You didn't tell me I'd have to dress up as a woman. That was a onetime thing. I'm not doing it again."

Jerry had dressed as a woman so he wouldn't be recognized when he met me at a rest area on the turnpike. He'd looked so good he fooled even me.

"I thought you wanted to help Eleanor."

He hung his head. "Okay. I'll do it, just this once… for her."

"Consider yourself lucky. You won't have to squeeze your feet into high-heeled shoes." I tossed him a pair of high-topped sneakers in red canvas. "These should fit." I pointed to the dressing rooms. "And be quick about it."

When he emerged wearing a pair of elastic-waist pants, a flowered blouse, the sneakers, and a brown wig, he looked very much like someone's mother. Anyone knowing Brenda would not have been fooled, but I didn't think Freddie and his goons had gotten a very good look at her in the swamp. They were too busy killing Henry to pay much attention to the woman shaking in terror at his side. I wanted them to believe the woman I presented to them was Brenda Montrose. I believed the tumbled-down shack in the shadows of the swamp would provide poor enough lighting that Jerry wouldn't be recognized. I wasn't planning on any of us settling in there for a long conversation.

I traded Brenda's blue cardigan for a sweater in the shop and tossed hers to Jerry. "Put this on too," I told him. He looked even more matronly in the oversized sweater.

"Not my choice for what a mother should wear, but it will do," I said.

Lionel almost grinned.

I hugged Grandy and told Brenda I would be back with her daughter and mother. She gave me a confused look, but Grandy put her arm around Brenda's shoulders and the woman leaned into her. "You look very much like someone I know, but I can't remember who."

"That's okay, dearie. It will come back to you," Grandy said. "Eve—"

"I'll be fine. Don't worry."

Lionel, Jerry-as-Brenda, and I got back into the tribal police car and began the short journey to the airboat business where we would take the boat out to the shack. There was no way to get there by road. I took my cell from my pocket and called Frida.

"What are you doing, Eve? I'm sitting here with these tribal guys guarding me until they get the word from Lionel to let me go."

I told her what was happening. "I can't give you precise directions to the shack, but I'm guessing you can track my phone to locate me. Am I right?"

"It's not as easy as you think, Eve. I guess the techie back at the office can get a read on your phone and convey it to me, but—"

"You'll have to come by canoe from the airboat business location. It's closest to the shack. Don't use an airboat or any other motor or Freddie will hear you."

"I'm not an idiot, Eve. I can figure that out."

"Okay. Sorry. We're getting into the airboat now. Freddie is expecting me in," I looked at my watch, "less than thirty minutes."

"Can you drive an airboat, Eve?"

"No, but…." I wanted to say that Jerry or Lionel could, but I was supposed to be with Brenda and no one else. Suddenly my clever plan went all to pieces.

I stood at the edge of the canal and looked at the airboat. Lionel seemed to catch on to what was happening.

"I don't have the time to paddle my Brenda stand-in and me out to the shack, and Freddie knows I can't run an airboat. We are so screwed."

TWENTY-THREE

"THE RILEYS DOWN THE ROAD have a motorboat. I'm sure they would loan it to us," Lionel said.

We jumped back into the car and sped out of the drive and onto the road. A sod truck pulled in front of us. Lionel steered into the passing lane and managed to get around the truck, playing an unintentional game of chicken with a pickup coming from the other direction. We pulled up in front of the Rileys' house to find no car there.

"The Rileys aren't home," I said, kicking the dirt at my feet.

"Leave a note. We'll just borrow the boat." Jerry grabbed his wig off the car seat and ran to a small boat pulled onto the canal's bank.

"I'm not leaving a damn note," I said. "And put your damn wig back on."

"It's hot."

"Too bad." I jumped into the boat. Lionel pulled the starter cord and the engine sputtered, caught for a moment, then died.

"Check to make certain it's not out of gas," said Jerry.

Lionel grunted and ignored him, pulling the cord once more. Again it sputtered and died.

I looked at my watch. We were almost out of time.

"Once more," said Lionel.

I nervously played with the amulet I wore around my neck, the charm Grandfather had given me for protection.

The engine came to life, and we were off down the canal. Would Frida be far behind?

At the bend just before the shack, Lionel turned the boat over to me, slipped over the side, and waded to shore.

"I wonder how many goons Freddie has with him?" asked Jerry as we pulled back into the waterway.

"I'm guessing at least two. He came across as a pretty arrogant guy, so I bet he thinks a skinny gal along with three other women plus a couple of Indians will pose no problem for three men with guns."

"Your plan is set up to include you, me, Lionel—all of us with no weapons—and your family—also with no weapons and undoubtedly tied up or restrained in some way—to do what? Our firepower comes from Frida and her men…if she finds us in time. Maybe we should rethink this."

"You got anything better, buddy?" And there it was. Jerry and I sounded just like we did when we were married. Isn't it wonderful how some things never change?

I pulled the boat into the small landing that led to the path up to the shack. I knew we were being watched. I could feel it. Something moved just to one side of the pathway as we got out of the boat. I was prepared to see Freddie step in front of me, blocking my way and demanding that his men frisk us for weapons. Instead I caught sight of the mama gator who liked to hang out here. She moved farther into the underbrush, but I knew she continued to watch us. She must be riled up with all these humans around. I wondered if she had a nest nearby. Babies to guard made her unpredictable. Behind me something made a splash in the water. Jerry heard it too, and we both turned. Nothing was there except the widening circles where an animal had dived. I had hoped it might be Frida arriving.

"Don't worry, my dear," I said as if speaking to Brenda. "It's a turtle."

"That better be all it is," said Freddie, stepping onto the path in front of me.

"We're here," I said. "Now, where is my family?" I stood in front of Jerry, as if protecting a frail woman.

"Can't you do better than that, Ms. Appel?"

"What do you have in mind?" I asked.

"I'm sure you know my intentions. I have a contract with a very rich man. He has no intention of sharing his family wealth with his father's bastard daughter and her offspring. But this doesn't have to involve your family."

"You know they're part of my family, so of course this involves me, but maybe we can find a way around this." I was stalling for time, waiting for Lionel to appear, followed by Frida and her gang.

Behind Freddie stood two men holding handguns. I couldn't tell what kind, and I didn't know if they had other weapons.

"I need to determine if you're armed," said Freddie, signaling to one of his men.

"Just a minute. I need to see if everyone is all right."

Freddie laughed. "Sure. Why not?"

He nodded to one of the men, who turned toward the shack at the exact moment Lionel Egret rushed him and knocked the goon's gun from his hand. The other man turned and fired his weapon at Lionel, who sank to the ground with a groan. Freddie continued to point his weapon at me, ignoring the person he thought was Brenda behind me. Suddenly Jerry pulled a gun out from under his skirt and fired at Freddie. And missed. But the distraction gave Lionel enough time to grab the gun on the ground and fire at him as well as get a shot off at the man who had shot him.

"What the...?" said Freddie, surprised to see Brenda aim a gun at him. The shot whizzed by his ear and found a target in the second goon. Both of Freddie's men were down. I hesitated only a moment. With Freddie's attention divided between Jerry and the men behind him, I realized my opportunity. In that second, I delivered a kick to Freddie's midsection. With an "oof," he doubled over, but still held his weapon. He aimed at Jerry, but I gave him another kick with my other foot. This one knocked him backwards, but he still held his gun, unable to aim as he worked to regain his balance. I grabbed the gun Jerry still held.

"Give me that," I said, and without hesitation, I shot Freddie. My aim wasn't very good, the bullet having been delivered, as was my usual firing stance, with my eyes squeezed shut. But it did the trick. Freddie let go of his gun and grabbed for his thigh, where my shot hit him.

"You crazy bitch!" he yelled, "Another couple inches to the left and I wouldn't be a man anymore."

"Huh. I never thought you were much of a man to begin with," I said. I looked in Lionel's direction. Freddie's two sidekicks seemed to be out of commission. Both lay on the ground, one groaning in pain, the other face down in the dirt, unmoving. Jerry had grabbed both their guns and was standing over them.

"Is Lionel okay?" I asked. I bent down and picked

up Freddie's gun, which I aimed at him. I was worried he might have another one concealed somewhere, perhaps under all that bleeding he was doing.

Freddie seemed to have lost his lust for gunplay once he saw his buddies were no longer in the game. He began to crawl off the side of the path into the woods. Suddenly I heard a hiss. The mama gator was cutting off Freddie's retreat. Freddie saw her too.

"Shoot the damn thing, will you?" yelled Freddie, his voice several octaves above its normal already high range. Was that from fear or had I injured his manhood?

"Don't you know the kill area on an alligator is on the top of the head between the eyes, and it's about the size of a quarter in diameter? You just experienced how lousy a shot I am. I can't help you, I'm afraid," I said, pleasure almost making me giddy enough to jump up and down.

It sounded to me as if Freddie was crying. "For the love of…" he said, choking on his fear, "help me."

"Glad to," said a voice from behind me, "but I'm not tackling a mad gator." It was Frida.

"Nice timing. Where were you?" I asked.

"It took us a while to find the paddles to the canoe at the airboat business. We got lucky and located them under the counter in the chickee hut. Otherwise we'd still be searching." She looked down at Freddie and across the clearing at his men. "I guess you didn't need my help after all."

Freddie and the gator seemed to be at a standoff. Maybe the gator was just fascinated by the sound of a man sobbing and begging for mercy.

"I'm guessing she wonders what mobster tastes like," said Frida.

I decided to leave Freddie's fate to the alligator. "Just keep calm and don't let her sense your fear. And don't make any sudden moves. I think she's worried you're after her young," I told Freddie as I moved beyond him to give the alligator a wide berth. Frida followed me to where Lionel was sitting up, holding his arm.

"How are you doing?" I asked. He growled something at me that I interpreted to mean "fine." I rushed into the shack, afraid of what I might find, but Sammy ran to me and hugged me while the boys surrounded us and joined in. I smiled at Eleanor and Irene. "You two all right?" I asked, holding out a hand to them, which Irene grabbed. Eleanor smiled at me for a moment then caught sight of Jerry, who ran to her and gathered her into his arms.

Irene stepped forward and said to Jerry, "You're not my daughter. Where is she? That Freddie guy said she would be here."

Eleanor withdrew from Jerry's arms. "She's okay, isn't she?"

"She's with Grandy at the shop," I said.

The only one in the shack who seemed to be unsurprised to see me was Grandfather Egret. He was happy—that I could tell—but he looked as if my appearance confirmed what he already had known would happen. I smiled at him as he walked over to us to join in the group hug.

"Hey, everybody," said Sammy. "Back off. You're squishing my baby." Did he mean me or the little one?

"WHO'S THAT?" I ASKED, pointing to a man sitting as far back in the shack as he could manage.

"Oh, him," said Sammy. "That's another of Freddie's

men, but he's so terrified of being in the swamps that he's been back there trembling and talking to himself for hours. I think he's in shock."

Frida entered the shack and checked to see if the man in the corner was armed. She removed a handgun and called to one of her men to cuff the frightened man.

Then she grinned at everyone. "Are we okay here?" We nodded. "Good. Lionel's wound is not life-threatening and neither is Freddie's, but I've called for a helicopter to airlift them both to the hospital. I should leave your father out here to the swamp critters instead," she said to Sammy. "He had tribal cops hold me and my officers at the casino while he made his getaway using a tribal police car."

"You're not going to do anything to him, are you?" I asked. "He risked his life for us, and he was doing what he had to for his family."

"I know that, but I'm not going to tell him I'm going easy on him. The man needs to be taught a lesson. He can't take police authority for granted just because we're on his land."

"I think it's far too late to teach Lionel Egret anything he doesn't want to learn," I said.

"She's right. He's too stubborn. Like someone else I know." Grandfather gave me a look and clucked his tongue.

I tried for a look of innocence, something I have yet to perfect.

WHEN WE WALKED into the shop, Grandy rushed over and enveloped me in one of her warm hugs. "Thank heavens you're all right."

Behind her, Brenda stepped forward, and Irene

stood for a moment as if too paralyzed to move or say anything. Then she held out one hand and said, "Brenda."

Brenda continued to hold back until Eleanor grabbed both hers and Irene's hands in hers. "Your mother, Mom."

A look of doubt crossed Brenda's face, but it soon brightened to one of joy. The three women came together in a clumsy hug, but it was a hug, and I was grateful for that.

Frida entered the shop and observed the reunion, her lips forming a half smile as if she, too, was happy to see the family reunited. Her eyes expressed something else—concern that she would have to interfere with their newfound happiness.

"I'll need to talk with all of you down at the station," she said.

"You're arresting us. But what for?"

"No, I'm not arresting you, but I do need the three of you to help me put together this story."

"We're being arrested?" asked Brenda. She looked at me, worry creasing her brow. "Are you arresting my other daughter, too?"

Oh, boy. There were some issues that still needed to be worked through.

"Eve is not your daughter, Mom," said Eleanor.

And then there were some issues that were resolved at last.

TWENTY-FOUR

SIX MONTHS AFTER that day in the swamp, things had settled back into what passed as normal in my life. Lionel Egret's wound was not serious and required some minor surgery, after which he was moved into the same hospital room as Nappi. The two of them became friendly, and when they were released within days of each other, they started meeting for lunch several times a week. Talk about strange bedfellows, huh?

I awoke that morning feeling energized and decided I'd spend the afternoon in West Palm, picking up consignment items for our shops. I grabbed a pair of pants and a matching red top—yippee for stretchy material— and looked at myself in the full-length mirror we had installed on the back of the bedroom door. I had gained weight, a lot of it, but it was all baby weight. I remained as skinny as ever and now looked like the neck of one of the snowy egrets who had swallowed a large fish.

Sammy came up behind me and encircled me with his arms, his large hands resting on my baby bump. I shared with him the egret image, and we both chuckled then broke into laughter, which made my stomach move up and down as my guffaws got stronger.

"Uh-oh," I said.

Sammy looked at me, his smile fading. "What's wrong?"

"Nothing, but it's time," I said. "My water just

broke, and if I'm not mistaken, that feels like a contraction."

By the time we arrived at the hospital, the contractions were strong, regular, and close together. Less than an hour later, I gave birth, not to the baby boy that Sammy's father had predicted, but to a baby girl.

"What happened?" we both said as I held her in my arms.

"You just had a baby," said the doctor, his brow wrinkled in puzzlement.

"It was supposed to be a boy," said Sammy.

The doctor patted him on the back. "You'll get used to it."

The family had gathered around my bed—my three boys, Grandfather, Lionel, Grandy, and Max. Madeleine and David joined us a few minutes later. Everyone was google-eyed with surprise. I guess we all counted on the ability of the Egret elders to foretell the future.

"I didn't want to hear the results of the amnio with respect to the baby's sex because we all knew it was going to be a boy. Because you told me it was going to be a boy," I said to Lionel.

"Anyone can make a mistake," said Grandy. "I, of course, knew it would be a girl."

"Did you? And you chose not to share that insight with me?" I said. The snappish tone in my voice must have alerted my newborn to my distress because she began to cry. Actually, her crying was more like howling.

Smiles wreathed my visitors' faces. "Just a chip off the old bloc," someone said.

"Too bad you let me name my girl Eve. It would be

a perfect name for her. She's got your sass and your lungs," said Madeleine. "What will you name her?"

Sammy and I looked at each other, puzzled for a moment, and then both spoke at once.

"Renata Adelaide after Sammy's mother and my Grandy," we said in unison.

"Are you certain you don't want to use your mother's name?" asked Grandy.

No. I didn't want the name Mary for her. It was a name that had been used by another. Now that everyone knew Eleanor's mother was Brenda, not Mary, I wanted Mary to be my mother's name and no one else's in the family.

Nappi and Jerry came to the door of the room. "Is there room for two more?" asked Nappi, holding a huge bouquet of roses.

"There had better be," said Crusty McNabb. He was in the company of Shelley, who had graduated from tailor for the consignment shop to partner, buying a quarter share of the business. We still had not decided how we would handle both the shop here in Sabal Bay and the shop on wheels, but we were in no hurry to make changes. Our lives had been rather full of late.

All our boys had ridden in the junior rodeo. Jason won second place in calf roping for his age group, Jerome a third place for his, and Jeremy got an attendance merit ribbon. He was a bit disappointed, but he was younger than most of the other competitors in his age bracket. He also said his horse didn't like him. I don't know about that, but Grandfather and Lionel decided that there was enough property near the airboat business to graze three to five horses. We were now looking for the right ones.

I still don't think Lionel trusts me or likes me, but we had shared some harrowing times and seemed to have developed a grudging respect for each other. I was kind of delighted he had predicted the sex of our baby incorrectly. It meant I had something on him.

We were almost finished building our own house right next to Grandfather Egret's. There are four bedrooms with room to expand if necessary. We asked Grandfather if he wanted to move in with us and leave his place to his son, but he declined. Sammy correctly read my feelings and did not ask his father to move into our house. Lionel seemed to be there much of the time anyway, spending it with the boys, teaching them Miccosukee traditions and outdoor skills.

"Renata Adelaide is quite a handle for a kid," Nappi pointed out. "What will you call her?"

I looked down into my daughter's eyes, and her gaze met mine. "How do you like the name 'Netty'?" I asked.

Her crying stopped and she let out a loud burp.

"I think she likes it just fine," I said.

* * * * *